DANGEROUS RESCUE

RILEY EDWARDS

D1028238

Copyright © 2021 by Riley Edwards

Cover design: Lori Jackson Designs

Written by: Riley Edwards

Published by: Riley Edwards/Rebels Romance

Edited by: Rebecca Hodgkins

Proofreader: Julie Deaton, Rebecca Kendall

Dangerous Rescue

ISBN: 978-1-951567-17-0

Print ISBN: 978-1-951567-21-7

First edition: October 26, 2021

Copyright © 2021 Riley Edwards

To my family - my team – my tribe.
This is for you.

CHAPTER 1

14 years ago

What an asshole.

I mean, what a seriously whacked asshole.

I felt my sinuses start to sting, and that just pissed me off.

The bastard was lucky I was frozen in my seat, or I would've punched him in his face.

Troy Blizzard, my unofficial boyfriend who'd been working hard over the last three months to take the *un* out of unofficial. Just last night—*last night*—he pushed me again, told me he was falling in love with me, and wanted to be exclusive. He told me there was no one more beautiful than me—which was a lie, but it still felt good to hear. He told me there was no one else for him, and he wanted a future with me. Obviously, that was another big, fat, whopping lie seeing as he was right then sitting on the patio of my favorite Mexican restaurant sharing a meal with a beautiful leggy blonde.

When I pulled into the parking lot I'd immediately spotted Troy. He was hard to miss; he played football in high school and now played for the Arizona State Sun Devils. He was big, huge really. Another dead giveaway was the maroon Sun Devils t-shirt, which I often wondered if he bought a size too small just so it would stretch tight across his chest.

I saw him walking out onto the patio and stupid, stupid me got excited. I thought he was there to surprise me. He knew Las Machados was my favorite. He also knew that since I'd moved to Tempe, every year on my birthday I treated myself to *Molcajete Mixto*. And since I was a stupid girl living in some silly romantic movie thinking the guy who'd been pursuing me was making a grand gesture to win me over by surprising me on my twenty-first birthday at my favorite restaurant, I'd started to wonder why I'd been keeping Troy at bay.

Then I saw him pull out the blonde's chair, something he'd never done for me. I watched as he kissed her on the lips—another punch to my stomach. Then I sat in my car in the hot Arizona sun and watched my unofficial boyfriend touch, kiss, and smile at the beautiful blonde.

Troy had excused himself and gotten up to go inside, and like any crazy woman scorned I didn't pull away and go home. I didn't call my best friend, Brooklyn, to rant about what dicks men were. I sat in the hot Arizona sun and compared myself to the blonde. She was everything I wasn't. She was wearing a cute strappy sundress and I was in shorts and a t-shirt. She had on cute wedge sandals and I had on Chucks. Her hair was long and blonde and mine was short and black. Just-black, to match my just-hazel eyes. Nothing special about my appearance. She, on the other hand, was something special.

I didn't drive away when Troy rejoined his date. I forced myself to watch them. I memorized every touch, every look, and every kiss. I tattooed them on my heart so I'd never forget.

This was why I kept to myself. This was why I lived in my books. This was why I had exactly one friend. People sucked.

Once I'd tortured myself to the nth degree I started my car, but then stopped. This was part of my problem, I was a pushover. I didn't like confrontation. I wasn't good at it so people walked all over me.

That was ending. Now. Brooklyn would be proud. She'd been forever telling me I needed to stand up for myself. So, that day, seeing as it was my twenty-first birthday I was giving myself a better gift than Las Machados.

I yanked my phone out of my purse, found my text messages, slid the screen open to expose the little keyboard, and furiously thumbed a message.

You're a supreme asshole. I hit send but then because I was so mad I decided that wasn't enough.

You said you wanted to be exclusive. I see you with her. I saw you kiss her. You're a total douchebag. I hope she gives you crotch rot. I hit send again but I was still so angry I couldn't stop myself from saying more.

I'm glad I found out what a lying dick you really are before I slept with you. Happy Birthday to me. I sent that and sat in my car waiting for Troy to check his messages but he didn't even glance at his phone.

That was it. That pissed me off.

Nice. You're out with me and you've got your phone glued in your hands. You're with her and don't check it. Total douche.

Since I was sending rapid-fire texts I decided I had one last thing to say.

In case I wasn't clear we're done, Troy. Do not ever call me again. And if you see me don't talk to me.

I was about to drive away when my phone beeped.

I'm guessing this is Troy's phone. I found it on the counter in the bathroom. I was feeling bad someone lost it, now not so much. Tell me what he looks like so I can give it to him.

Oh my God.

A stranger read my texts.

And what kind of moron doesn't have a password on his phone? The stranger messaged again.

Troy. He's too stupid to figure it out. I returned.

Well, Letty. I like your style. The crotch rot was a nice touch. Now tell me what the twat looks like so I can deliver the phone.

I glanced up from my phone and saw Troy walking back into the restaurant.

Maroon shirt. Sun Devils logo on the front. He's coming back in maybe to look for it. I quickly sent.

I see him. He's going back into the bathroom. Want me to kick his ass for you?

A hysterical bubble of laughter escaped. I had no idea what this stranger looked like but Troy was two-hundred-pounds of muscle and six-foot-one.

If you think you can take him sure.

Whoa. Did I really type that? I smiled at my phone, rereading my message. I totally did. This standing up for myself felt kinda good.

You got it. My birthday present to you.

Another message came in and it said, *BTW any man who takes you on a date so much as looks anywhere but at you is a loser. Dump his ass and move on.*

Wow. That was nice.

Wise advice. And I was kidding about beating up Troy. He's not worth your time.

Any man who lies and cheats is worth me taking the time to deliver a message. He's coming back out. Hope your birthday gets better.

I didn't wait in the parking lot to see if the stranger kicked Troy's ass when he gave the phone back. I picked up In N Out and drove back to the apartment I shared with Brooklyn. Then I sat on the sofa and ate a lonely birthday lunch waiting for Brooklyn to get back from class.

Three days later I was studying for finals daydreaming about what I was going to do with my life when I graduated in a few weeks, when my phone chirped with a text.

I nabbed it thinking it was Brooklyn, which was weird because she was in class.

A number I didn't know was on the screen and I didn't understand the message.

He's not bothering you, is he?

I'm sorry, who is this?

No need to be sorry. This is River from Las Machados. I'm the one that found Troy's phone.

My shoulders went stiff. It was nice this River guy was checking on me but he was still a stranger. And it was kinda weird. My fingers were a little shaky when I replied.

I haven't heard from him.

Excellent.

Excellent? I wondered what that meant.

You didn't really kick his ass, did you? I sent that and then a follow-up. *Not that I'm worried about him but I'd feel bad if you got in trouble.*

Didn't lay a hand on him but I made myself clear you were off-limits. Glad to know the idiot listened.

I stared at my phone and smiled.

I couldn't name the emotion that had taken over. I just knew it felt good.

You must be ten feet tall and wear a spandex leotard complete with a cape if you got through to Troy. He's a little dense and a whole lot full of himself.

River's reply came quick.

That's a negative on the spandex and cape. But even dense and cocky can be taught a lesson with the right motivation.

I closed the book in my lap and scooted down on my sofa so my head rested on the back and lifted my phone up so I could reply.

What kind of motivation?

The kind where he understood that long-lasting bodily harm would come if he contacted you again.

That was just insane. Which made me wonder if this River character was a little crazy.

Why would you do that? You don't know me.

There was a long pause and I started to think he wasn't going to answer me. Then I got worried he *did* know me. I was good with names; I never forgot one and I certainly wouldn't forget the name River. But he could be using a fake name.

Oh, God, what if this was a trick? I'd read about this.

Catfishing.

I don't need to know you. I have a pet peeve about men jerking around women. Especially on their birthday.

This was just bizarre. Texting a stranger that could be a total psycho.

So do you wear a leotard and cape? An Avenger to protect birthday girls who've been cheated on?

Why was I still engaging?

I'm ignoring the leotard comment. I read the text and

smiled. *I have to run. My flight's boarding but I wanted to check on you before I left. Glad all's well. Take care.*

Great. I was nosy by nature, now I wanted to know where he was going.

I refrained from asking.

Thanks again, River. Have a safe flight.

He didn't respond.

Three months later, I was officially a college graduate and getting ready to move home to Idaho.

Now what?

I had a degree in English—creative writing to be exact—and I had no interest in writing. When I started I did but I quickly learned my love for reading didn't translate to my mind forming stories of my own. I lived inside my books. I got lost in other peoples' worlds but I couldn't create them.

So now I was off to face the real world with a buttload of debt. Okay, it wasn't a buttload but I'd be paying off my loans for the next ten years. I should've listened to Brooklyn and switched majors. She had a plan. She'd filled her studies with business, marketing, and management classes.

Brooklyn was smart.

I was adrift.

That was what I was thinking about when I bumped into Troy. Literally ran right into him. I'd been looking down, digging through my purse looking for my wallet, and bam! My head hit his chest. I jerked back and opened my mouth to apologize but I didn't get the chance. Troy's eyes got huge then he shuffled past me like I had a plague—a nasty one that would eat your flesh if you came in contact with me.

Damn. Whatever River had said to him was effective.

So, due to my inherent nosiness and Brooklyn's encouragement, we tried to find River in the campus directory. There were no students enrolled at ASU with the name River. Then Brooklyn had this great idea of signing up for this thing called MySpace to see if he had a profile. After a few hours of searching, wondering why people would purposely put all their personal information out for the world to dissect, we gave up.

I never found River, which only cemented my suspicion the stranger had given me a fake name.

But since Troy's reaction was so comical I pulled up River's contact info I'd saved and sent him a text.

Ran into Troy. My fault I wasn't watching where I was going and slammed into him. Head first. Embarrassing. But he didn't utter a word to me. Just scurried away like a frightened mouse.

A month passed before he responded.

LOL. Glad to hear it.

The next time I heard from River it was my birthday. Exactly one year after the first text.

I hope this year's birthday's better than the last.

Had to find a new favorite birthday meal after last year's debacle. Can't very well enjoy my Molcajete Mixto while thinking about the asshole.

River's next message made me smile.

Why would you think of him at all?

Good question.

I guess I'm not really thinking about him, just about the memory that men are cheating bastards.

While I waited for a response, I saved the document I was working on. I'd put my degree and love for books to good use and got a job at a small publishing company. I didn't make a good living—I was entry-level—but I loved it, and I got to work from home.

A cynic. I'm not sure if that's smart or a little sad.

Then before I could stop myself I typed out the burning question.

Are you really a man?

Yep.

Three letters. That was all he had to say on the topic. He didn't offer a picture of himself. Interesting.

Is your name really River?

Yep.

Huh. Again no further explanation. Not that that really was an explanation to me asking him his name.

Have you ever cheated on a girlfriend?

Nope.

Well, then I'm sorry I lumped you in with the bastards.

Apology accepted. Happy Birthday.

Thank you, River.

And that was how it happened for the next three birthdays. Each year I heard from River. Each year it was a short exchange—him wishing me a happy birthday.

Until my twenty-sixth birthday rolled around and I didn't get a text.

I weirdly panicked. The next day I texted him to check in and got no reply.

I panicked some more.

Thirty-five days after my birthday I got a message.

Hey, sorry I missed your birthday this year. And thanks for checking on me. I was working on something and didn't have my phone.

That sounded like a bad lie. So I didn't respond.

∼

Next year on my birthday I was woken up at five a.m. by my phone beeping.

It was River.

Happy Birthday, Letty. I hope you have a great day.

Something happened that day. It was the morning of my twenty-seventh birthday. I was working the same job. I no longer loved, it mainly because I was still making crap money even after being with the company for five years. And once again, I'd been cheated on.

I was over it. Totally and completely.

At least that was what I told myself when instead of answering the text, I called him.

If this was some elaborate scheme or he was some crazy person I was putting an end to it.

The phone rang twice.

Then it happened.

"Letty?"

Suddenly despite it being five in the morning, I was wide awake. Wide and awake with a strange feeling bouncing around inside of me.

"You *are* a guy."

An equally smooth, rich, silky chuckle filled my ear.

"Indeed I am. Happy Birthday, Letty."

Holy crap. Now that I had him on the phone I didn't know what to say. I didn't even know *why* I'd called.

This was crazy. I didn't know River. We'd exchanged a

handful of text messages over the last six years. We weren't friends.

"You there, babe?"

I laid back down and stared at the white ceiling thinking I really liked his voice.

"Yeah, I'm here."

"Everything okay?"

No, everything was not okay but I'd been pretending like everything was perfect for so long I didn't know how to ask my parents or Brooklyn for advice. I didn't know how to tell them I hated my job, I was bored out of my skull, and if I didn't make a change soon I was going to lose my mind.

Maybe that's why I spilled my guts to a stranger at five o'clock in the morning.

And thank God I did.

That morning changed my life.

CHAPTER 2

"River! Are you listening to me?"

I looked up from my phone and watched my brother, Echo, continue to pace around my living room while alternately flailing his arms and running his hand through his hair.

"Dude, brother, you need to calm down. This was the plan. This is what *you* wanted to happen," I reminded him.

"She's not ready," Echo practically growled.

"Shiloh's twenty-two. She's the same age Phoenix was when he went into the academy."

Echo stopped wearing a hole in my carpet only to pin me with a dirty look.

I was correct and he knew it. Echo and I had been twenty-three when we'd gone into the academy, Phoenix did it a year earlier than us, and now Shiloh was going in. We'd planned this. We'd talked about it since we were kids. Graduate, community college, then join the police force.

"She's not ready," he repeated.

I felt bad for my brother. He was the eldest, only two years older than me but it might as well have been twenty.

He was more of a father to me than the piece of shit whose sperm made me. Actually, he was more of a parent to me, Phoenix, and Shiloh—period. Our mom took off when we were young and left us to be raised by a criminal. Echo didn't like that much—our house under constant surveillance by the cops, our dad always getting pulled in for questioning, and then there were the times when we'd sit on the front porch while the police executed a search warrant inside. He didn't like it in the sense our loser, criminal father was our only role model.

So, Echo did everything he could to teach us how to be productive members of society. And he'd succeeded. However, it came at a cost. He'd stopped being a teenager and started being a parent. He'd sacrificed his youth. In high school, Phoenix and I played sports—Echo had a job. He taught me how to drive, he bought me my first car, and he demanded I get good grades. By the time Phoenix was old enough to get his driver's license our loser father was locked up.

Fun times.

Then Echo found himself the legal guardian of two minor children. He'd assumed responsibility for our two younger siblings and wouldn't entertain the idea of me at nineteen helping him with the burden even though he was barely twenty-one himself.

"Why don't you think she's ready?" I asked.

There was a long stretch of silence and I knew my brother was trying to come up with a valid reason when there was not one to be had.

Shiloh was ready. The problem was, Echo had been a dad since he was sixteen and like any good parent, he was having trouble recognizing the baby was no longer a baby. So, the truth was, *Echo* wasn't ready.

"I think she should stay in school. Maybe go for her masters."

I did a slow blink as I tried not to laugh at the absurdity of my brother's statement.

"We're talking about Sunny. It's a miracle she got her bachelor's. She hated school. There's zero chance you're talking her into going another four-plus years."

"She's smart."

"No doubt. But that doesn't change anything. She's got fire in her belly, Echo. The same passion for the job that you have. That I have. That Phoenix has. You put it there, brother. We've been pushing for this since she was eight. This is all she knows. Like it or not, she leaves in three days and she's gonna kick ass."

Once again my brother lapsed into an uncomfortable silence and instead of continuing down the fruitless path of enlisting me to help him talk Shiloh out of leaving for the academy, he looked around my apartment.

"You're a slob," he grumbled.

I wasn't a slob, I just wasn't a neat freak like he was. Now, Phoenix—he was a slob. And he blamed Echo and his militant rules about the house being clean after our dad got locked up as to why as an adult he refused to run a vacuum.

"Brother, I just got off shift. I'm exhausted. I got all the time in the world for you if you need to work through your feelings about your baby sister joining the force. What I don't have time for is you bitching because I've got mail piled on my counter."

"How's the task force going?" Echo changed the subject.

Instead of answering I walked into my kitchen, went straight to the fridge, and pulled out two cold ones. On the way out, I nabbed the Thai menu. If my brother was staying, he was buying dinner. After I handed my brother a beer and the menu I sat in one of the two recliners I had in lieu of a couch and got comfortable.

Echo tossed the menu on the table and pulled his phone out.

"Subtle," he mumbled.

With the food ordered and both of us kicking back I helped my brother process his uncertainties about Shiloh by filling him in on my job. It was only a temporary fix. I knew as soon as Echo left, he'd go home and visions of Shiloh at ten would invade his memory and the worry would creep back in. So, really, all I was doing was putting a Band-Aid on the issue.

But for Echo—I'd do anything, including talking about work after coming off of a twelve-hour shift when all I wanted to do was shower and fall into bed.

"We got word the feds are coming in," Echo informed me.

"The shipment of gabapentin?" I asked.

"Yeah. Who's moving it?"

I had very few complaints about being a cop. No two days were the same, especially now that I'd officially been assigned to the gang unit. But one of my biggest grievances was the lack of communication between precincts and task forces.

"Jimmy Lone's crew," I told him.

Every cop in a hundred-mile radius knew Jimmy Lone and his crew he called the Lonesomes. They moved a shit ton of contraband. If it was illegal, Jimmy was moving it. Everything from narcotics to guns to cigarettes. The guy was a piece of shit. Unfortunately, he was a clever piece of shit.

The doorbell rang at the same time as my cell.

Echo went for the door and I pulled out my phone.

Letty.

It had been a week since she'd called me the morning of her birthday and I'd be lying if I said I hadn't been tempted to call her back every day since then. There was something about the woman's chirpy voice that had drawn me in. She was animated as she chattered away and in my mind's eye I could picture her being one of those people who talked with their hands. I would bet her facial expressions and body language matched the words she spoke.

I'd never been enthralled by a woman's voice before, especially one I'd never met in person.

Actually, I needed to rewind to the very beginning—to the stranger's phone I found on the bathroom counter in a restaurant in Arizona and the text messages I'd read: *You're a supreme asshole.*

That had piqued my interest but it was the second text that caught my attention in a big way: *You said you wanted to be exclusive. I see you with her. I saw you kiss her. You're a total douchebag. I hope she gives you crotch rot.*

Obviously the woman had caught her man cheating on her which was a huge pet peeve of mine. I hated cheaters almost as much as I hated liars. It was then I made a split-second decision to return the phone to the asshole along with a lesson about respect. I'd texted the woman back with the sole purpose of ascertaining a description of the dick-head. I don't know why I did it, I can't explain my thought process, and I was fully aware then as I was in the years that followed how bizarre it was that before I returned the phone I programmed Letty's name and number into my phone.

Then I proceeded to text her for the last six years on her birthday—the date we met, the date she'd found out her man was cheating on her. I'd even transferred her number to three new phones. I had no idea why I'd done it.

Nothing in those handful of texts had solidified a friendship, or even the start of one. But then Letty called me, and spent the following hour telling me all about her job and how she felt like she was wasting her time working a job she no longer liked. After she was done bitching about her job she launched right into a long tirade about how she'd been so busy working she'd forgotten her dream of opening a bookstore.

That felt like the start of something.

I'd wanted to connect with her again, yet I hadn't reached out because it felt strange to do so.

"Are you gonna answer that?" Echo asked.

Yes.

No.

I don't know.

Right before the call went to voicemail I swiped the screen and answered.

"Hey, Letty."

"I did it!" she shouted.

"Did what?"

It was hard not to smile when I could feel her excitement through the phone.

"I quit!" she whooped.

"Quit?"

"I thought about what you said," she rushed out. "And you were totally right."

I wasn't sure what I'd been right about but I was very cognizant of my nosy brother staring at me. But before I could tell her I had company and needed to call her back she went on.

"I gave my job two weeks' notice, talked to my parents, my dad gave me some guidance, then he and I talked to a buddy of his who used to live here in Idaho but now lives in Spokane."

Idaho.

Letty lived in Idaho. Unintentional or not, that was the first piece of personal information she'd told me.

"Brooklyn—that's my best friend," Letty explained. "Majored in business management so she helped me with a business plan and my dad's friend Lenny looked it over before I went to the bank to apply for a small business loan. And guess what?"

Fuck she was cute.

"What?"

"The loan was approved. I'm opening my bookstore and it's all because of you. If you were here, I swear I'd kiss you!"

Jesus, the girl didn't mess around. It had been a week.

Her ambition was damn impressive.

"Babe, I didn't—"

"I was spinning my wheels," she interrupted. "And I would've done it longer had you not pointed it out and given me a five a.m. pep talk."

"Nope. Not taking any credit," I told her. "*You* did it, Letty. *Your* accomplishment. *Your* reward."

Letty laughed and once again her excitement made me smile.

"Well, I haven't accomplished anything yet. I might still fall flat on my face and fail."

"You took the first step and that's a step most people don't take. And a failure's only a fail when you don't take the lesson and learn from it. And you don't strike me as a woman who lets an opportunity slip by. You'll do great."

I heard Echo rooting around in my kitchen which served as a reminder I needed to get off the phone.

"Listen, I hate to cut this short," I started. "But my brother's over for dinner. Can I hit you back after he leaves?"

"Damn, River, I'm sorry."

"No need to be sorry. I'm happy you called. No, strike that, I'd be seriously disappointed had you not called to tell me your good news."

There was a brief stretch of silence before Letty softly muttered, "You were the first person I thought to call."

Damn, that felt good.

But it wouldn't be for eight more years that I would fully understand the depth of friendship that started that day. Nor would I admit that as the months and years slipped by I was falling more and more in love with a woman I'd never laid eyes on.

CHAPTER 3

My phone chirped with a text and I smiled. I didn't need to look at my phone to know who it was. Seeing as it was after midnight, it was technically my birthday. But since I did know who the text was from I tossed my book aside and snatched my phone off the bedstand.

The big 3-0. Happy Birthday, sweet tart.

River's silly nickname made my smile wider as I texted him back.

TY! You're up late. Hot date?

Please say no!

My phone chirped again and irrational jealousy flooded.

Depends on your idea of a hot date. My evening did end with handcuffs.

At the end of his message, there were three purple devil emojis and a sideways happy face with tears.

River was being funny—this was not abnormal. The only person who was more amusing than River was Brooklyn, my BFF since forever. Brook called River my Pen Pal or my Male BFF but made it clear her position was Head BFF and that would never change. And Brook was right. River and I were best friends—*just* friends and nothing more. River dated. I dated. But I couldn't deny it was getting harder and harder to separate friendship and feelings. The feelings being the more-than-friendly kind.

I didn't know how to respond so I sent back a smiley face.

That was when my phone rang and my heart clutched.

River and I did not hide things from each other. We knew everything about the other person with the exception of our last names. That was something we'd decided on three years ago when we started talking on the phone. We'd also promised we'd never look the other person up on the internet or social media. And he did not know the name of my bookstore. But other than the clear lines we'd drawn he knew I lived in Idaho and I knew he lived in Georgia. He knew I had a sister by blood, Kiki, who worked my last nerve, and a sister of the soul, Brooklyn, who'd come to live with my family after her parents died. And I knew he had an older brother, Echo, a younger one, Phoenix, and a sister, Shiloh.

I also knew his deepest fears and his dreams. As well as he knew mine.

So, I stared at my ringing phone, scared to answer it. Scared that I was spending my thirtieth birthday alone and feeling weirdly vulnerable. I wasn't sure I could take hearing River tell me about a date that ended with handcuffs.

But I answered anyway and I did it in a fake-chirpy voice that sounded ridiculous even to my own ears.

"What good, Boo Berry?"

I heard River chuckle, then his smooth like honey voice coated my raw nerves.

"Happy Birthday, baby."

Baby.

God, I wished that were real.

"Thanks."

"Did I beat Brooklyn this year?"

"Indeed you did, my friend."

This was new, something that started on my twenty-eighth birthday—River and Brooklyn competing on who could wish me happy birthday first. Due to the three-hour time difference, River had an unfair advantage, so last year Brooklyn set an alarm and texted me at four in the morning, beating River's five a.m. text.

River's loud, exaggerated yawn reminded me it was after three in the morning for him and his night had ended with handcuffs.

"Long night?" I asked even though I didn't want to hear his answer.

"Just got home from a call out."

Did I mention he was a police officer? As were his brothers and his sister.

A family affair, as he called it. A noble profession—their drive behind it, heartbreaking.

"I thought you had the weekend off."

"I did but last night Echo's unit made a bust and my team was called in."

Handcuffs.

This knowledge didn't fill me with relief. River being a cop—more specifically part of the gang unit—was something that filled me with no small amount of fear.

"And get this," River continued. "Shiloh announced last night at dinner she was thinking about going out for SWAT."

"Wow! That's badass."

Echo was part of the drug task force, Phoenix was transferring to the gun unit, and Shiloh was still in uniform. She was the opposite of my pain-in-the-ass sister who couldn't be bothered with real life because it would cut into her bitching and moaning about how unfair the universe was.

My comment was met with silence so I prompted, "River?"

"It's dangerous work," he grumbled.

"Being a cop is dangerous work, honey," I gently reminded him.

River sighed and changed the subject. "Did Kiki decide if she was going to your birthday dinner tonight?"

"Oh, she decided all right," I huffed. "And in true Kiki fashion, she dramatically declined with the excuse she had to work since she now has rent to pay. She's being ridiculous about my parents asking their twenty-five-year-old daughter to pay two hundred dollars a month and threatening to move out of their basement. I mean, seriously, she's twenty-freaking-five. That's not a damn threat like she thinks it is. She should've already moved out of their damn house. But that's a bitch fest for another day."

"Sorry, babe. I know you wanted her there."

The hell of it was, River was right. I had wanted my sister to join us for my birthday celebration. But more, I wanted my sister not to be a raging bitch all of the time. I wanted a normal, healthy relationship with her. But her attitude made it damn near impossible.

"It's whatever. Kiki's Kiki. I'm used to it."

"What else is on your mind?" he asked.

"What do you mean?"

"You sent me a smiley face text instead of one of your snappy comebacks when I told you my night included handcuffs. I gave you the perfect setup and you dropped the ball. That's not *my* Letty. So, what's the deal?"

The deal was: I was thirty years old, single, I'd fallen for a man who lived in Georgia, one I'd never met in person and probably never would.

"Why haven't we ever met in person?" I blurted out.

"I don't—"

I quickly interrupted him, "Forget I asked."

"Babe, what's really going on?"

"I don't know. Nothing. Maybe I'm just feeling weird about leaving my twenties behind. Thirty feels like suddenly I'm a real adult and I should be looking into the future, making plans to settle down. You know, husband, kids, house—real adult stuff."

"You want to settle down?"

"Not right now. Besides, I haven't even been on a date in like six months. Maybe that's it, why I'm feeling weird. I just need to find a man and go out and have a good time."

That was a lie! I didn't want to find a man—I'd already found one.

"Right." River's clipped answer gave me hope, then that hope was quickly dashed when he continued. "You and Brook are in DC next month. Maybe you'll find yourself one of those book cover models you told me about."

We were indeed going to DC next month for a book signing and in an effort to get a reaction out of River I had stupidly told him there would be hot cover models there. It was juvenile and immature but all evidence suggested I was madly in love with River and I wasn't beyond childish antics to suss out if he felt the same way.

Clearly, he didn't.

And he'd avoided the topic of us meeting. Even if I'd cut off his answer, he never went back to my question and instead brought up the models.

I had to get my shit together and stop my imagination from running wild. This was not some happily ever after romance novel. River wasn't a hero who would rush in and save the damsel in distress. This was real life. He lived on the other side of the country. He had a job he loved and a family. I was a business owner and had my family here in Idaho.

We didn't work.

We never would.

I had to move on.

I was freaking the fuck out.

No, I wasn't freaking out, I was excited, scared, worried, happy, *and* freaking out.

My hands were shaking when I pulled up River's number and hit call.

I had a secret. A huge secret I couldn't wait to tell River about.

"Hey, Lets, what's good?"

Without preamble, I blurted, "I'm gonna be an aunt! Brooklyn's pregnant."

"Come again?"

I heard River's shocked reply but also voices in the background. I glanced at the clock behind the checkout counter and quickly did the math; it was after seven his time. I asked, "Do you have company?"

"No, I'm at the grocery store."

I steeled myself against wondering what River kept stocked in his pantry and how I'd never have firsthand knowledge of this and why that bothered me so much.

This was getting out of hand.

I needed to let go of the notion that one day River would be buying groceries for us, and that the food he purchased would be stocked in a pantry in a home we both lived in.

"Letty?" River snapped. "Brooklyn's pregnant? You didn't tell me she—"

"Don't get judgy," I interrupted him.

"Baby, you don't have to say that shit to me. You know I don't judge other people's life choices."

He was right; I knew that.

But...

"She met a guy in DC and they spent the night together."

"Christ, Letty, that's dangerous."

No, what that was, was interesting that apparently it was dangerous for Brooklyn to hook up with a stranger but months before, River had encouraged me to do just that.

"Well, obviously she didn't end up on a Dateline NBC Murder Mystery Special."

"I'm being serious."

"And so am I. She's pregnant, not sliced up."

She was also scared out of her mind to be a single mom.

"What's the guy say about her being pregnant? He's gonna do right by her and the baby, yeah?"

Maybe, if we could find him. So far, Brooklyn wasn't having any luck.

"So, what are the chances of you getting the name of someone who rented a hotel room?" I inquired and crossed my fingers for good measure.

"I don't understand what you're asking."

"Say, Brooklyn didn't know the guy's name but she remembers the room number and obviously the hotel."

River made a disgruntled noise and gave me the very unfortunate news. "I would need a search warrant for that information."

Damn.

That was the second no of the day. Earlier, Brooklyn had tried to hire an investigator in DC and the PI told her he couldn't help either.

"She doesn't remember his name?" River continued. "I hesitate to ask this since you're excited but was she drunk or—"

"No! She was one hundred percent sober," I cut in, not even wanting to hear the rest of his question. "And the one night, no-names was her idea. She thought..."

I trailed off, not knowing how to explain to River that Brooklyn, much like me, believed in love at first sight, soulmates, destiny. Brook had taken one look at this mystery man and had fallen in love. But I didn't know how to explain that to River. Or, I did know how, I was just too afraid of what his reaction would be.

"Letty?"

"I'm gonna be an aunt," I whispered. "Brooklyn's nervously excited. One day, I'll tell you the whole story but for right now I just want to be happy for her."

"Okay, baby. Boy or girl?"

I smiled at that.

"It's too early to know," I told him.

"Tell her I said congratulations."

And there it was, River was being River, giving me what I needed yet at the same time giving me nothing I wanted.

Such would be my life for the next five years as we grew closer and closer.

CHAPTER 4

"River, brother, you need to chill."

I slammed the beer bottle on Phoenix's table and narrowed my eyes on my younger brother sitting across from me. Then my gaze swung to my older brother who smartly kept his mouth shut.

Chill?

How had my life turned into absolute shit?

"I'm sensing you're pissed but I have to ask, is it really your place?"

Phoenix's question had my blood pressure skyrocketing.

"I don't know, brother, you tell me. Our sister goes to visit our father in prison and no one thinks to fucking call me? Not only that, she visits our bitch of a mother and no one fucking calls me about that either?"

"You were undercover," Echo cut in. "I stand by my decision not to tell you while you needed to be concentrating on the task at hand."

I'd heard that before—Letty said the same goddamn thing. It was the same fucking excuse she'd given when I questioned her about why she hadn't fucking called me when her sister, Kiki, went missing.

It pissed me off then and it pissed me off more thinking about it now.

But what really, seriously, fucking pissed me off was that shit was going down in Idaho and Letty was shutting me out. Her nephew Remington's father had shown up out of the blue, part of a force multiplier task force called Takeback, the U.S. Marshal Sex Offender Investigations Branch had set up. I'd worked with the Marshal service before. Their help had been invaluable in several cases. I myself had raised my right hand and been deputized a time or two. It was a well-known practice and the officers sworn in were known as force multipliers.

Letty had explained Takeback was working hand-in-hand with the Marshals on human trafficking cases and they'd shown up to rescue and dismantle an operation. This guy, Rhode Daley, was one of them.

Letty had not called when Kiki had gone missing.

She had not called when her parents were beside themselves with worry.

She had not called when she was struggling with her emotions.

She had not called when Remy's dad materialized.

She had not called me when Rhode was making moves to claim his family.

She had not called when Remy had been kidnapped.

The final goddamn straw was, she had not called me when her sister was murdered, even though I was home from my undercover assignment and would've been on the first plane to Idaho.

And in the months following Kiki's murder, Letty had pulled away and was dodging my calls and texts. Something she had not done *ever*. Not even after I missed my birthday text to her on her twenty-sixth birthday. She'd later admitted she thought I was lying about working when I was indeed training and had no cell service, and if I had, I still wouldn't have had time to text.

But now she was fucking ghosting me.

And I was goddamn pissed.

"C'mon, River, be honest," Phoenix started. "This isn't about Dad or Mom or what Shiloh did. This is about Letty."

I clenched my jaw to stop myself from lashing out. While I was doing that, I contemplated my stupidity. I had never hidden my relationship with Letty and the interesting way we met, and the entertaining albeit strange fact that I was friends with a woman I'd never clapped eyes on. Seeing as my brothers were not dumb they knew precisely when my feelings for Letty changed from a fun and amusing pal who lived on the other side of the country to something more. For the last five freaking years, Echo had been calling me out on my feelings for Letty, encouraging me to make plans to go to Idaho or have her come to Georgia.

But something held me back.

Fear.

I didn't want to shift our dynamic. I was too afraid of losing her, losing the only person outside of my siblings who understood me, knew all of my secrets. I couldn't fathom the possibility of Letty not being in my life. Her absence wouldn't crush me, it would destroy me.

I needed Letty like I needed air.

I couldn't live without her.

But neither could I bear the thought of losing her to another man. And that would happen. No man would want their woman texting and calling a male friend, at least not at the frequency we did. And no man would want their woman connecting with another man the way I connected with Letty.

My life was fucked.

The only good news was that Shiloh had found Luke Marcou, a former SEAL who worked for a local company called Triple Canopy. Luke had wasted no time putting a ring on my sister's finger. He was her perfect match, the one man on the planet who could give Shiloh Kent what she needed. So I wasn't even mad when Luke proposed while I was undercover.

I was pissed now though, at everything and everyone, especially Letty.

"It would take two seconds to find her address." Echo told me something I very well knew.

Over the years it had taken a great deal of willpower on my part not to look her up. Fourteen years ago when we first met, it would've been difficult to find her. Not impossible but it would've taken digging. Now with the internet and the information I knew about her, not to mention her sister's murder probably making the local news, I could have a full workup on Letty and her family in under ten minutes.

Yet, I refrained.

Part of me liked knowing my attraction to her was not physical. I loved Letty in the purest sense of the word. I loved everything about her and not one of those things was the color of her eyes or the shape of her body. Instead, I loved all the important things.

A few years ago she'd asked if I wanted to know the color of her hair. When I declined I heard the hurt in her beautiful voice. I couldn't explain that my denial wasn't an insult without giving away how much I loved her.

Her.

Just *her*.

Not the superficial shit.

"Holy fuck!"

Phoenix's outburst drew my attention. He was staring down at his phone and when his head tipped back and his wide eyes hit mine, I knew what he'd done.

He'd taken the two seconds I knew it would take and he looked up Letty.

"Don't!" I held my hand up and scooted the chair back. The sound of the metal legs scraping the hardwood floor irritated me even more. When was my baby brother going to grow up and buy real furniture instead of using folding chairs and a card table as a dining room set?

"Uncool, Phoenix," Echo grouched.

Instead of answering, Phoenix turned his phone in Echo's direction and I watched my older brother's eyes go big and round.

I didn't know if that was good or bad and I didn't want to know.

"I don't want to know!" I growled.

"Regardless of that picture, my opinion has not changed," Echo told me. "Boss up, brother, and get your ass on a plane before you lose her."

"What?"

"You've been in love with her for so damn long, I can't remember a time you weren't. So the question is, are you gonna continue to act like a baby or are you gonna go meet her?"

I'd never acted like a baby *in my life*. The Kent siblings never had the luxury of being juvenile or childish. At ten I was more mature than my father. Echo certainly had been. Shiloh was the only one who'd been minutely shielded from the bullshit that was our life.

"Fu—"

"Answer me, Riv, you willing to lose the woman? You've been home months, her sister was murdered, she's been pushing you away, and your ass has been crying in your Wheaties. What you have not done, which you should've done even if—no, scratch that, *especially* when she told you not to go out there for the funeral—was get on a plane. Now, you're still jacking around. Trust me, brother, you think you feel like shit now. You think your chest hurts and it's hard to breathe, wait until she finds a man and she's lost to you forever. Then you'll know what pain is."

Christ.

He was right.

So damn right.

But I had a job and a family here in Georgia. She had the same in Idaho.

Don't put the cart before the horse, idiot.

"Text me her full name, address, name of her bookstore, and the address to that. Also, find Rhode Daley and get me his contact information. He's employed by Takeback in Coeur d'Alene, Idaho."

I didn't bother clarifying who I was asking to get me the information; either of them would do.

"Do you want me to text you her picture?" Phoenix asked.

"Absolutely not."

"When are you leaving?" Echo inquired when I got to the front door.

"I'm going home to pack and then heading to the airport. I'll figure out a ticket when I get there."

"It'd be easier if you had a ride so you're not leaving your truck there."

Damn, he was correct. In my haste, I hadn't thought about parking.

"If you're up for it, let's go."

Echo stood, nodded at Phoenix, and we were out the door.

We jogged down the stairs. Before we separated at the parking lot, Echo slapped me on the shoulder.

"You're making the right call."

"I'm quitting my job," I blurted. "I'm facing a desk and you know that's not gonna happen. When I get back from Idaho, I'll sort something out."

"*If* you come back from Idaho," he returned.

"What?"

"If you come back," he repeated. "I love you, brother, we all do. But I hope you don't come back to Georgia, at least not empty-handed. But really what I hope is that you find what you're looking for and set up house out west and start living your life for *you*. Doing what makes you happy."

"What about you, Echo? When are you gonna start doing what makes you happy?"

"Shiloh's getting married soon. I predict you won't be far behind her. One day, Phoenix will pull his thumb out and realize it's time for him to start taking his life seriously and he'll find a woman. Then I'll find my happy."

Fucking hell, he didn't even try to deny he wasn't happy.

"Brother—"

"That's non-negotiable. That's the man I am and you know it."

Yeah, I knew the kind of man my brother was. The best kind there was. The kind who gave up everything for those he loved. The kind who would encourage me to move across the country to be happy.

Selfless. That was Echo Kent.

CHAPTER 5

For the first time in three—no scratch that, four months—I felt normal.

I'd rolled out of bed with a pep in my step and was ready to take on the day. It was the first morning since my sister died that I hadn't felt the crushing weight of guilt. I thought this was a good sign.

A healthy sign.

A sign I was ready to accept my sister was gone and having a normal, loving relationship with her was no longer an option for me.

That was the tricky part, the place where the guilt and near-constant regret came from. I'd never had a good relationship with Kiki. It was like she was incapable of being a nice person for more than an hour. And it sucked to think ill of the dead but it was the truth. Now she was gone and she'd died with me being furious with her, prepared to tell her she was figuratively dead to me. Then she became very literally dead.

But this morning, I'd woken up for the first time since she'd died and remembered she'd saved Remington's life.

The last breath she took had been for my nephew and I could no longer be angry with her.

My good day shit the bed when I opened up my kickass bookstore, Smutties, and Reese Turmel and Jack Donovan were waiting for me in the store—*in it*—when the door had been locked with the alarm set.

Reese and Jack worked with Rhode—or Dulles as I'd nicknamed him. And when Dulles decided he was staying in Idaho with Brooklyn and Remy, Wilson McCray—the leader of Takeback—didn't want to lose Dulles so he moved the operation to Idaho. Now all the guys—Reese, Jack, Wilson, Davis Wright, Cole Keniston, and Asher Noble lived in Coeur d'Alene. I secretly loved this. I adored how they were with Remy. And if I was being truthful I loved how easily they fit into all of our lives, which included my parents who had lost a daughter.

My nephew finally had his dad and with him came six new uncles to spoil him.

However, I still liked to give the guys shit, and since I was me, and had a flair for drama that meant I ratcheted it up whenever they turned their overprotective nonsense my way.

It was like having a horde of big brothers around.

"Why me?" I muttered as I walked across the store.

"Why not you?" Jack returned and I narrowed my eyes on him.

"You need better coffee, woman," Reese complained.

"You know who has awesome coffee? Treats Bakery two doors down."

A wide, lecherous smile formed on Reese's stupidly handsome face and at the same time, he wagged his eyebrows.

"Don't I know it."

"Please tell me you're not banging Sadie," I groaned. "She's one of the few people I really like."

Sadie Pierce was a sweet, quintessential girl-next-door type. She was pretty but not over-the-top made up or fashion-forward. Down to earth, salt of the earth, cute, and super nice. She also made killer muffins, cookies, and her cakes were out of this world.

"He wishes he was banging Sadie." Jack laughed. "He only knows how good the coffee is there because the last time he went in, Sadie dumped a very large caramel iced coffee with extra whip over his head."

"Noooo!" I chuckled. "Sadie did that?"

"Yup."

"It's called foreplay." Reese waved his hand like he was swiping the words out of the air. "She wants me. She's just not ready to admit it yet."

I could see Sadie wanting a taste of Reese. However, I couldn't see her actually going for it. Reese wasn't exactly her type. She liked quiet, reserved men. And there was nothing reserved about Reese—he was in-your-face outspoken. One of the many reasons I enjoyed Reese's company. He spoke his mind, much like I did.

"You're lucky you're hot, friend, because you don't have much going on between your ears."

"You think I'm hot?"

Reese smirked, and even that was hot.

"Please, you know you're hot. Too bad you're a pain in the ass and you have serious commitment issues."

Jack tossed his head back and laughed.

It must be said, Jack was good-looking, too, with the coolest coal-black eyes I'd ever seen. He was also a pain-in-my-ass big-brother type and too tall and big for my liking. I liked my men strong but lean, not giants that towered over me and looked like they could crush me with one hand.

Besides, for the time being, I'd sworn off men.

Without telling my hand to do it, I rubbed the ache in my chest.

"You okay?" Reese asked.

I was not okay.

I was heartbroken.

I missed River.

"No. You're in my bookstore bothering me," I lied.

"You love us."

It was a sad truth, but I totally loved them all.

"I have work to do," I declared haughtily.

"By all means, don't let us stop you."

A lightbulb moment struck.

"As long as you're here, put your muscles to work and help me sort the boxes of books I got in yesterday."

Two grown-assed, too-big-for-their-own-good men groaned like five-year-olds and stood.

The chime over the door rang, and I turned to see the finest, hottest, sexiest man I'd ever seen in my life walk into my bookstore.

Well, hello, handsome.

"Can I help you?" Reese boomed, and I wanted to kick him in the shins.

"Yeah, I'm looking for Letty."

Yes! Today was going to be an awesome day if this man was looking for me.

But before I could speak, Jack got in there first.

"And you are?"

"A friend."

My insides froze and my heart slammed into my ribs like a freight train.

I knew that voice.

I just didn't know the man.

"River?"

His icy blue eyes locked onto mine, and I shivered.

River. My Pen Pal, my Male BFF standing in my bookstore—something I never thought would happen—*ever*.

But there he was, and he was scowling down at me. And I say down because he was tall, *really tall*.

And he was gorgeous.

Sweet baby Jesus, I'd never seen a man so beautiful. And that was saying something since Dulles and his team of badasses were all so damn hot. But River? He was by and far better looking than any of them. He should've gone into modeling and not police work, though I could totally see him as Mr. July for the policeman's yearly calendar. With his uniform shirt unbuttoned, his hair glistening wet, with maybe some honey drizzled on his chest for good measure. And those ice-crystal blue eyes were incredible.

"Letty?" he muttered.

"What are you doing here?"

After knowing River for fourteen years, with seven of those fourteen being best friends, that was what I asked.

He couldn't hide his disappointment.

"I think you know why I'm here."

I did know why. I'd been putting much-needed distance between us. I needed to move on, and I couldn't do that while I was in love with him and lying to everyone. I'd laughed off Brooklyn's prodding so many times over the years then outright lied to her when I promised I wasn't in love with River. I'd evaded all of my mom's questions when she'd asked me about him and I told her we were just friends, that I didn't have any romantic feelings for him. My dad had even brought up River with me and I'd told him the same lie as I told everyone else. We were good friends and nothing more. Dulles and all of the guys—especially Reese —got in my face about how dangerous it was to talk to a guy I didn't *really* know.

Though I did know River, I knew everything about him, and there was a lot to know, which meant there was a lot to love.

And I'd been blowing him off more and more. Letting calls go to voicemail, not calling back for days, not answering text messages for hours after I'd received them, or ditto on the days. In the seven years since our relationship changed from texting once a year to daily phone calls, I'd never blown him off. I'd lived for those calls. I'd counted down the hours until I could speak to him.

"I needed—"

"Nope. No bullshit, baby. You forget I know you better than anyone. I know what you needed. I also know why you weren't letting yourself have it. I gave you time, hoping you'd sort your head. I waited for you to come to me. You didn't. You pulled further away. Time's up, Letty."

"Time's up?"

River didn't get a chance to explain.

A whole host of things happened at once. Reese moved closer to me, and River tore his gaze from me, and when it landed on Reese, it turned hard. Jack stood where he was, but his head turned toward the door. The chime sounded and in ran Remington with the exuberance of a very nearly five-year-old energetic boy. Dulles and Brooklyn came in behind their son at a much slower pace. I barely registered Brooklyn's wide-eyed shock when she caught sight of River before my nephew hit me full force and wrapped his little boy arms around my hips, then jumped up and down, jostling me with his excitement.

"Seven days until my birthday, Auntie Letty!" he shouted.

"Seven days? That can't be right," I teased.

"Auntie Letty!" Remy huffed. "Seven days!"

God, I loved my nephew.

"Well, it's a good thing I already bought all your presents then."

"Can I help you with something?"

Dulles' question pulled me from the awesome moment I was sharing with Remy, reminding me River was there. Not that I actually forgot, but I was stalling for time.

What was a woman to do when she was in the same room as the man of her dreams?

What was *I* supposed to do now that the man I was in love with was in my bookstore and I was facing imminent rejection?

I wanted to run and jump into his arms like I'd dreamed about a million times.

I didn't do that.

I stood frozen with my heart pounding in my chest and the breath stolen from my lungs.

I should've run to him.

I should've told him the truth, years ago.

It would've made the whole scene less painful.

CHAPTER 6

"Whoa!" Remington shifted away from his aunt and looked me over. "You're tall!"

The kid was exactly how Letty had described him. Every sentence he spoke was punctuated with an excited exclamation mark.

"My brother Echo's taller than I am," I told him.

"Echo? That's his name?"

"Are you River?" Brooklyn inquired.

My gaze went from Remington to his mother but before I could answer, Remy cut in.

"Your name's River?"

"Yep."

"Cool name! My name's Remington Steel."

I heard Rhode groan then gently reprimand his boy. "What'd I tell you about introducing yourself to strangers?"

Remy's head tipped back and his lips pinched closed as he stared at his dad and pondered the question.

"Not to do it," Remy muttered.

At that juncture, it wasn't my place to inform Rhode I

was not a stranger. I'd known Letty and through her Brooklyn and Remington long before he knew them. My line of thinking might've been a stretch to some, but in my mind, it was not. Throughout Brooklyn's pregnancy, I'd received almost daily updates. I was the first person Letty called after Remington was born. And throughout the years, I'd been kept up to date on all things Remy and Brooklyn. However, it would serve no purpose to tell Rhode any of that. It would also make me an asshole, bringing up all that Rhode had lost out on—by no fault of his own, or Brooklyn's. I also knew how hard she'd tried to find him to no avail.

"River Kent?"

My gaze swung to the man who'd said my name. It wasn't a question, so I didn't answer. Further, I found it interesting he knew my last name. Letty and I had never exchanged our full names, so she wouldn't have that information unless she looked me up.

"How do you know his name?" Letty rejoined.

"Babe," the man answered and my stomach revolted.

Babe?

What the fuck?

"Don't babe me, Reese. How do you know River's last name? I've known him for years and I didn't know his last name."

"And that right there is exactly why I looked into him," Reese returned.

Anger swelled.

This was not going as planned.

Reality finally sank in.

Rhode Daley had come into Letty's life months ago and when he did he brought his team with him. Letty had been pulling away since then. My gut clenched and a new wave of irritation rolled through me.

I was too late.

She'd found someone else.

Fucking hell.

My Letty. *My* best friend. She'd found a man and didn't tell me. Or maybe she had been telling me, not with words but with deeds, and I hadn't been paying attention. Gone were the late-night conversations. Gone were the sharing of our days, the whispered secrets, the bitch sessions when one of us had a bad day, the teasing, joking, and laughing.

She didn't fucking tell me.

That didn't hurt; that fucking *crushed* me.

Bitterness crept in and before I said something regretful —in front of Remy, no less—I needed to leave. I took a moment and glanced around Letty's bookstore. Immense pride at all she'd accomplished filled me with regret. The two warring emotions were too much to bear. She'd done it —everything she'd set out to do. Smutties was cool as hell and she'd made it a success. Yet I felt crushing regret that I'd never get to share with her how proud I was of her, how for years I wanted to be right where I was now—in the place she loved most in the world, finally meeting her face-to-face.

But not like this.

From the time I'd left my house yesterday, to the flight, to lying awake in a hotel knowing she was close, it had never entered my mind she could be with someone else.

I shouldn't have waited.

My gaze landed on an overstuffed purple velvet chair in the corner and seeing it felt like a stab in the heart. I could remember Letty's excitement when she found it at a yard sale and how her dad had grouched about it weighing a ton.

Looking at it now, I could see why; the thing was huge and likely was a bitch to carry in.

Thoughts tumbled through my mind in slow motion, one after another until it felt like I'd been standing there for hours but in reality, it was only seconds.

"That was really uncool, Reese!" Letty growled and I was jerked back to the present. "I trusted you with something that meant something to me and you went behind my back."

Meant—past tense? Again, what the fuck?

"Lets, I was—"

"She's right," Brooklyn interrupted. "I understand why you did it, but it was still uncool." When Brooklyn was done with Reese she looked over at Rhode and asked, "Did you know he was looking into Pen Pal...I mean, River?"

Pen Pal.

Christ, I hated that nickname only a step above Male BFF. Letty was my best friend but she was so much more than that.

"Sugar—"

"Rhode! How could you?"

"You asked me to talk to Reese. I did. He didn't feel like standing down so he didn't. That was months ago, and I'll remind you, neither you nor Letty have heard a peep out of him about it since. So, yes, I knew he'd looked into River. I know what he found. And I know that none of it was bad or we would've had a conversation about it. The last thing I'll say is this; you know what we do for a living. You know the cases we see. And, Sugar, you know damn good and well none of us are gonna stand by while Letty continues to talk to a man she's known for fourteen years but has never met. That shit is dangerous."

I bit the inside of my cheek to stop myself from lashing out. The cop in me agreed with Rhode. If the situation involved Shiloh, no way in fuck I wouldn't have investigated the man in her life. Hell, I'd looked into Rhode Daley and his team as soon as Letty told me about him. But Letty being who she was to me, it annoyed the fuck out of me that they'd looked into my life.

There was a lot of shit to find. Ugly shit that Letty mostly knew about, but I didn't like strangers knowing the details of my life.

"Reese!" Letty shouted.

"Oh, boy." Remy stepped away from Letty. "This is what Pop calls dramatized."

"Remington!" Letty snapped.

"What? That's what Pop says. When your face gets red like that and you start yelling Pop says it's dramatized. Not me. I don't say that. He thinks you should move to Holly-weird. Not me. I want you to stay here with me."

"Brooklyn's the brains. Letty's the fun," I murmured and smiled.

If I had a dollar for every time Letty good-naturedly complained about her dad calling her dramatic and Brooklyn her polar opposite—the calm and the brains in their friendship—my entire trip to Idaho would be paid for.

"How do you know that?" Remy asked me.

"Your Aunt Letty's a good friend of mine."

"Do you know my mom, too?"

I glanced at Brooklyn and as strange as it was, I did. It might've been the first time I'd laid eyes on the woman, but I knew a lot about her.

Thankfully I didn't have to answer.

"Remington Steel, no birthday presents for you," Letty humphed.

"She doesn't mean that, boy," the other man in the room said then stepped closer to me with his hand stretched out.

"Jack Donovan," he introduced himself. "That's Reese Turmel. We work with Rhode but I assume you know that already."

"I do," I confirmed. "Good to meet you."

We shook hands and when we separated Reese stepped forward.

Jesus, Letty's man was going to shake my hand.

"River," Reese stated.

"Reese," I returned and we shook.

Next, it was Rhode's turn and now that some of the shock of the situation had worn off it was plain to see Remington was the spitting image of his father. I couldn't see any of Brooklyn in the boy, which was a shame; she was a pretty woman.

"Was wondering if we'd ever get to meet you," Rhode said as he gripped my hand. "Good you're finally here."

Well, hell.

I didn't know what to say to that.

"I know!" Brooklyn exclaimed. "Since I'm here why don't I work the store today and you and Pen Pal...damn, sorry. It's gonna take me a minute to remember to call you River."

"Why would you do that?" Rhode asked. "Letty knows my name but she still calls me Dulles. Seems fair you call River, Pen Pal."

That wasn't going to happen.

"You should be grateful she settled on Dulles," I told Rhode. "They used to call you Ragnar."

"Why did Auntie Letty call my dad Ragnar?" Remy asked.

Damn. The kid was so quiet I forgot he was there.

"Because she thought your dad looked like a Viking."

"What's a Viking?"

Rhode chuckled and I explained, "They were big, strong warriors who ruled the sea."

Remington's eyes rounded and he smiled when he said, "I wanna be a Viking! Do they paint their faces and crawl through the mud to find bad guys?"

"We'll talk about Vikings later, bud." Then to Brooklyn, "I'll take Remy fishing and be back around at closing to pick you up."

"Perfect. C'mon here and give me some love before you leave."

"But it's Sunday," Letty weakly argued. "You don't work Sundays."

"I do today," Brooklyn contradicted.

"But Reese—"

"Nope." Reese held out his hand and backed away from Letty. "You're not throwing me under the bus. Go on and handle your business. We got the store for the rest of the day."

Wait.

What?

My eyes landed on Letty and it hurt to look at her. Actual, physical pain that made my chest ache. It was not her beauty, which was abundant. It wasn't her flawless skin. It wasn't her slender, tall frame. It wasn't her long black, shiny hair or pert nose, or her gorgeous hazel eyes. It wasn't even that she was more stunning than I dreamed she would be.

It was the fear I saw.

It was the way her eyes darted around the people in the room, silently begging one of them to rescue her from me.

Fuck that.

Anger surged and I was beyond done with the scene. I damn well deserved an explanation and I was getting one.

"But—"

"Letty," Brooklyn started. "River's *here*. He's here, *right here*. I'll handle the store."

Letty's face softened and some of the sour in my gut dissipated but quickly rushed back when Reese spoke up.

"Let me know if you need to cancel tonight."

Fucking hell, this couldn't have gone worse.

CHAPTER 7

What the hell was wrong with me?

I was Letty Leeola Welsh—named after my grand-mother on my mother's side who was known far and wide for being a precocious child who grew into a beautiful, clever, outspoken woman. When I was younger I'd spent a great deal of time studying her every move—all the things that made her, her. And since I had watched and learned I became exactly the woman I wanted to be.

And this unsure, skittish, cowardly woman was not me.

I was unpredictable, high-spirited, lively, but mostly I spoke my mind and lived life as bravely as I could with my heart on my sleeve. Consequences be damned.

Except when it came to admitting how I felt about River.

Boss up, Letty, and lace up your big-girl combat boots.

Not my best pep talk but as sucky as it was it worked on some small level seeing as I squared my shoulders and prepared to face time alone with River which would be excruciatingly painful. Talking to him over the phone had become damn near unbearable, especially after my sister died and he'd listened to me cry for hours. And the absolute worst part was he knew all the right things to say—or not to say, as it were. He hadn't offered me empty platitudes, he'd given me permission to be angry at Kiki. It might've sounded bad, but at the time I was furious that in life my sister had been a royal pain in the ass and at times downright mean, but her final act was so incredibly selfless and giving I hated her for it. I hated that in her final moments on earth she was the sister I'd always wanted, that her last breath proved she had it in her to be sweet, kind, and loving. And that was all I'd ever wanted from her.

But she robbed me of the chance to know that person.

In the days after Kiki's murder River had been my rock and it hurt—horrifically hurt knowing he could be that for me but only as a friend.

So I pulled away.

Instead of asking him to the funeral then waiting for the proper time and admitting I'd fallen in love with him, I'd turned into this cowardly twit.

No freaking more.

It was time I faced the music.

River had been a good friend to me, he deserved an explanation.

But first I needed to answer Reese. Then River and I could leave.

"Don't try to get out of poker night just because you blew your wad last week and now you've got three more car washes and two extra laundromat runs. I'm keeping a tally —that's seven washes and five turns at the Coin-O-Matic. Tonight's double or nothing; bring your a-game, big boy."

"Don't worry, babe, I'm *all* game."

River grunted, Reese smiled broadly, and Jack laughed.

"Brother, your game sucks. Maybe we should invite

Sadie and watch poor Reese go down in flames on multiple fronts."

"What's this about Sadie?" Brooklyn asked.

"Reese hit on her and she dumped a large caramel iced coffee over his head," Jack supplied.

"Sweet Sadie?" Brooklyn sputtered.

"I didn't hit on the woman. I just complimented her on her firm muffins," Reese defended.

"No game," Jack muttered and shook his head.

"Miss Sadie has the best muffins," Remy piped in.

"She sure does, boy." Reese chuckled.

His lewd comment which thankfully went over my nephew's head caused the men in the room to bust out laughing—everyone except River. He was openly staring at Reese with narrowed eyes.

What was that about?

River's gaze skittered from Reese to me and I couldn't quite read his look, but if I had to guess it would be confusion—which confused me.

"On that note, we're out of here," Dulles announced.

Father and son walked to the door. Jack and Reese gave me chin lifts but it was Jack who spoke. "We'll move those boxes and help Brooklyn restock the shelves."

"Thanks. I owe you."

"I'll take a batch of double chocolate chunk cookies and a pan of brownies and we'll call it even," Jack informed me.

Reese stopped at the mouth of the hallway that led to the back room and craned his neck to look at me over his shoulder.

"My payment will be an invite to your next book club meeting." He completed his request with a wag of his eyebrows.

"Never gonna happen."

"Never?"

"Are you gonna read the book?"

"Fuck no."

"Then, no, you're never invited, you creep."

"Letty?" Brooklyn called my name and when she had my attention she continued. "You and River *really* should go somewhere and talk, honey."

I glanced back at River. The confusion had dissipated and anger etched his handsome features.

Why did he have to be so damn good-looking? Not that it made a difference; I wasn't a shallow bitch, I'd fallen for him without knowing what he looked like. But River looking like he did rubbed salt in my fresh wound.

I could stare into those blue eyes forever.

"Ready?" River clipped.

Oh, yeah, he was pissed and I had some explaining to do.

"Yeah, let me grab my purse."

Brooklyn met me at the counter where I'd stashed my purse and she leaned in close.

"What's wrong with you?" she hissed.

"Nothing."

"Bullshit! Pen Pal's here and you look like someone who's stepped in dog shit."

"I do not."

"Sister, you're lying. You've been lying for so many years I think you've forgotten how to tell the truth."

"I am—"

"In love with him," Brooklyn finished my thought, adding her own twist, making that statement true when I was going to again lie and tell her I wasn't a liar. "And you haven't smiled at him once."

Brooklyn was right, I hadn't smiled at River. I was too

busy freaking the fuck out. It had taken a lot of energy and control not to run and throw myself into his arms. Not to touch him. Not to kiss him.

"I can't do this right now."

Brooklyn leveled me with a look that was full of censure.

"You have until tomorrow to pull your head out of your rear end."

"Brooklyn."

"Tomorrow, Letty. I won't let you blow this opportunity. I've kept my mouth shut and covered for you. I backed you up with everyone including Rhode and repeated the stupid lie that you're not in love with him. Either you tell him and straighten it out or I will."

"You wouldn't."

"Letty, my sister, my best friend since forever, you bet your ass I'll fix this for you before you do something stupid and lose him." Brooklyn's face changed from fierce to soft and sweet. "I love you and want you happy. I love you and want you to have everything you've ever dreamed of having. I know you, Letty. I've known for a long time that Pen Pal was your one and only. He's here so why are you fighting it?"

I didn't have time to fully explain how scared I was.

"I'll call you later," I evaded. "And thanks for giving up a golden Sunday to help me out. I appreciate you."

"You can show me how much by calling me later to tell me you're taking the next week off to participate in a seven-day sex-a-thon."

"Dulles and the guys are rubbing off on you."

Brooklyn rolled her eyes and smiled.

"Right. We'll blame it on the guys and pretend we're not surrounded by some of the hottest romance novels ever written and we don't avidly read them, live in them, and fantasize about the heroes."

I had nothing to say. Brooklyn was correct on all accounts. But life wasn't a romance novel.

"Why are you still staring at me when your happily-ever-after is standing by the door impatiently waiting for you?"

And there it was—Brooklyn had the HEA. Against all odds, the hero had found her. He swooped in and claimed his heroine and in doing so gave her everything.

But that was not my story.

River wasn't Dulles and I wasn't Brooklyn.

"Happy people suck," I whispered.

"Why? Because we want the people we love to be just as happy as we are?"

"Yes!"

"Stop your drama and go talk to River."

I didn't respond.

I hefted the strap of my purse over my shoulder and walked to the door. I didn't drag my feet *like I wanted to*, I didn't lollygag and waste more time *like I wanted to*, nor did I fake a heart attack which would've been over the top even for me *like I wanted to*.

"Ready?" River asked when I got close.

That was a loaded question with a thousand replies.

I settled on the simplest of them.

"Yes."

River held open the door and I held my breath. But before I could get it back the door to Smutties closed and River grabbed my hand and spun me around. I hadn't yet recovered from the miraculous feeling of River's hand around mine when he dropped his chin and leaned close.

"What the fuck was that?"

I was in a daze, too busy freaking out that his lips were mere inches from mine. I could barely think yet I managed to get a few words out.

"What the fuck was what?"

"You letting your man talk about—"

"My man?"

What in the world was he talking about?

"Reese."

The haze of River's proximity wore off enough for me to understand what he was really asking.

"You think if Reese *was* my man, which he is absolutely not, I'd put up with him flirting with the hot, shy baker who also happens to be my friend? And not only that but I'd stand idly by while this was happening and join in on the conversation?"

"Didn't think you would until I witnessed that shit firsthand."

I yanked my hand in an attempt to break free but River tightened his hold.

"Let me go."

"He's not your man?"

"Why would you even think that?"

River flinched and I watched as he wet his bottom lip and my mind went back to how close his mouth was to mine. Even in a snit with my feelings hurt I couldn't stop myself from wondering how he'd kiss.

"Fuck," he whispered and my eyes went back to his.

The blue of his irises was startlingly beautiful in the sunlight.

"I'm sorry, I fucked up and made assumptions," he said.

Straight out he admitted it and apologized.

It was hard to hold onto a snit when the other person admitted they were wrong, and the polite thing was to let it go. But I was Letty—therefore, I was well versed in drama and holding grudges.

"You should be sorry," I snapped. "First, you assumed I

was some sort of idiot woman who'd let her man behave like a monumental prick—if Reese was my man, him going to Sadie's bakery not to buy his coffee but to flirt with her would make him an ass. Then bragging about it, not only in front of me but with our friends would make him a bigger ass and me a chump. I'm not a chump. Neither is Reese an ass. And second, you hurt my feelings thinking I was that kind of woman."

"Said I was sorry, baby, and I am. I was an asshole. I've got no excuse and fucked shit up royally."

Again, he'd apologized but I wasn't ready to give up.

"It wasn't supposed to go like that," I told him.

"What wasn't?"

"Our first meeting."

A spark lit in those crystal blue eyes and my belly whooshed and my womb contracted.

"How was it supposed to go, baby?"

His words were light and breezy and they carried through the air until they wrapped around my heart but the hand he'd placed on my hip drew all of my attention as his fingers dug in and heat radiated through my t-shirt like a brand.

"You were supposed to see me and—" I caught myself at the last second and clamped my mouth closed.

"I was supposed to see you and what?"

"Nothing," I dodged. "You weren't supposed to do anything."

The light in his eyes dimmed and I hated that it was gone.

"Is there someplace we can go to talk?"

No, I didn't want to talk. I wanted to do a multitude of other things that would not include conversation.

But wisely, I didn't tell him that. Instead, I suggested,

"Treats is two doors down and Sadie does make the best muffins in CDA and I promise she doesn't normally dump coffee drinks on her customers."

"Somewhere private," he clarified.

My belly fluttered and the numerous things I wanted to do with River came rushing back. High on that list was getting the light back in his eyes. Another priority was getting my lips on his. Not far from that was making him laugh, something I worked hard to earn, something I hadn't heard in weeks. And I missed the sound. Actually, I missed everything about him.

"We can go to my place."

River's fingers flexed, then he let go and stepped away.

I immediately felt the loss.

"I'll follow you."

"I walk to work," I absent-mindedly told him.

River glanced up and down the very obviously commercial street. My bookstore was in the downtown area of CDA, right in the middle of all the action. Foot traffic during the spring, summer, and fall was amazing. I was three blocks up from the lake and one block over from my favorite Greek restaurant. Rent was a whack but worth it. I could walk to work most of the year—okay, some of the year I could walk to work comfortably and some of the time I walked to work freezing my ass off. But it wasn't until winter truly hit that I drove.

"You walk to work?"

"No sense in driving when I live less than a mile away."

River's head tilted and he studied me.

"How did I not know that?"

I shrugged and answered, "I don't know."

"So you walk home in the dark."

It wasn't a question and since it wasn't and he was now

giving me narrowed eyes I decided to avoid the topic and asked, "Do you want to walk or do you have a rental?"

"I have a rental." He pointed across the street to the mammoth SUV with Wisconsin plates.

"Jeez, River, were you planning on adopting a family while you were in Idaho?"

"Woman, I'm six-foot-three."

"How did I not know you were six-foot-three?" I muttered.

The corners of River's lips curved up and he mimicked my shrug. "I don't know."

After that, he grabbed my hand, waited for traffic to clear, then mostly dragged me across the street. I was thinking about how long his legs were, how it took two of my steps to one of his to keep up with him, and I was looking at his shoes. He had big feet, big hands, big everything. I hadn't yet stopped pondering his size when he beeped the locks and opened the passenger door. Wordlessly I climbed in. River shut the door and I lost sight of him when he rounded the back of the SUV.

How was this happening?

Why in the world was River in Idaho?

The drive to my apartment was awkward, the only conversation—if it could be called that—was me giving him directions. Thankfully the drive was short. River was parked before I could give in to my natural inclination and started babbling. I wasn't fond of silence, less fond of the uncomfortable kind. And normally I would fill it with useless jabbering.

My dad had often said I could talk to a brick wall and carry on a one-sided conversation with it. He wasn't wrong. But right then, and during the time I led River into my building, up two flights of stairs, and down the hall to my apartment, I was mute. I had too many thoughts rushing through my head which would normally have me talking a mile a minute; however, for once I was unable to speak.

I opened the door, gestured for River to enter, but before I followed him into my tiny studio apartment I steeled myself against what was to come.

River was there for a reason.

And whatever his reason was it was going to drastically change my life.

And *that* scared the hell out of me.

CHAPTER 8

I didn't bother looking around Letty's apartment. Though I did note it was tidy and her bed was tucked into a corner off the living space, and there wasn't a television in sight but instead a wall of bookshelves. That was my Letty. She didn't watch TV unless we were doing it long-distance over the phone, then she watched the show on her computer. She mostly read, something I'd always loved. As curious as I was to finally see where she lived there was something more important on my mind.

"Let—"

I got no more out before Letty abruptly interrupted. "How long have you known my last name and address?"

"Less than twenty-four hours," I told her.

"You looked me up," she accused.

"Technically, *I* didn't look you up, Phoenix did."

"Why would he do that?"

Because he was my brother, loved me, and he knew I was in love with her.

I didn't tell her that. Instead, I took her in. No, I drank her in. The woman I'd spent years getting to know, the woman whose sexy voice I'd spent thousands of hours listening to, the woman whose personality had hooked me, the woman whose kindness and loyalty I'd fallen for. It was a shit thing to think, but in my mind, I'd always pictured Letty as passably pretty. It was my experience the more beautiful the woman, the more of a pain in the ass she was. There were very few exceptions to this rule.

Letty was an exception.

"River?"

I did one last top-to-toe, uncaring I was openly checking her out and when my gaze landed on hers. I took another moment to soak in the beauty staring back at me.

"How did I not know you were so beautiful I'd forget how to breathe?"

I heard her swift inhale, I saw her pretty hazel eyes flash, and felt the vibe in the room change.

I needed to rectify my colossal fuck-up and the only way I was going to accomplish that was with honesty. But first I needed to know if I had a clear shot.

"You rightly set me straight about Reese and I hope you know my apology was sincere. It was uncool I lost my temper and made assumptions. I wish I could take that back and start fresh, but since I can't do that I'm gonna start now and ask, are you seeing someone?"

She shook her head and mumbled a no.

Perfect.

"I'm not making excuses, but you've been pulling away," I started and watched Letty shut down. "And when I heard Reese call you *babe* and admit he looked me up, I made the wrong call and thought he was your man. At the time, the pieces fit. You started backing away from me around the time Rhode and his team showed up. Just so you know that's where I was with that, that's why I made the assumption."

"Reese is a good friend."

I'm a good friend, too.

Letty's response did nothing to ease the tension in my gut. Reese was a good-looking guy; I could see Letty finding him attractive and I'd been treated to the familiar interaction between the two of them, teasing and comfortable. They very obviously knew each other well.

A nasty ball of jealousy formed.

"Why'd you pull away?"

"I didn't—"

"I've known you a long time, Letty, I've *never*, not one time lied to you. And as far as I know, you've never lied to me; let's not start doing it now."

"Kiki—"

"Oh, yeah, baby, we're gonna talk all about your sister after you explain to me why you pushed me away. Why you fucking crushed me when you refused to let me come to her funeral. Why you forced me to stay in Georgia and listen to you struggle with how she died instead of letting me come to Idaho like I wanted. Why after all these years you'd rip us apart and in the process tear my goddamn heart from my chest. *I'm* your best friend, not fucking Reese. *I'm* the one you turn to. *I'm* the one who knows the history. *I'm* the one that should've been at your side. And we're gonna talk about why you didn't fucking call me when you thought your sister had been taken. I'm a cop, Letty. My brothers and sister are cops. If I couldn't have gotten out of my assignment one or all of them would've been on a flight to Idaho to take your back and help look for her. But you didn't call."

"You were undercover. You told me you'd check in when you could. You told me not to worry if there were long stretches when I didn't hear from you," she weakly defended.

"That's your excuse."

I wasn't asking a question; I'd heard that explanation before and it still sounded like bullshit.

"It's not an excuse, it's the truth."

"It's shit, Letty. Fucking hell, you know you're more important—"

"I didn't want you to see it, okay! I didn't want you to see!"

The pain in her voice bounced around the room before it hit me in the chest and seeped in deep.

"See what?"

"None of it. All of it. Me breaking apart. I didn't want what we shared to be contaminated with you feeling sorry for me."

What the fuck?

I didn't get to ask what she meant by contaminated before her hands lifted and her fingers pushed into her hair at her forehead and she fisted it.

"I didn't want you to see me weak and falling apart. That's why I didn't call you. And after that, after we found out Kiki wasn't missing, that she was just behaving like a spoiled brat and not answering our calls, making all of us worry I was so pissed off I didn't want you to see that either. You're close with your siblings. You love them, and at the time I hated my sister for what she'd put my mom and dad through. They were beside themselves, in pain, scared to death, and Kiki was being Kiki, acting like a monumental bitch. The whole thing was messy and ugly and I didn't want you to see it. Brooklyn, she knows how it is. She grew up with my sister. But you? You were the only person I had who meant something to me that was clear of it, not touched by my sister's selfishness and I didn't want that to change. Then in the biggest mindfuck she could've ever perpetrated she threw herself in front of a bullet and saved Remington's life."

Fucking hell.

Letty sucked in a breath and her face twisted when she spat out, "Why'd she do that, River? Why'd she die saving him?"

"Because, baby, deep down she loved Remy. She loved you and Brooklyn and your parents," I told her softly.

"I didn't want to be loved *deep down*," she seethed. "I just wanted to be loved. I wanted to love her. I wanted a sister. Now I will never know if what she did was some type of fluke or if under all of that childish jealousy there was a good person. She took that from me."

"She did," I agreed. "But, baby, does it matter? She saved Remy's life."

"By giving hers."

"Yes, by giving hers."

Letty's movements were jerky and agitated when she pulled her hands free of her hair and dropped them to her sides.

"I didn't want you to see this. It's not supposed to go this way."

That was the second time she'd said both of those things.

"You've said that, but you still haven't explained how it was supposed to go."

"We weren't supposed to meet this way."

Well, that was clear as mud.

"How were we supposed to meet?"

Letty shook her head and changed the subject. "Why'd Phoenix look me up? Why'd you come here?"

Truth time.

"Because I've been acting like a miserable fuck and my

brothers aren't stupid; they know it's because you've been dodging me. Last night we were having dinner together and they called me on it and called me out for being an idiot. Phoenix had your information pulled up before I could stop him. Ten minutes later I was driving to my house to pack."

"Why?"

Now I was getting pissed. There was no way she was so clueless she'd have to ask why I was there four months after she'd suffered a loss. And not just a loss but a monumental blow that had taken her from me.

"You know why, Letty."

She'd lost the indignation but her eyes were still troubled as she continued to stare at me.

Without telling myself to do it, just needing to be near her, I closed the distance between us and didn't stop until I was in her space and my hands went to her hips.

"You know why," I repeated.

At that, those unusual, pretty eyes of hers widened.

"River."

So long I'd waited to watch my name form on her lips. So fucking long it felt like millennia.

"You're my girl and you've been that from the start. For fourteen years I've kept you with me. The first six years, I didn't get it, why I couldn't let go and forget you. Why every year on your birthday I reached out hoping you hadn't changed your number. Why I held back and would only allow myself to connect once a year. Then one morning you called and I knew why I'd held on yet at the same time holding back." My thumb stroked the bare skin just above the waistband of her jeans while my other hand traveled around then up along her spine until I cupped the back of her neck. "At twenty-two, I was too young but smart enough to understand I wasn't ready. And I was proven right at twenty-eight. Five minutes into our first phone conversation and I was drowning in you."

After all this time, all the years, all the waiting—I was done and it was time for Letty to know. I slid my fingers into her silky hair, wrapped the long length loosely around my fist, tipped her head back, and waited for the barest hint she was on board. This took effort and a good amount of it but when Letty's gaze dropped to my mouth I knew she was where I needed her to be.

"I'm gonna kiss you, baby."

I watched her lips part and her breathing accelerate. The vision of that small gesture scored through me and I felt my cock twitch.

Every day, sometimes dozens of times, I wondered what it would be like to have Letty's hands on me, my mouth on hers, what kind of sounds she'd make, what she'd feel like, how she'd taste. And seeing as she was right there, where I'd imagined her thousands of times I wondered what the fuck I was waiting for.

I dropped my mouth to hers and my tongue swept her bottom lip. Her lips parted and I felt the air rush past as she moaned. Couple that with her hands going under my shirt and finally having them on me I shivered—an honest to God full-body tremble.

Good Christ.

My hand on her hip lowered to the curve of her ass and hauled her closer until her body was molded to mine and I deepened the kiss with a growl. Her hands moved down my back, slipped out from under my shirt, then I felt them go between us. I had no choice but to break the kiss and drop my hand in her hair when she yanked her shirt up. Once it cleared her head Letty tossed it aside. My gaze dropped to her chest and I took my fill. The white lace of her bra screamed innocence but her full breasts spilling over the delicate material said something entirely different. The contrast had my cock throbbing, my mind reeling, and my body at war with itself.

"Fuck, you're gorgeous."

"River."

Hearing my name in that breathy whisper snapped what was left of my control.

"I feel like I've waited a lifetime to watch you say my name," I told her and lifted my hands to frame her face.

A slow, wide smile formed.

No, *now* she was gorgeous.

So fucking gorgeous my blood heated.

"A lifetime to see that smile," I continued.

"Riv—"

I didn't let her finish.

My mouth slammed down on hers. A moment later the kiss went electric, a second after that I was walking her to her bed, two seconds after that Letty was flat on her back and I was staring down at the most stunning sight I'd ever seen.

A dream fourteen years in the making.

CHAPTER 9

River Kent.

My real-life fantasy.

No—better than a fantasy. Better than a dream.

Too good to be true was more like it.

I watched as his heated blue eyes roamed my body. I watched as they grew hungry when they skated over my exposed stomach. They flared when he stopped to take in my breasts. They softened when his gaze skimmed over my face and locked onto mine.

I felt every place his eyes had lingered. My skin tingled, my heart pounded in my chest, and my mind blanked.

"Christ," he rumbled.

Then his hands went to the bed next to my hips and his big body curled deep and his lips were on my belly. It got better when his tongue swirled around my belly button before he made his way up, stopping to kiss, sometimes to nibble, other times to drag his teeth along the way until he got to the inside curve of my breasts. It got astronomically better when one hand lifted off the bed and yanked my bra cup down, giving River the access he wanted. But he didn't move.

As a matter of fact, his body had turned to stone.

"River?"

His head tipped up and when I caught his gaze my breath caught.

He was *amazing*. Everything about him perfect.

"Give me a minute, baby." His thumb swiped my nipple and I arched into his touch.

I wasn't sure why River wanted a minute but I'd give him forever if it meant he continued to look at me like we were the only two people in the world. Like there was no other place he wanted to be. Like we had all night and if we didn't he'd make it so we did. His gaze was so intense he made me forget how jaded I'd become. How the ugliness in my life had consumed my every thought. How I avoided my parents just so I didn't have to see their pain.

I wanted to forget everything. I wanted to rewind my life to a time where I still believed in happily-ever-afters. I wanted my family whole and my sister still breathing. I wanted to go back to a time where I was blissfully unaware of the evil that lurked.

"Baby?" River murmured.

I blinked until his handsome face came back into focus.

"You're here," I returned just as softly.

"Christ, Letty."

"It's always been—"

My words were cut off when there was a very loud knock on my front door. I lost River's eyes when he craned his neck to look over his shoulder. The knock came again, this time louder accompanied by my name being shouted.

"Shit," I muttered and pushed against River's chest.

"Letty? Are you in there? I need to talk to you," my neighbor called out.

"Crap."

"Letty? It's an emergency."

That did it. River rolled and shot to his feet, taking me with him.

"Who is that?" he asked.

"My neighbor. Well, downstairs neighbor, Mrs. Simpson. She's ninety but lies and says she's eighty-three."

River was across the room in a flash, stopping to tag my shirt off the floor. He lobbed it in my direction. Not waiting to make sure I was decent he opened the door.

"Everything okay?" River inquired, blocking the opening with his big body.

I smoothed my shirt down and rushed to his side just to hear my neighbor purr, "Why, hello there, young man."

I rolled my eyes to the ceiling and in my head counted to five. That was as far as I got before River spoke.

"Ma'am, you said you had an emergency. Is everything alright?"

"Yes, yes. Everything is just fine. I'll come back later."

I couldn't see River's face but I didn't need to, to imagine the confusion that must've been written on it. This, too, was my response the first few times Mrs. Simpson banged on my door claiming there was an emergency only to find out the woman simply wanted to share gossip or tell me about something she'd seen on TV. Last year when her grandson came to visit from California he'd set her up with the inter-net. Since then her "emergencies" had multiplied times a hundred.

It didn't matter how many times I explained ninety percent of what she read on the internet was untrue, she still came running.

"Mrs. Simpson," I called and River stepped to the side.

I'd been doing a damn good job ignoring the flutter in my belly his presence evoked until his arm lashed out and he tucked me to his side.

Why now?

After all this time why did he show up now when my life was in ruins? When my head was so screwed up I didn't know if I wanted to drop to my knees and beg him to stay or kick him in the shins and make him leave.

I could lie to Brooklyn. It was mean and she'd be pissed at me if she ever found out but she was rightfully caught up in Rhode and Remy and their new house. She was flying high and I would not be the one responsible for bringing her down. Not after everything she'd been through. Not after finally finding Rhode. And if I was being truthful as much as I loved my nephew and Brooklyn, I adored Rhode; he'd lost so much time with his son and Brooklyn was willing to do anything to ensure nothing invaded his happiness—that included lying to my best friend.

But I couldn't lie to River. Forget the tiny fact he was a police officer and could likely sniff a fib from a mile away; he knew me—every secret, every dream, every frustration, everything.

I couldn't hide from him.

I didn't *want* to hide from him.

Then there was the issue of me being in love with him. But if what had transpired was any indication, it was possible he felt something toward me—which would make him being there worse.

Can you say, basket case?

"I thought I saw you come in," Mrs. Simpson said, her eyes darting from me to River then back to me. "Though I missed your gentleman caller."

Gentleman caller. The old woman was a hoot. And any other time I would've laughed but right then with my stomach in knots, my heart in pain, and my mind on the fritz I didn't laugh.

"Mrs. Simpson, this is River Kent. River, this is Mrs. Simpson."

"Ma'am," River greeted her. "Nice to meet you."

"Georgia?" She noted his slight accent.

"Yes, ma'am."

Mrs. Simpson gave River a wide, licentious smile that had him stepping closer to me. The smile widened further until it practically split the old woman's face and she acknowledged River's maneuver with a wink.

"Well, are you going to invite me in or am I gonna stand out in the hall all night like a vagabond?"

There was no time to explain to River that if he invited Mrs. Simpson in she would indeed be there all night and it wasn't even three in the afternoon. Since I couldn't warn him I could do nothing when he shuffled us back and allowed her entry.

On a normal day, I didn't mind Mrs. Simpson's company. Actually, I welcomed it, as she was interesting and funny when she wasn't being paranoid the world was coming to an end. She was classy and worldly when she hadn't watched *To Catch a Killer* or a Dateline Special and had convinced herself that we had a serial killer living in our building.

But that day was not a normal day. That day I'd met the love of my life—in the flesh. And if that hadn't been enough to send my brain into a tailspin, kissing him definitely did it.

As mentioned, Mrs. Simpson was ninety, yet there was a reason she got away with telling everyone she was eighty-three; the woman didn't look a day over seventy. Not only that but I'd bet she could walk a 5K though she'd never do it because that would mean she might break a sweat and as she'd told me numerous times when she'd caught me in the lobby on a hot summer day sweat on a lady was unbecoming. Thus I paid no mind to her waltzing into my house, but River unhooked his arm from around me in preparation for an accidental fall.

"You look like one of those men," Mrs. Simpson announced.

I groaned and River went on alert.

"What men?"

"One of those men that Letty associates with."

River's eyes sliced to me and I quickly explained, "She means Rhode and his crew."

"*She* has a name and *she* is sitting right here," Mrs. Simpson corrected. "A beverage would be nice, dear." There was a pause before she looked at River and ordered, "Have a seat, young man."

I shouldn't have done it, but I couldn't stop the giggle from escaping when River's panicked eyes widened.

I couldn't blame Mrs. Simpson—ninety, eighty-three, or a hundred you'd have to be dead not to notice River's extreme good looks. But more than River being off-the-charts hot, Mrs. Simpson was a flirt—with everyone. It was how she got Mr. Lars, my upstairs neighbor who was sixty, to carry in her groceries. It was also how she got our mailman to hand-deliver her mail to her apartment instead of placing it in her mailbox in the lobby.

Not only was she a flirt but was the spitting image of Liz Taylor. Perfectly styled jet black hair with artfully placed streaks of silver, obviously painted by a hairdresser. Her makeup was done and heavy, including kohl-lined top lids complete with the bottom of her eyelids winged out, giving the corners of her pale blue eyes the appearance of being tipped up. And she was dressed—as in dressed to the nines like she was going out to dinner at a five-star restaurant. Eliza Simpson sat in her apartment dressed to impress, not because she would be going out but because it was deeply ingrained in her to always look her best.

So, there in my small apartment Mrs. Simpson had on a nice dress, a string of pearls around her neck, diamond studs in her ears, and a diamond tennis bracelet. She was also flashing River a sultry smile and come-hither eyes.

"Something funny, my dear?"

"Nope. Nothing's funny, Mrs. S."

"I really wish you wouldn't shorten my surname like that. It's so...common."

"Mrs. Simpson's a bit of a snob," I shamelessly told River.

"I am nothing of the such."

"Right, that's why I keep a two-hundred-dollar bottle of Cognac in my cabinet that only gets brought out when you come up for a natter."

"Letty Leeola Welsh, never in my life have I had a *natter*," she spat. "As I've explained, only the best passes my lips." She paused purely for dramatic effect, making a show of eyeing River from the top of his head all the way down to his boot-clad feet. "And I'm happy to see, you, too, have exquisite taste."

"Letty," River mumbled and shifted uncomfortably.

"Come, River, let's get acquainted."

"Oh, go on, she's harmless."

Mrs. Simpson gave an over-exaggerated sigh but didn't correct me referring to her as if she wasn't in the room. One of her many pet peeves.

I barely contained my laughter as River strode woodenly to the empty chair across from Mrs. Simpson.

I busied myself in my kitchen and asked, "What brings you up, Mrs. Simpson?"

"Oh, right." She waved her hand in front of her face. "I need to enlist your men and I'll pay."

I'd given up reminding her that Rhode and the guys were not my personal crime-fighting force. And I'd often wondered if introducing her to Wilson McCray, Takeback's team leader, had been a mistake that backfired. But a few months back she'd worked herself up into such a fit when the body of a missing woman was found in a National Park in Montana I had no choice. Mrs. Simpson swore she'd figured out who the killer was. Having Wilson speak to her was my way of stopping her from going to the police. But now, she thought the men were at her beck and call.

"Mrs. Simpson, they're extremely busy and I heard them talking the other day. They have a job in Las Vegas—"

"This is important," she cut me off. "I found something."

I poured a healthy measure of Cognac into a crystal tulip glass I bought especially for these occasions and tried to find the right words to put Mrs. Simpson at ease.

I didn't get the chance before River asked, "What did you find?"

Shit.

"I was on Reddit. Do you know the website?"

"Yes, ma'am."

Shit on a shingle. Reddit and Yahoo Message Boards were worse than a Dateline Special.

"Children are being sold," Mrs. Simpson said matter-of-factly.

"Come again?"

"They call it re-homing—"

"Mrs.—"

I started but River interrupted, "Hang on, baby, I wanna hear this."

And there it was, the cop's interest had been piqued.

"Some of the children are free to a good home, they said," Mrs. Simpson scoffed. "Can you imagine that? These are children, not animals."

Free to a good home? Surely the old woman misunderstood what she'd read. No one would give away a child on the internet.

Right?

The internet was monitored. There was no way children were being trafficked out in the open. I'd heard the guys talk about the months—sometimes years—of investigating it took to take down trafficking rings.

"Mrs.—" I tried again but got no more out.

"I'd like to see this Reddit," River told her.

"Of course." Mrs. Simpson smiled. "Let me go down and straighten up a bit."

Mrs. Simpson stood and River followed. She glanced over at me with a Cheshire Cat smile. She'd gotten what she wanted but it wasn't her I was concentrating on, it was the deep lines creasing River's forehead that had me worried.

This had to be another one of Mrs. Simpson's crazy emergencies. I couldn't believe people would be so brazen they'd commit something as terrible as giving away a child out in the open for anyone to see.

Right?

CHAPTER 10

It went against the man I was not to walk the elderly woman down to her apartment. But before we went down I needed a brief from Letty. It was obvious Mrs. Simpson was lonely. Further, it was obvious the woman viewed Letty as a companion. I had to admit as soon as Reddit was mentioned I was ready to dismiss the conversation until Mrs. Simpson brought up re-homing. That was not a term a ninety-year-old woman should know. Hell, most people didn't know what that is and would never come across any discussions on the topic.

However, before we got into Mrs. Simpson and what she might've stumbled into I had to get a few things straight with Letty. Or more accurately, clue her into where we were going.

"Something you should know about Mrs. Simpson," Letty started.

"Before we go there, we need to talk about something else."

Letty dipped her head, suddenly finding the glass she'd

filled with Cognac extremely fascinating. It was not the tactic I expected.

Letty was ballsy. She always spoke her mind. She was the one who quit her job to follow her dream of opening a bookstore and she accomplished that in a week. She was scary ambitious and got more accomplished in one day than most did in a week.

So, no, Letty diverting her eyes was not what I was expecting. Though something had changed in the last few months so perhaps I should've. That change was part of the reason I was in Idaho.

"Baby?" I called.

"Hm?" she mumbled but didn't look at me.

"Letty, look at me."

Slowly, so slowly that, if I didn't know better, I'd think she was shy. But I knew differently. I knew *my* Letty was lively and outgoing. So seeing her slowly lift her eyes to meet mine annoyed the hell out of me. Not because I was impatient but because it was then I realized something was seriously off.

After what felt like a year, her eyes finally caught mine, and my gut clenched at the pain I saw. Pain so stark she couldn't hide it. A moment of indecision hit until I remembered the woman who I'd spent years falling in love with.

This was not the real Letty.

This pale version of the vibrant woman wrecked me.

"Honest to God, baby, you're killing me."

Her shoulders jerked and her brows pinched but none of the hurt left her eyes.

Eyes that I'd dreamed of seeing. Hazel but more green than brown with an added hint of blue around the irises. A window to a soul so beautiful it was only fitting they'd be just as stunning.

Top to toe, inside and out, Letty was the most captivating woman I'd ever seen. There was no doubt she was attractive, but her allure was bone-deep, it was all-encompassing, intrinsic. It was a need that couldn't be denied.

"What?"

"I know you," I reminded her. "I know everything about you. I know every detail about your life from the smallest trivia to your deepest fears."

Those creases on her forehead deepened when she narrowed her eyes.

"Okay."

"What I'm saying is, you're not hiding it. You can't hide it from me."

"I don't understand what you're talking about."

"Don't lie to me."

Her hands came off the counter and went to her hips. Some of the pain faded and anger sparked.

"I'm not lying to you."

"Baby, you are. You've been lying to me for months. Excuse after excuse why you're pulling away. Why I couldn't come after—"

"Don't say it."

Fuck.

There it was; the pain resurfaced with a vengeance.

"Letty—"

Her hand shot up, palm outward, holding off my words. Her head was also shaking so violently her hair was whipping around.

It sucked I had to do it, but I wasn't letting her off the hook.

"We're talking about this. Especially the part about you not wanting me to see you as weak and falling apart. You're mine, Letty. *Mine*. And you fucking know it. You should've called me, you didn't, so we're moving on from that. But not before you understand there's not one goddamn thing weak about loving your sister, being scared that she's missing, being pissed off, sad, hurt, or confused that she's gone. That's love. That's family. That's not falling apart, that's fucking *love*."

"You don't understand," she hotly returned.

"I damn well do. My father's rotting in jail serving a life sentence for murdering a cop and he's dying. I hate the motherfucker with every cell in my body. I've wished him dead for over half my life. He's embarrassed me and my family. He's a stain on society. He's a piece of shit. He's mean and nasty. Yet, someplace deep inside of me, I don't want to acknowledge that he's actually going to die. I can't say that I'm sad, but I feel something for a man who doesn't deserve an ounce of emotion.

"Good or bad, that's family. It can be beautiful or it can be ugly. Your sister was complicated, but that's family, too. Sometimes it's messy and annoying but under that, it's based on love. That's what you had with her. She's gone, Letty, and you have to stop lying to yourself and the people around you who love you, and admit you're in pain."

"I'm not yours," she whispered.

"Really? Out of everything I said, that's the takeaway?"

"But I'm not."

"Hark back, Letty. Not even twenty minutes ago I had you on your bed with my tongue in your mouth, and if we hadn't been interrupted you know exactly where that was going. But even before I laid eyes on you, you were mine and you have been for years." Letty's eyes turned wild— panicked and wild—but I pushed on. "You were mine when you called excited about Brooklyn being pregnant with Remington. You were mine when you called me from the hospital when your dad had that spill and he broke his arm and the doctor found his cholesterol was so high he was courting a heart attack and you were scared out of your mind. You were mine when Gunner died and you were the first person I called after I left the vet's office. I could do this all night. I have fourteen years' worth of texts and six years' worth of calls. I've changed phones at least ten times and I still have every single phone because back then your old texts wouldn't transfer to my new phone and I couldn't bear to lose a fucking word you'd sent me."

"River," she breathed.

"Yeah, baby, you're feeling me now and I haven't even reminded you of the hours we've sat on the phone. The nights we watched TV together. The times we fell asleep on the phone. All the times you texted to check to make sure I was home safe after a shift. Our relationship might've started in the weirdest of ways but there is no denying we have a relationship. I know you better than I know Echo, Phoenix, and Shiloh. Christ, Letty, I've been in love with you for so long I can't remember a time I didn't love you."

From across the room, I heard her draw in a breath. I watched as her head dropped forward, her hands went to the edge of the counter, and her hair curtained her face, blocking my view. But I couldn't miss the way her shoulders shook.

"Letty?"

"You can't love me. Not now. Not after...not now." She finished with a shaky breath and my jaw clenched.

"Not after what?"

Letty's cell rang and her gaze sliced to the phone with a mixture of relief and hope. She thought she was getting out of the conversation.

"Don't answer that." I gave zero fucks my demand made

me sound like a prick. "Answer *me*, Letty. I can't love you after what?"

She remained silent but at least she was looking at me again.

Her phone continued to ring. She continued to stare at me with fire blazing in her eyes. Her posture was stiff and the air around us downright hateful. But again, I'd take Letty pissed and angry over sad any day.

The shrill ringing stopped and I remembered something I'd somehow forgotten—Letty was stubborn as fuck. I figured she could stand there all damn day and not say a word.

"All right, baby, since you're not gonna talk, I will. I think you're scared. I think you've been in love with me for just as long as I've loved you and now faced with something real you're afraid. Just guessing, but I think you saw Brooklyn and Rhode get together and it got you thinking about your life and what you want. Instead of coming to me, admitting your feelings, and taking a risk, you pulled away."

"Just to point out, *you* hid your feelings, too."

Right, there it was; the *too* in her rebuttal was an admission she likely didn't want to admit. But it was now out there and I was going to use it to my advantage.

"I'm standing right here in front of you. What's that say to you?"

"It says that your siblings got tired of you being grouchy and Phoenix looked me up and forced you into coming."

Damn. I had told her that and there was a tiny sliver of truth in her statement.

"In all the years you've known me has anyone ever forced me to do something I didn't want to do?"

She didn't respond because the answer was fuck no.

"I'll give you this, I waited because I was afraid of screwing up something important to me. I was scared if I told you how I felt it would change things between us and I wasn't at a place in my life where I could face losing you. You'd become everything to me, our friendship was everything. But something I realized when you pulled your shit and took yourself from me was, I will never be in a place where I'd be okay losing you. I'll never not look forward to talking to you. You'll never not be the best part of my day. So here I am laying it out. I can't tell you any clearer, I can't make it any more plain. I love you and I will not lose you. And, Letty, I know you love me. So whatever's fucking with your head, we're gonna straighten it out together. I don't know why you think I can't love you but I'm gonna figure it out. I know you and because I do I know you're gonna be stubborn, you're gonna fight me, you'll use that brilliant mind of yours to come up with thousands of excuses. But, check this, I'm gonna win. I'm gonna make you believe. I'm gonna fight harder than you and I'm not going anywhere. Strap in, Letty, it's about to get bumpy."

Letty's phone started to ring again and she reached out to grab it. When she saw who was calling she frowned and took the call.

"Hey," Letty greeted. "Everything okay?" The was a pause then all traces of her earlier agitation vanished. "Damn, this is the second shipment this month." Another break, this one longer before Letty went on. "Would you mind calling the customers? The invoices are on my desk in the red folder. Just let them know the books came in and were damaged and I'll call them when I have an ETA on the new shipment." She stopped speaking but was nodding her head to whoever was talking. "I appreciate you, Brook. I'm coming back to the store now—"

"Babe, we gotta go down and talk to Mrs. Simpson," I cut in.

"Crap. I forgot," she said to me then to Brooklyn, "Mrs. S came up and said she had an emergency. River and I are going down to her apartment to see what she found. Hopefully, it won't take him long to dissuade her of whatever calamity she's convinced herself is imminent. When we're done there I'll be in."

While Letty was finishing up her call I glanced around her living room and once again noted all of the books. There must've been hundreds. There didn't appear to be any rhyme or reason to their placement on the shelves. They were almost messy, like she picked one, read it, and when she was done shoved it wherever it would fit. For some reason, I liked that. A long time ago she told me she preferred paperbacks but due to space restrictions she'd invested in an ereader and had thousands of novels on the device. Seeing all the paperbacks, I figured she'd greatly understated what was on her ereader.

"Ready?" she asked, pulling me from my perusal.

"When was the last time you sat and relaxed with a book?"

"What?"

"How long has it been since you read a book?" I pointed to the shelves.

"Yesterday. A new-to-me author sent me a copy to read. She wants me to stock—"

"No, baby. Not for work. How long has it been since you read one of these?" I motioned to her collection again.

"I don't understand what you're asking."

I wasn't sure what I was asking either. But I knew Letty used her books to lose herself. She'd explained it hundreds of times but I never got it because I didn't particularly enjoy reading and it wasn't something I'd do for pleasure. I glanced around again, seeing hundreds of books haphazardly placed on shelves but there wasn't one on her coffee table, or on her nightstand, or on her kitchen table. Maybe she put it back between the times she was reading but I didn't think so. Which meant, my Letty, the woman who loved books, loved stories, loved all things fantastical, wasn't reading.

"When was the last time you sat in one of these chairs or laid in your bed and read a book to relax? Just for fun. Just to get lost in someone else's head and get out of yours?"

I watched Letty flinch then swallow and I knew it had been a while.

"I've been busy."

That was a lie. She'd been no busier than she normally was.

I let the topic drop knowing I'd already pushed my luck far enough and calling her on her lie would only make her retreat.

"We'll talk to Mrs. Simpson, then go back to your store. After that, we'll grab something to eat."

"River—"

"Then I need to go to the hotel and grab my shit so I can check out."

I waited, and I had to hand it to her; it took a whole ten seconds before she could no longer contain her alarm.

"You're leaving?"

"No, baby. I'm staying with you."

"Staying with me?"

"Yup."

"We need to—"

"We need to get to Mrs. Simpson's and you have important shit to take care of at the store and I'm starving."

Letty gave me an *eat shit and die* look.

I ignored that and walked to her front door and opened it.

"It's really uncool you keep cutting me off when I'm trying to talk."

She was absolutely right, it was a dickhead thing to do. But we didn't have time for another argument and until I puzzled out what was going on in her head, I wasn't listening to what she said. I was going to listen to what she didn't say. I was going to pay attention to her body language. But mostly, I was going to hold on to the knowledge that she loved me whether she was ready to verbally admit it or not.

The rest? I was going wing it.

What I wasn't going to do was give up.

CHAPTER 11

"River," I whispered as my heart clenched and my stomach revolted.

He continued to scroll down the webpage on Mrs. Simpson's computer, shockingly reading faster than I was capable of doing because I wasn't finished with the horrifying comment before it was gone and he was on to the next.

Sweet mother of God, Mrs. Simpson was telling the truth.

Free to a good home.

I read it with my own two eyes that were now in desperate need of bleach. I didn't want to know this kind of stuff really went on, much less did I want to read the *disgusting* comments asking questions about the child in question.

"Baby, go sit with Mrs. Simpson," River all but growled.

"Is this real?" I asked, still whispering.

"Yes."

My heart lurched and fury spiked. Something came over me that I'd never felt—a murderous rage, the need to find this person offering the child to strangers and rip their head off.

This was not adoption.

The child in question *had* been adopted but was being given away because the mother said he cried too much. Cried. The child was two. Two year olds cry. They also throw tantrums and have to be fed and probably still have accidents in their pants.

He cries for no reason and never shuts up.

Those nine words were forever marked on my heart.

"That's despicable," I hissed.

"It is that, Letty. It's also something worse. Go sit with Mrs. Simpson, I'll be done in a minute and we'll go to the bookstore."

I didn't want to know what worse was so I stood up from where I'd been leaning and reading over River's shoulder and walked into Mrs. Simpson's living room.

Unlike me, she had a two-bedroom. Her floorplan also had a separate dining area whereas my apartment was one big open room. The dining room wasn't so far away that Mrs. Simpson, who'd been perched on the edge of her couch, couldn't watch River and me while we were on her laptop and I knew she'd been watching with an eagle eye.

Mrs. Simpson was nosy. That was why she always had the best gossip. She was also watchful and that was how she figured out what angles to play to make people spill their secrets. She was a sneaky old broad.

"I know who he is," she informed me.

"You should, seeing as I introduced you to him not even an hour ago," I returned.

She glanced up toward the ceiling and shook her head before she looked back at me and shook it again. "Don't be common."

I couldn't stop myself from smiling at her snub.

But as amusing as Mrs. S was—and she was funny—I wasn't in the mood to talk about River and I had a feeling I knew where she was leading the conversation.

"When's Joshua coming for a visit?"

Josh was her grandson. Her much-loved and adored grandson who she could and did talk about for hours.

"You know he got a new job in Texas," she huffed.

I did know all about his new job working for an aero-space corporation as an engineer.

"Is he enjoying Texas? The heat's not too much for him?"

Mrs. Simpson leaned forward and pinned me with a disapproving stare.

"I know what you're doing and I know why. I also know that young man is the reason you haven't had a date in a very long time and why the men you have gone on dates with never get a second one. I'm going to tell you something, Letty, and I hope you open your ears and hear me—do not waste your life. Do not waste time. I had sixty-five years with Oscar and sixty-five years was not enough. I'd do anything to have one more day with him. I look back and I regret every day I didn't spend with him. I see you're still hurting and I understand the pain of losing family. But, dear child, you're wasting your limited number of days on this earth."

The ugly ball of guilt I'd just that morning thought I'd rid myself of came back with a vengeance.

I was hurting but that wasn't the problem. I was *angry*. So angry it ate away at me. And seeing the grief in my parents' eyes made it worse. They were mourning the loss of their child and all I could think about was if my sister hadn't been such an asshole when she was alive and hadn't gravitated to criminals she'd still be alive and my parents wouldn't be in agony. If Kiki hadn't insisted on being a hateful, jealous, ungrateful human my mom and dad wouldn't look like their world had crumbled.

Who thinks that?

Who hates their dead sister?

Suddenly I couldn't catch my breath. Unfortunately, this wasn't new. It happened every time I thought about my parents. My chest would get tight and the shame of avoiding them would set in.

"Baby?" River called and I slowly dragged my gaze to him. "Ready to go?"

There he was, my every dream come to life and I couldn't for the life of me allow myself to have him.

I will never be in a place where I'd be okay losing you.

I love you and I will not lose you.

I didn't tell River I loved him back. I didn't tell him if I lost him I would forever be devastated. I didn't say anything because I was a fool. For as far back as I could remember I was a diehard romantic, I believed in fairy tales; I believed with a certainty born from years and years of living inside my books that one day my Prince Charming would sweep me off my feet. But now I knew better. Now I knew that life didn't work that way—bad shit happened and I couldn't take any more.

I'm gonna win. I'm gonna make you believe. I'm gonna fight harder than you and I'm not going anywhere.

River couldn't win. I couldn't let him get wrapped up in all the ugly surrounding my life. Tonight I would tell him he needed to go back to Georgia and maybe one day...

"Letty?"

"Yeah. Right. I'm ready."

I ignored the disappointment on my neighbor's face—something else I was becoming skilled at doing—and said my goodbyes.

On the drive back to Smutties, River had the decency not to bring up what happened in my apartment. It had been a long time since I'd kissed a man but even if I kissed one yesterday River's kiss would've erased any memory—I knew this to be true because he had wiped my mind clear the moment his lips touched mine. Best kiss *ever*. There was no comparison. Within seconds I was desperate for more. I needed to feel every part of him.

"Do you think Wilson McCray would mind me giving him a call?" River asked.

"Is it that bad?" I stupidly inquired and rushed to correct myself, "That was silly, of course it's *that* bad. What I meant to ask is, shouldn't we report it to the police?"

"Yes, we should report it and we will, but I know how these things go. Local police will have to call in the Feds, and that takes time. Wilson's got direct ties to SOIB; if he calls his contact the ball is set in motion a helluva lot quicker."

"What's SOIB?"

"Sex Offender Investigation Board. Wilson's team works with the Marshals SOIB and Missing Children Program. They're force multipliers and have the capability to move fast."

I had no idea how River knew so much about Takeback, so I asked, "How do you know all of that?"

River didn't make me wait for his very thorough, very scary answer. "Letty, did you think I was going to let anyone into Remington's life, or Brooklyn's, or yours, without a background check? As soon as you told me Dulles showed up and I had a name, I ran him. Once I found his involvement with Takeback I ran every man on the team and looked into their operations."

I didn't know how to feel about that. Actually, that was a

lie—River looking out for my nephew made my heart swell. Looking out for me and Brooklyn from the other side of the US made my stomach flutter. It also made me nervous.

"You looked into them?"

"I've worked with the Marshals warrant squad a few times over the years and I've kept in touch with them. And you know I was undercover in Florida."

It wasn't necessarily a question. Of course I knew he was undercover but I answered anyway, "Yeah."

"My unit was tracking a gang that we thought was distributing drugs they were smuggling in through Miami. Our source got me in with the guys in Miami. The drugs were a sliver of what they were doing. The real money came from transporting guns to Puerto Rico. The Marshals Fugitive Task Force was already tracking the shipments and asked that we hold off on our arrests until the guy they were gunning for made an appearance. And they already had their Gang Enforcement Unit in play. I got close to a Deputy Marshal so when I asked him what he knew about Takeback and Wilson McCray he got me the information I needed to put my mind at ease that the men who had inserted themselves into your life and Remington's were good men. After that, I left it alone."

River had occasionally breached the surface of his job. But he was careful with the information he divulged about his work. I never really thought about how much he was holding back until right then. I wasn't a dumbass, I knew being a police officer was dangerous, and working with gangs would up the danger factor by a hundred, but I still hadn't grasped the risks he took. Especially going undercover.

"Did the Marshals get the guy they were after?"

A beat of silence passed and as River pulled into a

parking spot close to the bookstore I was beginning to think he wasn't going to answer.

He killed the ignition and turned his head to look at me. His expression was blank and his voice was flat when he said, "Yes."

That sounded good so I didn't understand why he seemed almost haunted.

"Did you get the guys you were after?"

"Yes."

"Then why do you look upset?"

With absolutely no inflection or emotion River explained, "I got word an exchange was going to take place. Everyone would be in one place. The fugitive the Marshals were after was buying the crates of weapons my guys had smuggled to Puerto Rico. I was able to call it in and make an excuse why I wasn't going to be at the drop."

"Wait, you were in Puerto Rico?"

"Yep. I'd been there almost a month. We were all on edge because negotiations were taking so long. The longer we were there the more of a chance the fugitive caught wind the Marshals were there and the harder it became for me to communicate with them. Everyone was getting antsy when a price was finally agreed on. The takedown was planned, everyone was in place, then at the last minute, the location was changed. We didn't have enough time to vet the new location and when we went in, shit went sideways."

When River trailed off I quietly asked, "What's that mean?"

I held my breath, unsure if I wanted to know but needing to understand because River was now openly troubled.

"The new location was the fugitive's packaging site. Later, after the hell of that night was over and only one person from the gang was alive we would learn that part of the payment was to be made in drugs."

"Only one person?" I whispered.

"It was a bloodbath. The fugitive, six members of the gang I was tracking, and all sixteen of the fugitive's workers. The fuck of it was, the fugitive took out his own people. He mowed them down, that was his priority. Kill anyone who could implicate him and testify."

"I'm sorry, honey."

River had been looking directly at me the whole time he was talking, hadn't taken his eyes off of mine, yet he was now staring at me like he'd never seen me. His head tilted just a tad, his right eye twitched, but barely just enough for me to notice and his big body relaxed.

"Never shared that side of my job, baby, but you have to get what I do. The life I lead when I go undercover isn't pretty. For months at a time, I'm with the dregs of society."

"I get that," I confirmed.

"But still, I'd never seen a man so ruthless. There wasn't a moment of hesitation. So what I really mean when I say we *got* the guys we were after is they're all dead, and we *killed* them."

The emphasis on killed wasn't lost on me. Nor was the way his face hardened when he said it.

"I get you're trying to convey something important, River. I'm just not understanding what it is. I don't mean to be insensitive, but I learned something recently, and that is, criminals when pushed into a corner, do not care who they hurt—they kidnap children and murder unarmed women. So you and your fellow law enforcement officers didn't kill anyone as much as you protected yourselves and potentially saved countless good people who could've had the unfortunate occasion of running into a member of the gang. I understand the result was death, but honey, it sounds like you're holding on to something that you shouldn't be."

"Yeah, baby, I'm holding onto a lot of stuff that is mine to carry. I called in the location. I missed that drugs were part of the negotiation, and I sure as fuck missed the part about those drugs being packed by mostly women and a twelve-year-old boy. They're all dead, too, and baby that's on me."

I couldn't stop the gasp that tore from my throat. More evil I didn't want to know about. More disgusting, vile evidence that there was something seriously wrong with the world we lived in.

"You're getting it," River muttered.

"Yeah, I'm getting that people suck. That somewhere out there, right now, a child is packing up drugs for a dealer. That a mother is giving away a little boy because he cries too much. That revolting atrocities are happening all around us, and there's more evil than I ever imagined, and there are not enough people like you to make them stop. I also get that it's totally fucked-up that the good guys who protect and serve have to live with the marks on their souls when they're forced to take a life while the bad guys don't give two fucks. Trust me, River, every day, it's becoming clearer and clearer. I've spent my life with my head in the clouds, not paying a lick of attention to what's really happening."

"I can't argue that people suck," River agreed softly and lost some of the hardness around his eyes before he continued. "But Letty, you're forgetting that I do what I do—Rhode, Wilson, Jack, Reese, Davis, Cole, and Asher do what they do, my sister and brothers do what they do—so the population as a whole doesn't have to walk around in fear. I'm not saying you shouldn't be aware of your surroundings but you cannot dwell on the bad shit. It will drive you crazy.

I'll also agree you and your family were hit with tragedy, and baby, we have to talk about that—"

"No, we don't. You know what happened and there's nothing more to say."

River narrowed his eyes and leaned in close when he delivered a verbal blow that stole the oxygen from my lungs. "You know, Letty, you did nothing wrong. Your parents did nothing wrong. Kiki made every decision that led to her death. I know this sucks and it fucks me to say it but Kiki bought her end. Now, I'm not saying she deserved to die but she made the choice to run with a motorcycle gang and not a good one. She decided to hook up with the president, then lie to him and get her ass tossed out of the club. It was her choice of friends that stole from a pimp. A fucking *pimp*, Letty. The man was selling ass and I don't care the women he pimped called themselves high-class call girls, the man was a pimp and there's never a good kind of those. It wasn't like Kiki didn't have a good, loving family offering to pull her out—she did. You all tried. So in the end, what happened to her was on her. But she died saving Remington's life and that has to account for something. But up until that, every choice she made was wrong."

"I can't talk about this."

"You can but I get that you don't want to. But you need to understand now that at some point we'll be talking about your sister."

River got out of the SUV, leaving me winded and gutted.

He was right about what he said but he was so very wrong.

I hadn't tried to help my sister.

I'd turned my back on her.

CHAPTER 12

An hour later I was sitting in an overstuffed purple velvet chair in the corner of Smutties watching Letty and Brooklyn talk to a customer while Wilson, Reese, and Jack sat in nearby chairs with their tablets out looking over the internet links I'd sent them.

As soon as we'd walked into the store, Letty had called Wilson then handed the phone to me while she dealt with a box of damaged books. Five words into me introducing myself, Wilson had cut me off admitting he knew who I was and that Reese had shared the file he'd put together about me with the rest of the team. I returned the favor and told him that I'd looked into him personally as well as every man who'd be spending time with Remy, Letty, and Brooklyn. To Wilson's credit, he tried to mask his irritation—*turnabout's fair play*. I explained what Mrs. Simpson had stumbled on, what I'd read, and what I found when I dug a little deeper. Twenty minutes later he was at the store with Reese and Jack.

Now, they all had identical scowls of disgust.

What I hadn't told Letty—and wouldn't—was that 'free

to a good home' was a line of bullshit. Nothing in the world of human trafficking was free. But you had to know the marker words to decipher the code these scumbags spoke in. The child in question was being offered in trade. And if you knew what you were looking for you'd find the original poster was leading commenters to a message board. It was a sick and twisted game played out in the open and the fuck of it was on the surface it wasn't entirely illegal. It appeared the mother was at her breaking point, needed a rest, and was offering to give guardianship over through power of attorney for a specific period of time until she could get back on her feet. A mental break is what the mother was claiming.

"Jesus," Jack ground out. "These sick fucks never cease to make me want to puke."

He was not wrong.

"How'd you know what you were looking for?" Wilson inquired. "I would've missed the message board."

"A few years ago we had something similar to this in Georgia. Wasn't my case but the whole station was talking about it. The case in Georgia was a Facebook support group for adoptive parents. A father came in and reported some of the posts creeped him out and gave him a bad feeling. The officer taking the report agreed and referred it to our sex crimes unit. What the father thought was parents making arrangements to rehome their children without using the courts and child protective services was actually a cover for trafficking. Just like with this Reddit group the Facebook users were directed to another site, a Yahoo group. It was beyond sick what these fuckers were doing. My captain at the time instructed the sex crimes unit to educate all of us on what to look for in case something like that ever came up again."

Wilson continued to study me then asked, "Right, but how'd you figure out the name of the message board?"

"That, friend, was good old-fashioned detective work." I smiled. "Original poster made mention of the child crying uncontrollably. She went further and said she was open to ideas about how to make the boy stop. Any time the mother replied to a comment she used the phrase open to ideas. It took me five minutes to find a board hosted in Russia called Open To Ideas. I made an account and had access to the site but not the topics. I needed a password which was easy to guess."

"Original poster's Reddit user name," Reese surmised.

"Yep."

"How long are you staying?" At Wilson's question, my gaze went to him.

I waited three long beats contemplating how to answer before I said, "A while."

"How long's a while?" he pushed.

Curious but not aggressive—even still I wasn't going to give him more.

"Why don't we curb this line of questioning until I've had a chance to discuss it with Letty?"

"Fair enough." Wilson tipped his head to Reese and said, "I'm gonna call this in. Until we know what direction we're going I want you monitoring the message board but don't engage. Jack, I want you on Reddit. Same thing—monitor the thread, but look for more like it. I'll send Davis to go talk to Mrs. Simpson; she has a soft spot for him."

"Yeah, because he flirts back," Jack mused.

"He's also the only one she bakes brownies for," Wilson returned. "Seems to me like he's the smart one."

It had been a long time since I was the odd man out. Even when my sister Shiloh hooked up with her man,

Luke, and with him came his team of badasses who worked for Triple Canopy, they all welcomed me and my brothers.

I didn't know Wilson so I wasn't sure if his slight was intentional or if this was simply how he worked when he got a lead. I was hoping for the latter because the former pissed me right the fuck off.

"I'm gonna be staying with Letty," I informed Wilson. "So there's no need for you to send anyone to Mrs. Simpson's. Seeing as she lives down stairs from Letty, I'll talk her to and find out if she's run across anything like this before. The woman doesn't know how to clear her cookies or her browsing data. If she has, it'll take me ten minutes tops to find it. Not only that, she has an obsession with bookmarking pages. I'm not sure she understands the meaning of favorites."

Reese leaned back in his chair and let out a low whistle. "You're staying with Letty?"

"Yep."

"Does that mean you're coming to poker tonight?"

Damn, I forgot I'd overheard Letty and Reese talking about a poker game earlier. Which meant I needed to wrap this up and get back to the hotel to grab my stuff and take Letty someplace to grab a bite to eat.

"Yep."

"You any good?"

"Not even a little bit," I admitted.

A wide smile appeared and Reese clapped his hands together. "Great. Tonight we're playing at Wilson's condo. Make sure you don't wear holey socks; Wilson makes you take your shoes off."

"Appreciate the warning."

Jack had been quiet but he hadn't taken his eyes off me.

And I'd understand when he asked, "You gonna sort our girl's head?"

"Absolutely."

"Right and after you do that are you gonna skip out back to Georgia?"

"Like I said—"

"Yeah, River, I heard what you said. And I mean no disrespect but I think you get that Letty means something to all of us. And it's not lost on us, what you mean to her. So, I'm asking and I hope you get why I want an answer. Are you going back to Georgia?"

It was on the tip of my tongue to tell Jack to fuck off but then I thought about my sister and the shit we gave Luke when he came around. As far as I could tell from what Letty had told me, each of the men had taken a shine to her and Brooklyn. They'd become protective—case in point Jack demanding an answer.

So I didn't tell Jack to go fuck himself. I told him the truth.

"I told her today I was in love with her. I know she feels the same but after what happened to her sister she's pulled into herself. I know you all think you know Letty but what you know, what she's shown you since you've been here, doesn't scratch the surface. The woman I spent time with today is not my Letty. I heard her joking around with y'all when I came in, but that doesn't begin to touch the beauty that is her. So I mean no disrespect when I say I'll be around awhile and how long that's gonna be is not your business until after I've discussed it with Letty. What I will tell you is I've waited years to be right where I am, looking around the bookstore she loves, being in her presence, being in her home. I'm not all fired up to leave."

"Your job?" Wilson asked.

"I quit."

Wilson's shoulders jerked and his gaze turned shrewd.

"You quit?"

"I was facing a desk until I could be transferred and I didn't become a cop to sit my ass behind a desk. I also wasn't real happy about being transferred out of my unit. But my cover was officially blown, meaning I would be ineffective for any further undercover assignments. One of my brothers works narcotics and the other works firearms and my sister's SWAT so those units were out. With my choices seriously limited I decided it was a good time to bow out."

"You have something lined up?"

"You offering me a job?"

Wilson chuckled and shook his head. "No."

"Hey. Sorry to interrupt," Letty called. "Could one of you help Kira carry a few boxes of books out to her car?"

Letty might've framed her question to the group but she was staring right at Jack. The man proved to be smart when he narrowed his black eyes on her before he glanced across the room. My gaze followed his and in an effort not to smile I pinched my lips when I saw a very pretty, curvy woman talking to Brooklyn. Curves that bordered on voluptuous. I looked back to Jack and watched him take Kira in. He wasn't missing a single curve. Letty was matchmaking and Jack wasn't missing that either.

"Letty—"

"Kira runs a book club," Letty rushed to explain. "There are three boxes of books. They're heavy. You'd save us a trip if you helped."

Reese made a strangled sound and choked out, "Yeah, Jack, you'd save them a trip if you helped."

"Fuck off," he muttered to Reese and stood. "Lets, darlin', don't start."

"I'm not starting anything." Letty feigned innocence.

Jack blew out a resigned breath and followed Letty, proving again that Letty had these men's devotion.

Now that I understood the dynamic I didn't feel a stitch of jealousy. I was grateful she'd had these men to help her through the bullshit her sister had put her through even as I wished it had been me.

"Letty's barking up the wrong tree with that one," Reese announced and I tore my eyes off the sway of my woman's ass and looked back at him. "One look at that woman over there and there's no missin' she's a slight shy. Jack likes 'em... frisky. Letty'd have better luck hooking the shy ones up with Davis. He likes the challenge of coaxing the shy ones outta their shells."

"I think you're mistaking Jack's preference with yours. Heard about Sadie. Didn't take her for the excitable type. Seems you touched a nerve with your muffin comment," Wilson shared with a hint of humor in his tone. "Have you met Sadie yet?"

"No, though I have to admit I'm now curious," I answered.

Wilson's smile was a little on the evil side when he said, "The woman is fine and I mean that in looks and class. And Reese was right about one thing; her muffins are the best around. Though I'm talking about the ones she bakes. Can't say I've ever seen her flustered, sweet as sugar through and through."

"Where's my girl?" a loud, jovial male voice boomed through the store, and my attention was pulled to the front.

"Michael!" a woman snapped from beside him. "Stop yelling."

I didn't need an introduction. The woman was unmistakably Letty's mom, Tallulah. I knew she'd celebrated her sixtieth birthday two years ago but Tally could easily pass as forty. Stylishly dressed and even from a distance, I could see that, like her daughter, she wore minimal makeup. Not that either woman needed to artificially enhance her beauty. Michael was tall, broad, and not stylishly dressed. He looked like he was ready to go out into the woods for a week and set up camp, something I knew he did often. He used to take Remy and the two of them would go out for the weekend. Now that Rhode was there, sometimes the three of them went out, other times Michael still took Remy for Pop and grandson bonding. Letty had told me that her father had worried that he'd lose his time with the boy and was grateful when Rhode made an effort to continue to include him in Remy's life.

"Hey!" Brooklyn called and Tallulah's attention went to her but Michael's gaze had zeroed in on mine. "Letty's out back helping a customer."

Tallulah made her way to Brooklyn but Michael was on the move in my direction. When he got to our huddle we all stood and Michael didn't delay.

"Wilson, Reese, good to see you." Then Michael turned to me. "Don't think I know you and it's safe to say I'd remember you if I'd ever seen you. Michael Welsh, Letty's father."

"Nice to meet you, sir. River Kent," I returned.

Michael's gaze turned sharp and his torso swung back before he righted his posture and narrowed his eyes.

"River, you say?"

This wasn't starting the way I'd hoped.

"Yes, sir, River."

"Don't need that sir-shit." Michael waved a hand in front of him like he was knocking the offensive word out of the air. "You're River from Arizona?"

I'd first met Letty in Arizona, but she knew I lived in Georgia. What was interesting was Michael brought up where we met, not where I lived.

"I live in Georgia," I told him. "But, yes, I met Letty in Arizona. On her birthday before she graduated college."

I threw out the last two tidbits as a reminder I'd known his daughter for a long time.

"You married?"

"No."

Michael's gaze dropped to my hand as if to verify the truthfulness of my statement.

"And you're a cop."

Michael's remark didn't sound much like a question but I answered anyway. "I was, yes."

"Was?"

"Turned in my resignation before I came here."

"Finally smartened up," Michael muttered.

Reese chuckled low then threw me right under the bus.

"River's here to sort Letty out."

Michael visibly relaxed. Unfortunately, Reese wasn't done.

"He's so committed to the task, he's moving in with her."

Jesus. Shit.

"You're moving in with my girl?"

In my life, I'd met three of my girlfriends' fathers. All of those men liked me, though I'd never been close to moving in with one of their daughters. I'd never contemplated even clearing out a drawer at my place for one of them to use. Nor had I so much as left a tee or razor at any of their houses. Which in turn meant I'd never been serious about any of them.

So being blindsided, not knowing what Letty would want me to tell her father, I did the only thing I could do.

I told the truth.

"Yes, I'm staying with Letty while I'm here."

It would seem fatherly concern outweighed propriety when Michael's mask fell away and a father's grief and worry shone so bright his pain seeped into my pores and filled me with dread.

Fucking hell, he was mourning the loss of one daughter and desperate to help the other. So desperate he wasn't going to say a word about me moving in with Letty. Obviously, he knew about our friendship, which meant he knew Letty and I had a long-distance phone-only relationship and I knew how that would look to a father. I also knew Michael Welsh and his family had recently learned a painful lesson about the fucked-up world we live in. And knowing the lesson he learned wasn't one he'd ever forget I wasn't so sure he'd accept me into Letty's life. However, if the worry etched on his face was anything to go by, he was not only going to accept me but task me with helping him bring Letty back to herself.

"And how long's that gonna be?"

For the love of God, not this question again.

"For as long as she'll allow."

"Shit," Reese muttered, glancing over Michael's shoulder.

"Dad?"

At Letty's sharp tone, Michael's eyelids slowly drifted shut. He took a moment to let the pain of that wash over him before he opened his eyes and blanked his expression.

Michael turned to face Letty and with fake happiness, he greeted his daughter, "Hey, honey, your mom and I were downtown and thought we'd drop in and say hello."

I watched Letty flinch.

She actually flinched at her dad.

Yeah, she knew he was faking it and what the fuck was up with that? Letty was close to her parents. She'd waxed poetic on more than the rare occasion about how much she adored her father. She'd called him the best man she knew. And her adoration went beyond anything I'd ever witnessed when it came to her mother. With the exception of Kiki's annoying sibling rivalry she'd declared her childhood perfect. No, she'd gone further and described it as ideal.

There was so much not right about the situation it scared the fuck out of me.

Letty hadn't just pulled away from me, she'd taken herself away from everyone.

That shit was going to stop.

Starting now.

CHAPTER 13

The agony I saw on my father's face was the slap back to reality I needed.

That look was why I needed to keep River at arm's length.

How selfish was I?

My family was broken, my parents' whole world had been torn apart, and there I was with my head in the clouds again wondering if I'd made a mistake cutting River out of my grief. All it would've taken was a phone call and a plea for help and River would've come. He would've held my hand through it all. He would've propped me up when I was crumbling to my knees. He would've done *anything* I needed and I knew I wouldn't have had to ask, he'd simply *know*. Because he knew me.

Kiki did what she did and she shattered our family. Now I had no right to be happy while my parents were in pain. That would take selfishness straight to vile.

"There's my girl," my mom said. "Brooklyn said...oh my..." My mother's words trailed off as her eyes went to River.

I was sensing this was a reoccurring theme—young, middle-aged, old—River stole your ability to speak. It could've been his height, or his pool blue eyes, or his large, muscled frame, or his handsome features, or his smile, but it was probably all of the above mixed together into one devastating package.

"Tallulah, nice to meet you, I'm River."

I felt the heat of his body as he came to stand next to me before I felt his arm slide around my lower back and his hand come to a rest on my hip.

I couldn't stop the tremble. River didn't miss the shiver and gave me a squeeze.

This was not right.

So not right, it was *wrong*.

I tried to pull away but his arm tightened. I had two choices—stay where I was or make a scene. I was no stranger to drama, thus no one in the room was a stranger to it either. It was my go-to emotion when I was annoyed, pissed, or had a point to make. If a statement needed to be made, I was under the thought—go big or go home.

Yet, I remained where I was.

My father almost looked disappointed I hadn't shoved River away and behaved badly. My mother, however, took us in—complete with River's arm around me—and smiled hugely. I was the way I was in part because of her. She, too, lived with her head in the clouds and believed in things like fairy tales and romance. My love for happily-ever-afters came from her, my attitude came from my grandmother, and my ambition came from my father.

Therefore, my mother seeing the handsome, strapping River with his arm around me would give her ideas of rainbows and butterflies and good things to come.

I couldn't let that happen.

"River," I hissed and tried to pry his fingers from my hip. He ignored me.

"River." My mom smiled broadly. "Brooklyn said you were here. It's a pleasure to meet you after all these years."

Seriously?

Was it really a pleasure?

Why would River showing up in the middle of a family crisis be anything other than a disaster?

"Dinner at our place," my dad boomed.

Pain assailed me.

"Actually, Dad, we have plans. It's poker night."

"So? What's stopping you from playing poker at home after dinner? Besides, I have a brisket, I'll throw it in the smoker."

"Dad—"

"There. Settled."

His tone left no room for argument. Well, it did leave room—plenty of room. But fighting him would only make me look like the horrible daughter I was. There was a place for theatrics and there were times when I knew to throw in the towel. My father using his Dad Voice was one of those times when I knew it was time to shut my mouth.

"River, it was good to meet you. We'll see you tonight." My father issued a demand instead of extending an invitation and I couldn't help my sigh. "Seven sharp and as always, door's always open. More the merrier."

That last part was directed toward Wilson, Jack, and Reese. But it was Wilson who replied, "Appreciate it, Michael, I'll spread the word."

With that, my dad ushered my mother out the door so fast she barely had time to lift her hand and wave.

"What was that?" I muttered.

"That, darlin', was your father's way of telling you he's

putting a stop to you bagging on dinner at his place," Wilson informed me.

I felt my body string tight. River pulled me closer, Brooklyn looked at her feet, and Reese made a grunt that sounded a lot like he was agreeing with Wilson.

"I don't bag on dinner at my parents'," I bold-face lied.

"Letty," Brooklyn murmured, using my name as a quiet rebuke.

"What? I've been busy," I weakly defended.

Busy hiding.

"Honey, you canceled on the last three get-togethers," Brooklyn gently reminded me.

But I didn't need the reminder. I could vividly recall the hurt in my mom's voice when I'd told her I was canceling. Of course, she let me off the hook without calling me out on my lame excuse but she hadn't hidden her discontent.

"You're avoiding them." Her censure was delivered in a way only a best friend could pull off—tone sweet and full of concern but full of accusation.

"Why are we talking about this?"

"Because we've been dancing around it for three months and it's time."

It damn well wasn't time. It would never be time.

"I'm sorry if me getting over losing my sister isn't fitting into your time frame," I lashed out and immediately wished I could yank the words back. "Damn, Brook, I'm—"

"Nope, don't say you're sorry," Brook cut me off. "Tell me why you're canceling and not just on your parents. I invited you over last week and ten minutes before you were supposed to be at my place you called to tell me you weren't coming. And you've canceled book club meetings indefinitely. And you bailed on me and your mom when we're going to take Remy to the mall. And that's just the tip."

Brook lifted her hand and jabbed a finger at River. "I asked you if you were going to ask River to the funeral and you told me no. That right there, sister, was the red flag I should've paid attention to but I didn't have the heart to say anything so soon after Kiki passed. But then you stopped answering his calls and that wasn't a red flag, it was a big, honkin', flashing sign that you were not okay and I let that slide, too. So, honey, I'm the one who needs to apologize to you for being a shitty friend when I saw all the signs but let you pull into yourself. Clearly, that was the wrong thing to do, but I was afraid if I asked too many questions you'd push me away and that would leave you with no one. But now things have changed."

At some point, my body had locked tight and begun to revolt. The first thing to go was all the oxygen from my lungs. Next, a chill raced up my spine, and closely following that, my heart got into the rebellion and tried to explode from my chest.

But more than my body having a negative reaction to my best friend since forever calling me out in front of a bunch of people—one of them River—my eyes started to blur and my mind went hazy.

I wasn't sure if I was pissed or having an anxiety attack. No, wait, I knew; I was pissed. Irrationally, off-the-charts pissed beyond belief.

"I cannot believe you'd say that to me." My voice sounded funny but I was fairly confident that my ears were ringing and that might've been the cause.

"You should believe it, Lets. I screwed up and I'm telling you now, I won't let this go on any longer."

"Maybe you could've staged this bullshit while we didn't have an audience."

"That's where I went wrong to begin with—waiting for

the right time, waiting until we were alone, *just waiting*. And if you think everyone doesn't see it, you're wrong. We all feel it, Letty. You're slipping away and it *hurts*!"

That was when I lost it.

"Hurts? You don't think I don't hurt? You don't think that seeing my parents hurts? They're broken, Brooklyn. Wrecked. I can't look at my dad without seeing how much he's hurting and you know what happens when I see that pain on my dad's face? I hate Kiki more. When I catch my mom staring off into space lost and heartbroken that hate grows exponentially. I fucking hate what she did to them, to you, to Remington, to our family. Now I can't have anything good in my life because she was a selfish, jealous, immature bitch and stole everything from me."

Then suddenly I wasn't standing. I was in River's arms being carried across my store. I shoved my face in his throat uncaring where he was taking me as long as I didn't have to get myself there because all my energy had drained away.

I was bone tired.

Months of pent-up emotional baggage piling up and I was crumbling under it.

"I'm sorry," I mumbled against his throat.

"Shh, Letty."

"I'm so sorry for everything. I'm sorry she ruined everything."

"Shh, baby."

"She's dead and now I can't have you."

"Baby, quiet."

I stopped talking mainly because I'd already embarrassed myself enough for one day. Now, River knew what a basket case I'd become. He'd witnessed firsthand what a shitty person I'd become.

Fresh air hit my face, River shifted me in his arms, then I

heard the alarm on his rental beep. After that, I closed my eyes like the coward I was and didn't protest when he set me in the SUV. I didn't help when he buckled me in and slammed the door.

It was utter silence on the drive back to my apartment and we went through basically the same process when he parked in front of my building, only in reverse. River unbuckled my belt, scooped me up, and carried me into the complex, up the stairs, and set me on my feet in front of my door so he could reach above the frame and pull down my spare key.

While he was unlocking the door he said, "Will be talking about you keeping a key to your front door above your fucking front door."

"How'd you know it was there?"

"Babe, I'm six-three. The key was practically eye level."

"Well, most people aren't giants like you so it's not eye level for them."

I didn't think it would be in my best interest to tell him the spare key was a necessity since I'd lost my keys three times in one year. In his current mood, I was actually surprised smoke wasn't billowing out of his ears.

Once he had the door open, he ushered me through, pocketed the key, and shut the door. After that, he scooped me back up and carried me directly to my bed.

I didn't have a chance to voice my objection before I was on my back and River was next to me. After that, he yanked my arm so it was across his stomach. With no other place to put my head, it came to rest on his chest and he bracketed me to him with his arm tight against my back.

"Now we're gonna talk about why you can't have anything good in your life."

"What?" I whispered.

River didn't whisper when he said, "After that, you're gonna explain what exactly Kiki ruined, and why you can't have me."

I was finding it hard to breathe again and even harder to think.

"Letty, slow down before you hyperventilate."

Perfect. Next, hot-guy River was going to pull out a brown paper bag and make me breathe in it.

I sucked in a deep breath and concentrated on slowing my pounding heart.

Why was this happening now?

"Baby, breathe."

River's arm locked and he gave me a squeeze, making it damn near impossible to do what he asked.

I slowly exhaled and started to come back to myself. On the next inhale I caught the scent of River's cologne, something I'd missed earlier. Which, lying there with the spicy masculine scent filling my nostrils, I wondered how that had happened. The soft cotton of his tee under my cheek registered and I nuzzled closer. I closed my eyes and took in the feel of being in his arms.

It was a dream come true.

I'd literally had hundreds of dreams over the years of River in my bed holding me.

And River, *my* River, was in my bed for the second time that day.

Yes, this was a dream come true.

In real life, he was bigger than I'd imagined. He was taller and sexier, but he was still River. *My* River, the man I'd had countless conversations with, the man who'd listened to me—really listened and offered honest advice. He'd never, not one time in all these years, let me down.

"I miss my family," I whispered the truth.

River's hand curled around my hip but he stayed silent.

"I don't go over there because it hurts to see them."

"I gathered that, but have you thought about how much *they* miss you?"

I had but I still couldn't stop myself.

"I can't face them when every time I see them upset it makes me angrier at my sister. Then I feel guilty and I get more pissed at Kiki. She's their daughter, they love her, and I feel like a horrible person for hating her so much. It's not right and if they knew how I felt, they'd hate me."

A moment passed then I was no longer resting on River's chest. I was on my back with River propped on one elbow, looming over me. His other hand shifted my hair off the side of my face. When he was done doing that, he slid his hand lower before it came to a rest on the side of my neck.

"Baby, that would never happen."

With my mind muddled I could do nothing but stare into a pair of the bluest eyes I'd ever seen. They were mesmerizing, intense, gentle and I wanted to stare into those eyes for the rest of my life. I wanted my children to have those eyes. And I wanted those two things with a perverse desperation I'd never felt before.

"It would if—"

River's face dropped closer to mine and he didn't let me finish.

"There is nothing that would make your mom and dad hate you. Not. One. Single. thing. Now let's talk about what Kiki ruined."

That was easy, she'd ruined everything.

"She shattered the illusion."

"What illusion?"

"Of happiness. That in the end, everything works out."

"Letty, honey." River's soft tone sliced through me.

"It's fake. All of it. Happiness doesn't last—"

"Yeah, baby it does. But you're thinking about it all wrong. Not every moment of every day is gonna be happy. Hell, not every week or month or even year is gonna be a great one. Sometimes the whole first half of your life is clouded in darkness, tarred by nothing but shit, but baby, that doesn't mean happiness is an illusion; it just means you haven't found it yet."

I closed my eyes to block out the anguish in River's eyes. I knew what he was thinking about. His life had been shit. His mom had abandoned him and his siblings, leaving them to live with a father who was a criminal turned cop killer. River didn't have much good in his life and very little happiness.

"Are you happy now, River?" I asked with my eyes still closed.

"Yeah, Letty, I'm happy now. And when I was younger Echo found ways to make sure Phoenix, Shiloh, and I had happy times. He worked his ass off to show us that life wouldn't always be shit. If we worked hard at it and earned it we'd find our happy. And I worked hard at it. I was proud of my accomplishments, proud I was a good person, but it wasn't until I heard a sleepy voice say, 'You *are* a guy,' did I truly understand what happiness was."

My eyes shot open but before I could respond River went on. "Sucks, baby, but sadly in the end things don't always work out the way we thought they would or how we wanted. But that doesn't mean you give up or stop dreaming. And this anger you're feeling is never gonna work its way out if you keep it bottled up. You've mentioned it twice now; you feel bad for being mad at your sister, but what you're failing to get is—that isn't normal. And maybe if you talked to your parents about it you'd find they're pissed, too.

They're just as angry and hurt as you are and they're doing the best they can. But even if you don't talk to them about it you have to talk to Brooklyn about it."

I shook my head and followed up with a verbal answer, "No way in hell am I bringing Brooklyn into this."

"Letty—"

"No, River, she has Remy and Rhode to worry about."

River's fingertips pressed into the back of my neck and he whispered, "That's fucked up, and if she knew you felt that way it would gut her. This is just a guess, but an informed one. When she lost her parents you were there for her, your parents were there for her. She's your family and she was already that while her parents were alive."

Of course, River was right. When Brooklyn's parents died my parents became her guardians. But before that, she was already family.

But still...

"I don't want to be a burden," I admitted.

"That's just as fucked-up."

He was probably right about that, too.

But I wasn't going to change my mind so I kept my mouth shut.

"Now, tell me why you can't be with me."

I sucked in a breath, and even though I was lying on my back with River mostly on top of me, my legs started trembling so badly they turned to jelly. I wanted to have this conversation even less than I wanted to discuss why I wasn't going to talk to Brooklyn. So I ignored River and started scanning my ceiling. He gave me a few moments to do this before he dropped his weight on me and rolled us back to our sides. This time, my back was to his front and his arm was slanted over my belly, holding me taut against him.

I liked River holding me.

I liked it so much I started to relax.

I should've known better.

"Tell me, give me all of it so I can start fixing what needs to be fixed."

"You can't fix this."

"Baby, you and me, we can do anything."

River said that like he believed it and I wished that were the case. But it wasn't.

"How am I ever supposed to be happy when my parents are miserable?"

River didn't answer. He just held on tight.

CHAPTER 14

"I really don't want to do this," Letty grumbled.

We'd been in my rental for thirty minutes and that was the second time she'd complained. And before that, when we stopped at the hotel for me to grab my stuff and check out, she'd tried to get out of dinner at her parents' by telling me she was tired. Which after a three-hour nap, I doubted this was the case. Though I did learn something about Letty; she mumbled in her sleep—which was cute as hell. She also moved around a lot. So much so I had to pin her legs to the bed with one of mine, which meant her ass was pressed firmly against my crotch. Under normal circumstances, I would not mind this—actually, I would highly encourage it. However, after what happened at her bookstore, followed by our talk, it didn't take a genius to know Letty was emotionally exhausted. Furthermore, she'd fallen asleep so quickly I wondered how much sleep she'd been getting in the last few months. The fact I no longer knew what was going on in her life cut deep and was a reminder of just how much she'd cut me out.

"River?" Letty snapped indignantly beside me.

I wouldn't've been able to stop my smile so I didn't bother trying.

"Yeah, baby?"

"You're ignoring me."

"Yep."

"And smiling," she pointed out.

"That I am."

"Why?"

"Why am I ignoring you or why am I smiling?"

"Both. And you turn right at the stop sign up ahead."

I put on my blinker, checked my mirrors, and changed lanes. What I didn't do was answer her.

"River," she growled and shifted in her seat to look at me.

One of the good things about Letty being worked up about not wanting to go to her parents' house for dinner was, she didn't give me shit about checking out of my hotel to stay with her. I learned a long time ago one of the best ways to cure Letty of a drama was to distract her with something else. The woman could get herself into a lather but she couldn't multitask. She could only focus on one trauma at a time, which meant her snapping at me meant she wasn't fretting about dinner.

"I'm smiling because you're cute as hell when you get peeved. And I'm ignoring you because you've told me three times you don't want to go but we're going so there's no point talking about it."

"Just to point out—we didn't actually talk about it."

I made the turn at the stop sign and was immediately taken aback by the neighborhood. It was obviously an older development; the houses were large, and even in the dimming light, I could see the landscaping around each house I passed was well-maintained and manicured. Either there was an HOA that dictated the park-like setting or the owners took immense pride in their homes.

"Take the next left," Letty instructed.

"You grew up in this neighborhood?"

"Yeah. My parents bought this house after Kiki..." she trailed off and I glanced over at her to see she was now looking out the window. "I was five when we moved here."

Fuck.

I made the left and before I could think of what to say, Letty continued to give me directions. "The house is on the left. Cole's big-ass black Hummer is parked in front."

I spotted the Hummer as well as a bunch of other vehicles lining the sidewalk and debated dropping her off at the driveway. That would've been the gentlemanly thing to do if I wasn't afraid in her current state she'd hotwire a car to flee.

I didn't want to ask my next question but I still had more pieces of the puzzle to put together so I had no choice.

"Does being here bother you because the house holds memories of your sister?"

I found a place to park a few houses up. While I was pulling in, Letty answered.

"Yes and no. Weirdly, all the memories that used to piss me off, like Kiki cutting my hair because she was being a brat, don't bother me now. Those are actually bittersweet. It's when something catches my attention, like the vase she made my mom for no reason. It wasn't her birthday or Mother's Day or a special occasion. Kiki just made our mom something nice. Those are the memories that bother me. It doesn't make any sense. Like I'm mad at her for all the sweet stuff she did but forgive her for the mean, nasty shit she did and said."

Actually, it made perfect sense.

"She loved you, Letty."

"How—"

"Listen to me, baby, your sister loved you. She might not have known how to show you, but in the end, she proved it. I'm gonna keep telling you this until you believe me. She loved you, your mom and dad, Brooklyn, and Remington so much she died protecting Remy. That's both tragic and beautiful. Words are just that—words. That vase she made your mom? That's proof. The bullet she took for Remy, the ultimate proof. Her life ended and you feel that pain, you all do, but she did that so Remy didn't lose his. Kiki loved Remy. She loved you. She loved your mom and dad and she loved Brooklyn."

A car door slammed, followed by another one and I looked over to see Rhode opening the back passenger door and Brooklyn rounding the hood of a silver SUV.

"Before we go in I need to talk to Brook."

"You want me there for that conversation?"

"Probably not," she murmured.

Remy jumped out of the back of the SUV and looked up at his dad. The boy's mouth was moving and Rhode was smiling.

"Kiki did that, baby. She gave them that. So, tonight when you're struggling to get through dinner, I want you to think about that."

I didn't give her a chance to respond. Not that I needed one; I knew she got me when her hand shot out and squeezed my bicep.

"Let's get out so you can talk to Brooklyn."

Letty released my arm and unbuckled. I did the same and we got out.

"River! You're here!" Remy shouted.

Damn, the kid was cute. Of course, Letty had bragged about her nephew all the time—from the time Brooklyn had pushed the kid out, in Letty's eyes Remy was the best at everything. It was a strange feeling to be a part of Remington's life but from a distance. Through Letty, I knew everything about Remy—when he first crawled, when he started to walk, his first words, when he caught his first fish, when he learned how to ride a bike.

Finally being there was surreal.

"Hey, bud," I called back.

Letty came to my side as Rhode, Brooklyn, and Remy crossed the street.

"Guess what?" Remy continued to shout even though he was now two feet in front of me.

"Inside voice, Rem," Brooklyn said. "River's right here."

"But we're outside. Why would I use my inside voice when we're not inside?"

The kid had a point.

"Cheeky boy." Brooklyn laughed. "What I meant was you don't need to yell, River's not hard of hearing."

"He might be," Remington shot back. "Pop says you never know so you never judge. I haven't asked River if he's hard of hearing so maybe he is."

I tried, I really did, but the kid was damned funny, so I couldn't stop the roar of laughter. When I finally had it under control, I let him off the hook. "I'm not hard of hearing, bud, but your pop's right; you shouldn't assume. You asked me to guess something so I'm thinking you have something important to tell me."

It took a moment before Remy remembered what was on his mind. But when it hit him he smiled huge and nodded. "I caught four fish today."

"You did?"

"Yep." Remy semi-shouted excitedly. "But we only kept two. Mom doesn't eat crappie so we throw them back. Can I go in so I can tell Pop?"

Remy looked up at his dad but I answered, "I'll go in with you. Let's give your mom and Aunt Letty a minute to talk."

Rhode caught my eye and gave me a chin lift in understanding.

I shifted to my right, hooked Letty around the waist, and pulled her front flush to mine, then bent down.

"You good?" I asked quietly.

Letty tipped her head back, caught my eyes, and nodded.

"Okay, baby, I'm going with Dull...Rhode and Remy."

Her lips twitched and she told me, "You can still call him, Dulles. I do."

"A man doesn't call another man the name of an airport when he knows his real name unless that nickname was earned. Seeing as I only called him Dulles because I refused to call him Magnus and didn't know his real name, I'm now off the hook calling him that, too."

"Dulles is a cool nickname," she defended.

She wasn't wrong but I still wasn't calling the man Dulles, and since it wasn't worth continuing the conversation, I moved on to something else.

"Make things right with your girl, Letty, and I'll see you inside."

I bent farther and gave her a quick, closed-mouth kiss that wouldn't leave Remy scarred or asking questions, then I let her go and followed Rhode and Remy to the sidewalk.

It happened when we were out of earshot of the women and close enough to the Welshes' front door so Rhode could keep an eye on Remington when he instructed, "Go on in, Son."

Remington took off like a shot across the lawn, and like the exuberant boy he was, he jumped well before the steps up to the porch, landed on the second one, then skipped up the third, and swung open the door.

"Letty okay?" Rhode cut straight to it.

And since I didn't have time for bullshit I told Rhode the truth.

"No. She's feeling guilty for being pissed at Kiki. She says that Kiki dying means that she can't be happy. Part of the reason is that her parents are grieving and broken and I think she feels like it would be unfair if she's happy and they're not. She's in pain and doesn't want to discuss this with Brooklyn. My guess is because after all these years, you're back in Brooklyn's life and Brooklyn's finally happy and Letty doesn't want to jack that up."

"That's fucked-up," Rhode grunted.

"I already told Letty if Brooklyn knew that was the reason she was holding back, holding everything inside, suffering alone, it would kill Brooklyn. I've encouraged her to talk to Brooklyn and even reminded her that Brooklyn knows she's suffering and doing it alone. Evidence of that is Brooklyn calling her out on it today at the bookstore."

Rhode took in a long deep breath, then he gave me his honesty.

"Brook's been wanting to say something for a while now. It's eating her, seeing Letty pull into herself, but she was afraid that if she said something and Letty pushed her away Letty would have no one. Now that you're here, Brook feels safe to say what's been on her mind. She trusts you'll have Letty's back." Rhode paused and I didn't like the way he clenched his jaw before he went on. "Heard you caught some shit from Reese and Jack today. I hope you get Letty's grown to mean something to all of us. They meant no disrespect, and I mean none now, but I have to ask; you sure you have this?"

Again, since we were laying it out I didn't hesitate to give Rhode what he needed.

"I absolutely have Letty's back. And it's a good thing y'all have grown to care about her. That means, y'all will take my back when shit hits the fan."

"What's that mean?"

"You've been around Letty enough to know she's stubborn as shit; how do you think this is gonna go?"

"Right," he mumbled.

"Today I scratched the surface of the issue. Tomorrow I'm gonna start the task of pulling her out from all the shit she's piled on top of herself so she can get down to grieving the loss of her sister. Which means she's gonna try to retreat further and I'm gonna have to pull her kicking and screaming back to me. It's likely gonna get messy and I'm gonna need all the firepower I can get."

Rhode's eyes turned troubled before he said, "Michael's had enough of Letty pulling away from the family, so I don't know this for sure, but I'm thinking he'll have your back on this but more, I'd bet he plays it like Brooklyn, and now that you're here to take care of Letty, he's gonna give her some fatherly wisdom he's been keeping in his pocket."

"Noted."

"That's a lot of weight—"

"I told you I got Letty. By that I mean, I *got* her; no matter the weight, I'll see her through."

Rhode nodded. "Glad you're here."

I was, too.

Rhode's mouth curved up into a smile, then he said, "Hope you don't mind but I'm warning the team to brace."

"Might be a good idea."

"Might be? Brother, Letty on a tear; there's no might be about it."

I returned his smile and agreed, "True."

"I gotta get in there before Remy talks Tally into giving him dessert before he eats dinner."

We started walking and were on the porch when I told Rhode, "They love Remy like crazy. From the day Brooklyn told them she was pregnant they loved your boy."

Rhode reached for the screen door and nodded.

"Something I've learned about the Welshes, their love is endless and they always have room for more. Their door is always open for a meal, a cup of coffee, a chat, or if you're in need of wisdom they'll take the time to give that, too. When they open that door and you step into their home you're family and they don't shy away from letting you know it. How Kiki never got it, I do not understand. Whatever was twisted in Kiki's head was of her own making. But in the end, Michael and Tallulah raised a daughter that had it in her to protect my boy. So Kiki proved she was a Welsh—selfless, loyal, with endless love to share. Brook sees it. Michael and Tally see it. It's just Letty who needs to recognize it."

Damn if Rhode wasn't right.

I heard a loud peal of laughter. Michael was sitting across from me and I glanced over his shoulder and found Remy dancing around holding a football over his head. Rhode and Reese were both smiling at the boy. The three of them were in the grass tossing a ball. Brooklyn, Letty, and Tallulah were sitting in folding chairs at the edge of the lawn watching the excitement.

"Touchdown!" Remy yelled.

Tallulah and Brooklyn smiled, but it was Letty's wide, carefree smile that held my attention.

It was the first time I'd seen her happy. I heard her excited and happy over the phone. I'd imagined what that smile would look like. I'd even seen a few smiles today but none of them were like the one on her beautiful face right then. It was captivating and so damn mesmerizing I could get lost in that smile forever.

"And...he's a goner."

"Can't really blame him."

I snapped out of my haze and looked around the table. Michael, Cole, Jack, Asher, Davis, and Wilson all had their eyes on me. All of them smirking, except for Michael. He looked thoughtful.

"Seems I know a lot about you," Michael started. "Thought it was strange when my girl started talking about you. I never got it, even when she explained it was like the two of you were pen pals only electronically instead of on pen and paper. Thought you might be one of those predators you hear about on TV. But as the years slipped by and you never asked my girl for money or tried to lure her to a hotel room I figured you might be okay. But I still had my reservations. A man talking to a woman over the phone for so many years and not wanting to meet, I started to think you were married and just jerking her along."

It would seem we were now at the interrogation portion of the night. I was actually surprised Michael had waited until dinner had been consumed before he started asking his questions.

"I can see how our relationship would give a father pause. Do you know how we met?"

"Wrong number text or something like that," Michael incorrectly shared.

"I was on my way back from Lake Havasu. I was starting the police academy the next month and went out to Arizona to meet up with some friends. One last vacation before I buckled down and got serious about my life and my career. We stopped in Tempe for lunch and before we sat down I went into the bathroom to wash my hands. I found a phone on the counter and the thing was blowing up with text messages. I picked up the phone and flipped it open and, thank God old school tech was not what it is today because there was no password. A text string was open and someone named Letty was rapid-firing angry text messages. *I hope she gives you crotch rot* was the sentence that caught my attention."

I chuckled at the memory. "So, I admit I got nosy and scrolled up. From what I gathered some asshole had cheated on his girlfriend and she'd caught him and she was breaking up with him over text messages. I knew she had to be close because she said she saw him with this other woman. And I knew it was her birthday. So I texted the woman back and asked her what the asshole looked like. Then I asked her if she wanted me to kick his ass. Before I gave the guy back his phone I put Letty's number in my phone. Can't say why I did it, except there was something about this woman telling her lying, cheating boyfriend she hoped his dick fell off that amused me." More like captivated me but that might sound creepy. "I found Troy and had a few words with him and explained that he and Letty were over and if gave her any hassle he'd be seeing me again. Troy didn't like this, we had some more words, and eventually, he understood if he fucked with Letty, me and my boys would have no problem fucking with him. And that's how I met Letty."

"She was there. Did you see her?" Cole asked.

"Nope, never saw her."

"But you texted her again," Asher pointed out.

"Yeah, a few days later before I flew home I texted to her to ask her if Troy had given her any trouble. She reported Troy had left her alone. Three months later she texted to tell me she'd run into Troy and the asshole did the smart thing and put his head down and scurried away from her. For the next year, I was busting my ass through the academy getting my shit sorted, feeling overwhelmed helping my brother raise a sixteen-year-old girl and helping my younger brother stay out of trouble and getting his ass into college. But I couldn't get Letty out of my mind. So when her birthday rolled around I had the perfect excuse to connect and not feel like a stalker."

All those years, the months between her birthdays, I'd battled with myself. Forced myself not to contact her, telling myself that she had my number and if she wanted to connect she'd contact me. Years of knowing something was missing from my life.

Michael was staring at me with curiosity which I thought was better than him looking at me like I was crazy for stealing his daughter's phone number out of her ex-boyfriend's phone.

"Heard a lot about your brothers and sisters. Letty talks about them, says they're all police, too. Says you're close with them but she never mentions your parents. Mind me asking where they are?"

Fucking, *fucking*, shit.

Lester Kent.

"I don't have parents," I told Michael. "I have an older

brother who raised me. Our mom took off when we were kids. And our father was a low-level criminal until he graduated to stealing cars and running a chop shop. From there he decided it would be a good idea to add drugs into the mix. If that wasn't enough he found there was money to be made in weapons and added that to his inventory. By the time I was a teenager I was well-versed in how a search warrant was executed. When I was nineteen my father went to prison. He's serving a life sentence for killing a cop."

"I can see you're waiting for my judgment," Michael began. "You can relax, you'll get none from me. There are a lot of lessons to learn in life. And there are many different teachers. The most valuable of those are the ones that knock you on your ass. Those are the ones that build character, give you perspective, and make you into the man you want to be."

I let go of the breath I was holding and let Michael's acceptance wash over me.

"I appreciate your honesty," Michael continued. "And that will be the last we talk of them."

Thank fuck.

My phone vibrated in my pocket, and as rude as it was, I had three siblings in law enforcement; I never let a call or text go without checking who it was from.

"Excuse me," I said, pulling my phone out. "Gotta check this."

I glanced at the screen and saw it was from Letty.

The familiar feeling of excitement hit my chest when I entered my password and opened her message.

Thank you for making me come.

I rushed to type back my response.

I haven't yet, pop tart, but you're welcome in advance.

I hit send and avoided Letty's father's gaze. Three beats later Letty's loud roar of laughter filled the backyard.

Only then did I look at Michael. His eyes drifted closed and he smiled. When they slowly opened they were full of that endless Welsh love. "Thank you."

"You'll be hearing more of that soon. You have my word."

CHAPTER 15

"Well?" Brooklyn asked.

I looked up from my computer and found my best friend bouncing from foot to foot in front of the counter.

"Well, what?"

"Letty!" she snapped.

"What?"

"It's been five days. Five! And I feel like you're holding out on the goods."

Unfortunately, I wasn't holding out.

River was.

And something I'd learned in the five days we'd been living together was that River Kent was more stubborn than I was. He was also good at flirting and better at cuddling.

"Nothing's happened," I told her.

"Nothing? How's that possible?"

Oh, it was possible—frustratingly possible.

I should recap the last five days.

I'd apologized to Brooklyn for snapping at her. She'd explained she was genuinely worried and didn't handle the situation well. Dinner at my parents' went better than I thought it would and while I was there I did what River had suggested and gave into the good memories of my sister.

When Monday morning rolled around, River went to the Takeback office to talk to the guys about what Mrs. Simpson had found and I went to work. At closing, River came to the bookstore and picked me up. We went to dinner, talked about what was going on with his family, which was a welcomed change in topics. Then we watched a movie on my laptop and went to bed. That was it; we went to sleep with me on my side, River behind me holding me close.

Tuesday, Wednesday, and Thursday were much of the same with slight variations.

No kissing. No touching. No big heart-to-hearts.

Nothing.

Light conversation, good company, and cuddling.

It was weird.

"Okay, so this morning he came out of the bathroom after his shower without a shirt on."

"And?"

"And nothing. He was shirtless."

"That's all you're gonna give me?"

I rolled my eyes. "Seriously, you have a hot guy in *your* bed and you want more?"

"No, I want to know how *you* felt seeing *your* hot guy come out of the bathroom shirtless."

I'd felt like running across the room, pushing him onto the bed so I could explore every ridge and valley of his abs. I wanted to climb astride him and ask him what had changed since that first day in my apartment when he'd kissed me stupid.

But I didn't tell Brooklyn any of that. Instead said, "He's changed. He's affectionate but he's careful. He teases me like he always has, he even flirts with me, but he won't even kiss me. The strangest part is, his being there feels normal. No, not normal—it feels like he's always been there."

"He has always been there, Lets. You just have him in a new way."

That was weird but true.

"Do you think he's changed his mind?"

"About wanting to be with you?" she asked and I nodded. "No. I think he's slowed things down because he wants more from you and he wants to make sure you're in a place to give it to him."

The pain that had been in my chest since Kiki had died clawed its way to the surface.

"I want to give him more," I admitted.

"I know you do, honey. And I understand what's holding you back." Brooklyn leaned forward and put her elbows on the ledge of the counter and held my gaze. Something she did when she was going to deliver a blow. "I don't agree with you, Letty. Tally and Michael want nothing more than for you to be happy and I think right now they need that more than ever. I think it would help them knowing that you're moving on with your life after what you all lost. But I love you and I'll stand by you no matter what. So you take your time working all this out. However, I'm putting it on record right now, if you ever try to cut me out again, I'm resorting to physical violence. It's always been you and me and it will always be you and me."

My eyes narrowed and I snapped, "Don't you have a book to narrate?"

"Yep."

"You should go do that."

"And you getting snippy is how I know I got through."

Brooklyn smiled and walked away. I watched her do it thinking there was no better friend in the world.

Around two o'clock my phone chimed with River's ringtone and I picked it up, happy for the distraction. I'd been answering emails and placing orders between helping customers.

You hungry?

Yes, for some hot, steamy bedroom action.

I didn't type that but I did answer.

Yes. Starving.

When I didn't get a reply back right away I went back to my email. I was reading the third one that had come in that day asking when the Smutties book club would start back up when my phone pinged.

Maybe it *was* time I got on with the business of living my life.

As River had pointed out the first day he was there, I hadn't read a single book with the intention of getting lost in a wonderful world of make-believe since Kiki had died. When she passed I'd stopped believing in happily-ever-afters. My desire to be swept away into the magic of the written word had vanished.

If ever there was a time I needed a great book to take me out of my head and place me inside a fantastical fairy tale where the heroine always comes out on top it was now.

Yet, I couldn't get myself to open a book.

My phone beeped again and I picked it up to see two texts from River.

Tell me what you're hungry for and I'll bring it by.

Then...

You got two minutes until I leave and you'll have to eat whatever I get you.

I was starving but not for anything in particular so I messaged him back with...

I'll eat whatever you bring me.

That got me an immediate response.

Burger Joint?

Since I'd introduced River to the magic that was the Burger Joint we'd had it twice for lunch. This would be our third and he'd get no complaints from me. I could eat there every day and I was ashamed to say some weeks I had indeed had it every night for dinner.

Yes! Jumbo Jack with extra sauce and a choc malt. I hit send then quickly sent another one. *And please don't forget to ask them to make it thick. So thick I can't suck it through a straw. Just tell 'em it's for me, everyone knows how I like it.*

A moment later I got...

You're hell on a man's resolve, baby.

I was hell on his resolve? I think not; he was holding out just fine, killing me with his cuddling and walking around shirtless. Okay, so he'd technically only walked out of the bathroom once without a shirt on but it was hell on my lady parts. Especially when he hadn't fully dried off and there were still droplets of water dotting his chest. I didn't believe for a second River hadn't done it on purpose.

What can I say, I'm a woman who knows how I like it. The thicker the better.

There, take that!

It's good you think that, honey.

Tease.

Not me grinding my ass on you all night.

Not me grinding my hard-on on your ass all night.

What can I say, you gotta great ass, I like having it pressed up against me.

Ugh!

I DON'T LIKE TO BE TEASED, RIVER.

You'll get used to it.

I didn't want to get used to it. I wanted the teasing to be over but then I remembered what Brooklyn had said about River wanting more and how that was likely true and I stopped being irritated with River and started to be annoyed at myself.

I don't want to get used to it.

Just saying, the longer we jabber on about this the longer you gotta wait for lunch.

And because I could get spiteful and mean I sent him...

Fine, tease all you want. But tonight I'm taking a long bath and don't come knocking when you start hearing my vibrator.

I tossed my phone on the table and jumped when I heard it ring.

I saw River's name and smiled.

"Yes?" I chirped.

"Warning," River growled through the phone and I shivered. "You think to take your vibrator in the tub and get yourself off without me, I'll break the fucking door down. Then I'll haul your ass and your vibrator to your bed and I won't let you up until the batteries are dead and I've wrung so many orgasms out of you you're begging me to stop."

If he thought that was a threat he was dead wrong.

"They're fresh batteries so good luck with that. Unless you want to give yourself carpal tunnel wielding my vibe for hours."

"Letty."

Another growl, another shiver.

"You started it, River. Don't get salty when I best you at your game. It's been a long, lonely dry spell. My toys have seen so much action I had to start shopping at Costco to buy batteries in bulk."

So that was a small exaggeration; I didn't go through *that* many batteries.

"I know precisely how long it's been," he reminded me.

"You know, it's annoying you know everything about me."

Motion caught my eye and I watched Brooklyn come out of the back area of the bookstore. She'd been in her recording booth for hours.

"Right."

"Hey, Brook," I called. "River's stopping at Burger Joint to get me a nice, *thick*, yummy malt. Do you want anything?"

My friend scrunched her face and raised one eyebrow.

"Um. Not anymore I don't."

"You sure? You know how thick and tasty they are."

"Yeah. I'm positive. And I think I might need a shower because you're being really gross."

She forgot immature, but that's what best friends do when they know you're being weird—they don't call you out on your childish behavior.

"River, honey, Brook doesn't want anything."

"I might smack your ass for that," he informed me.

"Will that be over the knee, sir, or do you prefer over the couch?" I purred.

"I'm leaving," Brooklyn muttered and did an about-face.

"Tonight it's gonna be over my knee so when I have your ass nice and pink, and you're so wet your excitement is soaking through my pants, I'm gonna keep you like that for a long fuckin' time before I let you get yourself off, and you're gonna do that in front of me."

River hung up and I squeezed my thighs together. Which did nothing to quell the ache River had created. A few minutes later with my legs still clenched together, I realized I'd made a huge mistake. River was much better at the teasing and flirting than I was.

I answered a bunch of emails with my mind on work and not what River had threatened to do. After ten minutes, I yelled for Brook.

"Is it safe to come out or are you still having phone sex?" she asked from the doorway.

"That wasn't phone sex."

"Might as well have been. Sheesh, girl, I read books for a living. Deliciously naughty books. And the way you were purring your words I thought for a second you were either gunning for my job or interviewing for a sex phone operator position."

I rolled my eyes at her exaggeration.

"I've decided to start the book club meeting back up. But I was thinking of doing them Wednesday nights instead of Fridays. Does that work for you?"

Brooklyn's face went funny and I fought against the guilt of seeing my friend look at me with surprise over something as trivial as our weekly book club meetings.

I did that.

My closing down had caused that look and it sucked, but I had to work to climb back out of the hole I'd dug for myself and take the hits while I did it. Because the bottom line was, I had to do it.

Not for River, not for Brooklyn, not even for my parents. I had to do it for me.

"Yeah, Wednesday works for me," she said and schooled her features.

"And I'm going to make them twice a month instead of every week."

"Sure. Great. Whatever you want to do."

I sighed and shook my head.

"Stop being careful with me, agreeing with everything I'm saying. Honestly, does that work for you?"

"Yeah, Letty, it works for me in a big way you starting back up the book clubs. As far as the day of the week, any day works, and twice a month is great."

After months I'd finally taken the first step in the right direction.

CHAPTER 16

I woke up with a jolt when Letty's knee came dangerously close to nailing me in my balls. Instead, it glanced off the inside of my thigh as she rolled to her side. I rolled with her and threw my leg over both of hers to pin them down. One near-castration event was one too many in my book.

My arm went around her waist, her ass nuzzled back into my crotch, her hand found mine, and, oh, a sigh as she threaded our fingers together.

"Just in case I haven't told you, I'm happy you're here," Letty mumbled sleepily.

Before I could respond I felt her body relax and she was back asleep.

Still, I told her, "I am, too, baby."

Then I laid in the dark holding Letty, hoping her restarting her book club was a good sign.

I did not get to redden my woman's ass before she fell asleep. That was because after we'd finished dinner her mother had called, and during the conversation I watched a bevy of emotions play across Letty's face. She didn't tell me what they'd talked about but from this side of the conversation, I heard the Welshes were going to go through Kiki's belongings and start the process of keeping what they wanted and giving away what they didn't. After that, the mood was broken so I took my girl to bed and she fell asleep twenty minutes into a movie.

Now it was sometime in the middle of the night and I had my girl in my arms; thus I had not one thing to complain about even if my dick thought differently.

Letty was not some woman, she was *the* woman, and being that there would only be one *last* first time for either of us, I was waiting until the time was such that the memory would be perfect.

On that thought, I drifted back to sleep.

"So hot," Letty groaned and shuffled her legs under mine.

I laid frozen while she continued to move, rubbing her ass against my quickly hardening dick.

Was she talking in her sleep? Dreaming? What the hell was happening?

I opened my eyes and blinked them shut when the blinding early morning light shone directly in my face.

"River," she groaned again.

I shifted my hard-on away from her only to give her more room to thrust her ass back.

Torture.

"You awake?" I whispered.

"Yes. So hot."

I smiled into her hair when I realized she was talking about actually being hot.

Christ, I had sex on the brain.

I moved my leg and she instantly kicked the covers off.

"You're like a heater when you sleep."

I had no response to that so I said nothing but I did allow my gaze to travel down the length of her until I caught sight of her bare legs lying next to mine.

I can't explain why that was so fucking sexy other than I'd spent years waiting for it to happen.

And now since we were both awake I had to get the fuck out of bed.

I started to let go of her hand but her fingers tightened and she pulled our hands up to her chest and held them there.

"Time to get up, baby."

"Not yet," she mumbled in a husky voice that made my dick pulse.

Yesterday, Letty had reminded me she'd had a long, lonely dry spell. What was left unsaid was mine was actually longer than hers, and under normal circumstances, with any other woman, there would be no issues. However, with Letty's body fitting into the curve of mine, our hands resting on her breasts, with my dick rock-hard and ready to pound her into the bed, and her phenomenal ass still moving against me...I definitely had issues.

Shit was about to get messy. Something that hadn't happened to me since I was a young buck copping my first feel. At that age, not understanding how my body worked, I was embarrassed as fuck. At thirty-six, having a great understanding of not only my body but a woman's, I'd still be embarrassed as fuck if I came from just Letty's ass grinding on my dick.

"Letty."

I said no more but she read my tone and stopped moving. Problem one solved.

She brought our hands away from her chest and I

breathed a sigh of relief only to have my lungs fill with fire when she shoved them under her sleep shorts.

Christ.

Fucking, shit, goddamn.

"Letty."

She shifted her leg until up over mine, opening herself up in the most beautiful invitation I'd ever received. She pushed my hand between her legs and the moment my fingertips encountered wetness my control snapped.

"You want my fingers, baby?"

"Yes."

I brushed my fingers over her opening and her hips jerked.

Jesus, she was primed and ready.

"River."

Her hips moved, communicating need, the same need I felt. I pushed a finger through her wetness and had to close my eyes against the onslaught of emotions.

I slowly dragged my finger out and pushed two back in and Letty rocked her hips encouragingly. It was a wasted effort. I needed no encouragement.

"Yes," she hissed as I fucked her with my fingers nice and slow.

"I want your mouth, baby."

Letty craned her neck and I didn't delay taking what I wanted. I also didn't delay taking the kiss straight to wild. Our tongues swirled and I fucked her faster until she was moaning in my mouth as the walls of her pussy tightened. Wild turned to out-of-control when Letty started grinding down hard on my fingers.

I tore my mouth from hers and her breath hitched.

"Ohmigod."

"Christ, Letty."

"River."

Hearing her moaning my name set my heart pounding and my body on fire.

Years.

Fucking years I'd dreamed about hearing her moan my name in pleasure.

Years I'd waited to have her.

I didn't care if it took me the next fourteen years to pull her out of the cloud she was living under; she was mine and I was stopping at nothing to prove it to her.

Her back bowed, her face pushed into my throat, and her body locked.

"So fucking beautiful."

Her excitement coated my fingers, her pussy clamped, and I stroked her through the rest of her orgasm.

Once Letty's body sagged I stilled my fingers but left them inside of her.

I was in the midst of preparing for any reaction to our festivities when Letty shifted and kissed the underside of my jaw.

"You know I do, right?" she whispered.

"I know what?" I asked just as quietly.

She didn't clarify but she went on to tell me, "Please be patient with me. I'm trying."

My eyes closed and I rolled just enough to give her some of my weight.

She was telling me she loved me, too.

Fucking hell.

"Baby, you take all the time you need. And while you're taking it I hope you know I have your back. Anything you need."

"I do know."

"Good."

"And you know, I do, too."

"Yeah, Letty, I know you love me."

"Good."

"Time to get up. You've got books to sell and I need to get to Wilson's office."

"Will you tell me what's going on with that?"

"I'll tell you on our way into Smutties."

And when my dick wasn't throbbing and ready to explode.

Letty pressed her lips to my throat and started to roll away. Unfortunately, that necessitated me sliding my fingers out from her wet heat. It was worth losing her pussy to hear her disgruntled whine. When she sat up and looked over at me, her smile was sweet and sexy but most importantly it was real.

"You're good at that, honey. Way better than a toy."

I waited a beat then busted out laughing.

By the time I was done, I had just enough time to catch a few sways of her ass before she disappeared into the bathroom.

Then I got up to make coffee.

"Wilson got approval to look into the message board I found and the Reddit thread. With approval comes money, so Wilson outsourced the computer work to a guy named Shephard," I told Letty once we were on the road.

"I'm still shocked it was right there, out in the open," Letty grumbled.

Nothing criminals and scumbags did shocked me anymore but I wasn't going to get into that with Letty. Actually, I didn't want her thinking about it at all. She had romance books to sell and a business to run. Both of which were much more pleasant than knowing the details of children being traded and sold.

"What do you have going on for today?" I asked.

"Before I let you change the subject can I ask you something?"

"What's that?"

"Have you talked to your family?"

"Yep." I smiled. "Echo called yesterday to check in. I've texted with Phoenix a few times. Both of them are good. Nothing new. Sunny called to inform me that she and Luke set a date for the wedding and my attendance is required, as is yours. She reports that Luke put his foot down when she told him she wanted to go to the courthouse and he told her no to eloping. He wants a big wedding, which really means he wants Sunny to have something special."

"I think it's cute you call Shiloh Sunny."

My sister's nickname was ironic. She'd never been sunny, she'd always been tough and stoic. And she grew into a woman who was hardworking, dedicated, loyal, and jagged. At her station, she was known as Killer Frost. Until Luke, no one penetrated the thick wall of ice she'd built around herself. No one but, me, Echo, and Phoenix. The four of us had always been close. Our bond was such that nothing could ever break it.

"I'll tell her you think it's cute," I teased.

"You tell her that and I'm never talking to you again," she huffed.

"Right."

"What about your job? When do you have to go back?"

I'd been waiting for her to ask me about leaving. I was actually surprised it had taken nearly a week for her to bring it up.

"Quit my job."

"What?" she screeched and shifted in her seat so she was sideways and facing me.

"I told you about what happened on my last case and how that ended. What I didn't tell you was that I was going to get transferred. I couldn't go undercover again and word travels fast on the street. Any contacts I had were drying up. Snitches don't like to be seen with cops and any anonymity I had was gone. I didn't join the force to be a paper pusher and sit at the station. That's not the type of cop I am. So, I quit."

"Just like that, you quit?"

"Took a page out of this smart woman's playbook and evaluated my situation, realized I wasn't going to be happy and didn't dally making a move."

A moment later she quietly told me, "It's not the same thing. When I quit my job to open Smutties, I hated my job. You love being a cop."

"I hated the direction my job was taking me. I didn't need to spend five years learning I hated it. So I did something about it before I became bitter. Yes, I love being a cop. And lucky for me there's police work in Idaho."

"You're staying?"

I heard the hitch in her voice. This time it was different than the first time I'd heard it. It wasn't a sexy, pleasure-filled tremble but it was still full of emotion.

"I've waited a long time to be right where I am, Letty. There's no way I'm finally here and I'm not staying."

"When were you going to tell me?"

"I'm telling you now."

"Why did—"

"Baby, I was waiting until you were ready to hear it. And since you asked, I'm taking that as my cue you're ready. But even if you hadn't asked this morning, you gave me the green light to push forward so I was going to bring it up tonight. So before you ask why I was hiding it from you, I wasn't. You have a lot going on, important stuff you need to sift through and I wasn't going to pile more on. Now you know; I'm unemployed. So it's a damn good thing my woman's a successful business owner and can take care of me."

"What, I'm your sugar mama now?"

"No, Letty, you're my hot, sexy, smart, stubborn, beautiful, sugar mama."

The sound of her laughter filled the SUV and my heart clenched.

My eyes were on Davis placing a sticky note on a very bare whiteboard.

Rhode had explained this was Davis's way; he was either drawing connections on the board or he was sketching them in a notebook. It was a trait I appreciated and a technique I used myself.

"Shep's working on getting us real names," Wilson announced. "He's matched three to the kids; Rhode, I need you to run what he's found. When we have something, Reese, you and Jack will take the first name. Asher and Davis will take the next. Cole, you're with River on the third. I want everything you can find but most importantly, I want to know about the kids. Are they enrolled in school, sports? If so, talk to teachers and coaches. If they're not, talk to the local PD and ask if they've been called out to the residence for any reason. Then we'll call in wellness checks. Depending on what we find, we'll take the next steps and plan to go in. But as you all know that takes coordination and time—something my gut tells me these kids don't have. So with this, we're gonna rely on the locals to do their jobs and be the boots on the ground. Any questions?"

When Wilson was done he looked around the table and waited.

Last Sunday night during dinner at Letty's parents' house Wilson had asked me to come into the Takeback office to discuss the Reddit case. After that, no further conversation about my continued involvement had taken place. No one on the team had said anything about me being there. Cole had simply pointed to a desk next to his and told me to make myself at home. I couldn't say I was happy about being behind a desk—reason one I quit my last job—but I could say it felt damn good to be welcomed into the group.

"Brasco on board?" Rhode asked.

"Yeah, forgot to mention I talked to Brasco yesterday and explained what was going on," Wilson replied.

"Who's Brasco?"

Wilson's gaze came to me when he answered, "Jet Brasco, detective with the CDAPD. We worked with him on Kiki's case. Good guy. Since we moved Takeback to Coeur d'Alene he's become our point of contact with his department. It's highly unlikely we'll be working in his jurisdiction, however, I've given him a heads up as a courtesy. And while we're on the topic of things you need to know. Kiki's ex, Trevor Lawrence, better known as Zeus, president of the Horsemen MC went quiet after Kiki was murdered. But word is since Tug Anderson went down that left his business up for grabs and Lawrence felt like expanding into prostitution and picked up Tug's stable. Brasco's keeping a close eye on that but like everything Lawrence does, he's keeping three degrees of separation between himself and the girls. So as frustrating as it is, it's known Lawrence has control but no one can prove it. We've offered our services to Brasco, which means if you're up for it, you'll be put on rotation. Light surveillance and you don't have to be stealth about it; we want Lawrence to know we're watching him."

Tug Anderson, the motherfucker who murdered Kiki. The motherfucker who'd taken aim at Remington and was poised to pull the trigger. It was a good thing the fucker was dead, and by the look on Rhode's face, he wholeheartedly agreed.

"Letty hasn't said anything so I'm assuming Lawrence is keeping his distance?" I inquired.

"Yeah, Rhode made it clear Brooklyn, Remy, and the Welshes were off-limits. The rest of us showing just put a line under it. Lawrence is a piece of shit, but he ain't stupid. He knows he doesn't want the full force of Takeback raining hell down on him," Wilson assured me. He paused a moment and took me in. When he came to a decision he carried on. "This is need-to-know. And the only people who need to know are in this room."

"Got it."

"The DEA's gotta man inside the Horsemen. He's a patched member and has been there a good long while. He gave us what he could when Kiki hooked up with Lawrence and he'll find a way to get word to me if he hears something we need to know. There's a delicate balance—us keeping Lawrence on the defensive and us not fucking the DEA's case."

I let out a low whistle. "DEA plays the long game. Gotta friend back in Georgia who used to be DEA, and my brother, Echo's coordinated with them a lot over the years.

Takes commitment and patience to be an agent. Any idea when they'll be wrapping up their case?"

"No clue, but you're correct, they play the long game, so best guess however long it takes to get what they need on the whole MC and make a clean sweep."

That was the best way to dismantle an organization— lock everyone up so there's no one left behind to rebuild.

"I got nothing else on this," Wilson announced. "But River, if you've got time, I'd like you to look at the case Cole's working."

"Sure thing."

I glanced at Cole to make sure he was cool with me looking over whatever he was working on. He gave me a lift of his chin and said, "Got the file on my desk."

With that, the meeting was over and everyone was up and moving out of the large space they'd fashioned into a conference room. If two long plastic tables that looked like they'd come from Lowes, metal folding chairs, and three whiteboards nailed to the wall constituted a conference room.

No muss, no fuss. Which was exactly how Takeback operated as a whole. Something I appreciated after years of jumping through hoops and being hamstrung by red tape.

I saw Cole waiting for me by the door and I'd be lying if I said I didn't seriously like Wilson and the rest of the guys.

CHAPTER 17

I knew before I did what I did it was a bad idea.

A horrible, crazy, stupid idea.

But I couldn't stop myself.

It was also a horrible, crazy, stupid move on my part not to tell River what I'd done. Like, say, earlier when he was driving me to work and I had the perfect opportunity to admit my lapse in sanity.

It started when I had some downtime at the store on Monday and I couldn't stop thinking about the Reddit post. In a moment of extreme idiocy, I made a Reddit account. And because I was so enraged and disgusted by what I'd read, I had a lapse in judgment and made a comment.

Then I got busy and honestly, a little freaked out I'd commented and decided I needed to forget about what I'd read and let Wilson and River handle it.

I've been known to be impulsive. I also had a reputation for being a tad bit on the wild side. But as impulsive and crazy as I was, I wasn't stupid.

So, I didn't know what had come over me and further, I didn't know why I allowed my curiosity to get the best of me, but right then I was staring at my laptop screen with my Reddit account open, and the little chat icon indicated I had a message and the bell icon next to that meant I had notifications. My cursor was hovering over the bell but I'd yet to find the courage to click on the icon when the front door opened.

In walked River with a face full of thunder, followed by Cole, Dulles, and Wilson. The three men behind him didn't look as pissed as River but there was no mistaking their anger.

I shut my laptop and moved around the counter.

"Everything all right?"

"Have you lost your mind?" River roared and I jerked back, thankful that even though it was a Saturday late in the day the store was empty.

"River," Dulles muttered.

"Answer me," River pushed.

Fury infused my spine as I stared into his glittery blue eyes.

"I'm not sure why you're asking *me* that, but I know you've lost yours talking to me like that."

"Forget to tell me something?" River continued.

I wasn't a big fan of sarcasm directed at me and his tone did nothing but ratchet up my anger, therefore, I didn't try to hide the acid when I sneered back, "I'm sure I've forgotten to tell you a lot of things but I'll warn you now—"

"Oh, no, honey, you don't get to—"

"You just *honey'd* me," I snapped. "Are you serious right now?"

River leaned in and with a ferocious, angry snarl he told me, "I'm deadly serious right now. You made a fucking Reddit account. And if that shit wasn't whacked you went a step further and commented. So, yeah, Letty, oh, fuck yeah I'm deadly fucking serious."

I felt my blood start to cool. My breath crawled into my throat and stalled until I felt like I was going to choke.

Oh no.

Oh shit.

"Um...I...uh."

"Letty," River growled.

I glanced at Dulles and quickly realized I'd get no help from him. And then he verbally confirmed what I'd read on his face.

"Love you, Letty, but Brooklyn pulled this, I'd hit the fucking roof."

I didn't bother looking at Cole or Wilson so I opted for my shoes.

"I waited fourteen years," River whispered. "Fourteen years for this, baby. Every day for the last six living to hear your voice. Every. Single. Day and that's no exaggeration. When I was undercover I'd listen to your voicemails just to get my fix. Never thought it was possible to love anyone as much as I love you. So, tell me, why in the fuck would you do something to put yourself in danger?"

Danger? How was I in danger?

"I didn't think—"

"No Letty, you did not!"

Oh boy, I was getting pissed again.

"Stop cutting me off and listen to me."

"Are you gonna tell me why you invited some sick fucking predator into your life that now wants to open negotiations with you?"

Invited? I didn't invite anyone to anything.

Negotiations?

"What are you talking about?"

"That comment you posted, how'd you know what to say?"

What to say? I thought back to my comment, which in my opinion was nothing to get upset about. Okay, making an account and commenting at all was pretty dumb but I didn't think I'd said anything dangerous. And besides, how would the person know it was me? Reddit was anonymous, wasn't it?

"Letty?" Wilson called.

"I don't understand." I put my hand up when River started to interrupt. His mouth snapped shut and I went on. "I get you're pissed, I did something stupid by making that account, but I don't understand why you're asking about how I knew what to say. And I don't get how what I said was dangerous."

Wilson pulled his phone out of his pocket but it was Cole who spoke. "'If you're open I have some ideas. Rocking, singing, or long car rides should do the trick. But if not then lots of cuddles and kisses while he cries it out.'"

That was my comment.

Innocent and non-antagonistic. I didn't know what I was trying to accomplish. I hadn't come up with a well-thought-out plan. Okay, so I thought maybe I could get one of the people to engage with me, possibly slip up and say something damning. Thinking back on it, my comment was ludicrous, and frankly hearing it read back was embarrassing.

"See? The comment was dumb. I didn't say anything that would remotely put me in danger."

My attention had turned back to River so I watched him do a slow blink and blow out an irritated breath.

"You used every possible marker word that would ping their radar," he said.

And once again, I was confused.

"I don't know what a marker word is, River."

"Fucking Christ," River ground out and looked at Wilson. "Now what?"

Now what? What did that mean?

Cole cleared his throat and when I glanced at him I knew I was in trouble, big, *big* trouble.

"Now she plays."

Um. What?

"No fuckin' way," River grunted. "Call in a female marshal, pull a female detective from the CDAPD, or hire a fucking female PI to stand-in. No way in fuck is Letty getting any more involved."

Say what?

"River, she's already in it."

"What am I in?"

"Have you checked your Reddit messages?"

Oh, shit.

I shook my head and Wilson's face went funny—not funny ha-ha, funny like he was on the verge of committing murder, possibly mine.

A low, gravelly rumble came from River and when my eyes sliced back to him he looked ravaged.

My heartbeat spiked and my stomach pitched.

"River?"

"They found you, Letty."

Fear rippled through me.

Found me?

CHAPTER 18

Red hot anger coursed through my veins.

And seeing the fear on Letty's face only enraged me more.

"Found me?" she whispered.

The terror in her voice finally broke through my fury. I dropped my head and stared at my boots while my hand went to the back of my neck and I dug my fingers in.

"Fuck," I told the floor. I lifted my head, my hand fell away and I told Letty, "Come here, baby."

She didn't dally; in two strides she hit me full frontal and planted her forehead on my chest.

"I don't understand what's happening," she muttered.

"Cole, you mind locking up?" I asked.

"I still have an hour."

Cole ignored Letty's weak protest and headed for the door. Wilson jerked his head to the back corner and moved in that direction. I shifted Letty to my side and guided her to the couches. She was no less tense when I sat and pulled her down next to me.

"I came in here and acted like a dick," I admitted. "Why

don't we start at the beginning and you explain why you made a Reddit account?"

She shook her head and I felt her body tighten.

Goddammit.

"Letty, baby, I'm sorry I fucked up and lost my cool. But I need you to trust me and explain what happened."

"It was stupid. I wasn't thinking."

"What was stupid?"

She gave me incredulous wide eyes and I understood why. I'd come in, pissed as fuck, and I ran off at the mouth and had essentially called her stupid. Now I was asking her what was stupid.

Then in a very unlike Letty move she didn't bust my balls for acting like a prick—as she should've—she didn't hold on to her grudge and rub it in that I'd been a dick. She let it go and answered, and for some strange reason, that scared me.

"I couldn't stop thinking about the boy. I was just going to take a peek and see if there were any new comments and when I saw another fifteen people had commented it freaked me out so I made an account. I guess I wanted to see if someone would reply and I could...I don't know, engage them."

Jesus.

"And your comment, how'd you know what to say?" Wilson entered the conversation.

"I don't know what that means, either."

"These people have their own language. Code words or phrases. Open to ideas is one phrase this group uses. The other one that's pretty much universal for these sick fucks is cry it out," Wilson told her.

"Cry it out? That's what all parents say when they've tried everything and can't soothe their baby."

"Right, but to them, it means something different."

Letty jerked back. Her face was bleached of color and my anger swelled.

"What does it mean to them?" she asked.

"It doesn't matter," I cut in before Wilson could answer.

No way in hell, did I want Letty's head to be filled with this kind of garbage. Beautiful Letty, with her smart sense of humor, great laugh, and pretty smile should be thinking about her book club, running her store, and her nephew's birthday coming up. She should never have to think about alternate meanings of innocent phrases parents use.

"There's a lotta shit you can protect her against, but River, this might not be one of them," Cole informed me. "She hit their radar in a big fuckin' way and we're talking about kids here. Not that that should make a difference; a life is a life, but it fucking does and you know it. Before more kids get moved *we* have to move, and right now she's our best shot."

Cole was right; we had to make a move and do it quickly. But Letty would not be using herself as bait.

"No."

"Your best shot at what?" Letty asked.

"At getting that boy before he goes to someone else. Someone that will hurt him," Cole told her.

There was no hesitation, no thinking, no contemplation, not even a moment to consider what Cole said before Letty blurted, "I'm in."

"No, you're not."

Letty went solid beside me. Then she sat up straight and I saw the stubbornness infuse her frame.

Christ.

"Yeah, River, I am. If I can stop a child from getting hurt I'm doing it."

"Letty—"

"If this were Remy," she started and Rhode grunted. "And he was in a bad spot and there was a woman out there who could save him I'd want that. If the unthinkable happened and my nephew was being harmed and there was someone out there who could've helped but didn't I'd wish death on them. So, what kind of person would I be if I turned my back on a child who could be someone's nephew or brother or grandson, but even if he isn't those, he's someone's child and I will not turn my back on him if I can do something to save him."

"We're not gonna leave this boy, Letty. Rhode's got names and he's tracking them down."

"How long's that gonna take?" she fired back.

I clenched my jaw and she didn't miss it.

Rhode was doing what he could with the names that Shephard had found and was hitting dead ends. Then his searches came to a screeching halt when Shephard had called—not emailed which supposedly was his way—to inform the team that Letty's name had come up on the post. She'd made it damn easy for him to do since she'd used her internet connection at work and didn't do a damn thing to mask her IP address, which meant it was easy for Dora Thomas, the original poster of the thread, to find her as well.

"River's right, Letty," Rhode told her. "We're not gonna do everything—"

Letty cut him off, too, and said, "I get that. I know none of you would ever turn your back on a child, but Dulles, I've heard you and the guys talk. I know every minute counts. Every day that passes is a day those kids are living in hell. I'm not going to make them live an extra day in that nightmare if I can do something to stop it."

Arguing with Letty was a waste of time. When she got something in her mind there was no stopping her. This was another way I'd fucked up. I shouldn't have lost my temper for a variety of reasons. Losing my shit and coming to Smutties enraged and laying out exactly how mad I was meant she now knew more than I wanted her to know.

"What can I do to make you see how dangerous this is?"

Letty looked incredulous when she answered my question with one of her own.

"What kind of woman do you take me for?"

"A compassionate one, who would hear about the possibility of a boy being abused and wouldn't think twice about jumping in. A stubborn one, who won't listen to logic. But baby, I hope like fuck you're a smart one, who wouldn't put her life in danger."

Her face softened, her shoulders sagged, and some of the tightness in my chest loosened.

I should've known better.

Letty was Letty.

Her resolve was one of the things I loved about her.

But right then I learned something new about a woman I thought I knew everything about—she could be manipulative as fuck.

"I won't be in danger," she whispered. "You'll make it safe for me."

You'll make it safe for me.

I felt the trust those words stab through me and I knew I was screwed. Not just with this but in the future, because she was right; I'd always make it safe for her to be anything she wanted to be.

But still...

"Letty, danger comes in many forms. Trusting me to protect you means something to me, more than I can explain. But with this, I cannot protect you from the emotional fallout. Once you know, you know. You cannot unsee or unhear these things, which means I can't shield you from harm here." I tapped her forehead. "I won't ever be able to take it away. So, I can't protect you from this danger unless you actually allow me to do it and stand down. We'll get someone who looks like you to take your place—"

"Looks like me?"

I bit the inside of my cheek until I tasted blood. I didn't answer her. I was still contemplating how stupid I was when Rhode picked up her question.

Unfortunately, he was thorough in his explanation.

"We've got a computer hacker we use, Shep. I know you've heard us talk about him, he's good at what he does and found the real names of some of the people commenting on the Reddit post. One of the people he found was the woman who started the post. There's also a message board, the same woman runs that, too. The thing is, when you answered her post about her son who doesn't stop crying and you used the proper verbiage of someone who's, let's say into that lifestyle, she did her own digging. And since you didn't do anything to hide your identity she found you. And Letty, I had Shep hack her computer; she found a lot. Now, the good news is there's no information about me on the internet and Brooklyn doesn't have any social media accounts in her real name. One of the things I had Shep do when she and Remy came into my life was make sure there was nothing that could link them to me, and that included you and your parents. You don't have any personal social media either but you do have accounts for your bookstore and your name is attached to that and there are pictures of you on the internet—book signings, the store opening, book club pictures, your promo video. You're out there and exposed. So this woman has your name and your picture.

"And she wants a face-to-face meeting. In the message she sent, she didn't use your name—which she knows. She didn't reference you living in CDA—which she knows. All she said was she liked your parenting style and was conducting interviews for potential guardians and would like to meet with you immediately."

"Set it up."

My eyes drifted closed and my gut twisted.

Letty wasn't going to let this go. She was never going to back down. Again, her determination was something I loved, one of the first things I'd come to admire about her. But right then, I despised the fire I'd heard in her voice. I hated the grit and steel that made her the perfect woman for me. But mostly, I fucking hated that Letty was right; she was our best chance at rescuing a boy from a nightmare that was so hideous that one extra day meant indescribable horror.

I opened my eyes and focused on the task at hand.

"Have Shep scrub my records," I told Wilson. "And how fast can he construct a new profile?"

"Best guess, it'd take him a few hours to get rid of River Kent. Maybe a day to get a new life in place."

A few hours to get rid of thirty-six years' worth of existence. I wasn't sure if I was impressed or concerned.

"New profile should have some criminal activity," Cole noted, picking up on my plan. "Petty shit. B and E, theft, trespassing. It's too late to add anything for Letty. She's a clean, upstanding business owner, no record. But we can dirty her up using River."

"Have Shep give me a juvenile record and seal it. Give them something to spend their time on."

"Nothing drug-related," Rhode threw in.

"What's going on?" Letty asked.

"She might want a trade," Wilson rejoined.

"Then we'll convince her she wants to do business with us and offer her a shitload of money," I told him with great difficulty considering I was choking down bile.

"A trade?" Letty gasped and the bile I was trying to swallow made its way back up.

One of the many things I wouldn't be able to shield her against.

"This is the shit I can't protect you from. The shit I don't want your head filled with. How these people operate is disgusting. It wears you down until you have no choice but to harden yourself and disconnect. This is what I don't want for you. It's the devil's work, baby, and it gets under your skin and eats away at you."

"They want to trade the boy for another child," she rightly surmised.

"She might," I confirmed. "It's common practice."

"And who is *she*?"

"Right now we're focusing on a woman named Dora Thomas," Wilson answered. "It's looking like she's the organizer for this group."

The look on Letty's face could be described as horrified. And seeing that coupled with the sadness in her eyes had me making mental plans to scrap the operation and kidnap her. I could take her back to Georgia and lock her in my house. Or I could take her to Hawaii, buy her a bikini, and do my best to make her forget the website Reddit existed.

"Dora Thomas?"

There was disbelief in her tone and none of us missed it.

"Do you know who that is?" Wilson leaned forward and asked.

"Anyone who grew up here knows Greg and Dora

Thomas. They live in Kellogg and own an RV park. But it can't be the same Dora Thomas."

"Where's Kellogg?" I asked at the same time Cole asked, "Why don't you think it could be the same Dora?"

"Kellogg's about forty minutes east of here and it can't be the Dora I know because she and her husband are in their sixties and she makes and sells jam. Every Christmas she also makes these big wreaths and sells them at the Christmas bazaar."

Yet another fucking reminder of why I didn't want Letty involved in this; she was already struggling with the loss of her sister and with that a whole host of emotions including the reality that sometimes life knocked you on your ass. The last thing I wanted or she needed was to learn that a woman who makes jam and Christmas wreaths could also be the scum of the earth.

"Do the Thomases have children? Grandchildren?" Cole inquired.

"They had three but when I was in high school their eldest son shot his younger brother then killed himself— murder-suicide. That's how I know who the Thomases are."

That sick feeling in my gut started to swirl.

"You said three," I reminded Letty. "What about the third?"

"She was a year older than me. We went to school together but Brianna was shy. She didn't have a lot of friends. I had some classes with her but the only reason I knew who she was, was because of what happened to her brothers. I think after graduation she moved away."

Fuck yeah, the sick in my gut was turning to acid.

"If they live forty minutes away how'd you go to school with them?"

At Cole's question, she blinked, then her gaze went

around the room until she focused back on Cole and quietly said, "They moved after Brianna left."

"Why do you look so freaked out?"

Letty zeroed in on Rhode and with a pale face, still speaking quietly she said, "I remember a rumor that Sean—that's the younger of the two Thomas boys—was touching Brianna and that's why Joe, the eldest, killed his brother. But there were other rumors that both boys were touching her. Honestly, even when I was younger I didn't pay any mind to gossip. But after a tragedy like that people talk more than usual and what they say isn't always nice."

Damn, that was something I hadn't thought of, therefore, I hadn't brought it up. But now that she'd mentioned people talking shit after a tragedy, I wondered what was being said about Kiki and if it was being said directly to Letty or her family.

"Baby, are people saying not-so-nice things about Kiki?"

"What? Why would you ask that?"

Defensive.

Fucking hell—they were.

"Because the way you said that makes me believe you got personal experience with it and not just experience from hearing the nasty shit people can say, but being on the receiving end of it."

Letty started to move away but I reached out and hooked her around the waist, making it impossible for her to put distance between us.

"Answer me, Letty," I demanded gently.

"Kiki was Kiki. Everyone knew how she was."

"What does that mean?" Rhode cut in.

I could feel the waves of anxiety rolling off Letty and for a moment I wondered if pushing her in front of Rhode, Cole, and Wilson was a good idea. Then I remembered how much she'd held back, how she'd pulled away from everyone, not just me. But mostly, I remembered the look on Michael Welsh's face. And lastly, I remembered the shit people said about my father. It didn't matter if half of what had been said was the truth. The rumors and the nasty looks dug under my skin. No one had ever said anything to my face, certainly no one had said anything to Echo, but Phoenix had been suspended for fighting more times than I could remember. He and Shiloh had both been harassed about our dad's criminal activity. Shiloh internalized it until she built her fortress, then she kept herself locked behind it and suffered in silence. Phoenix defended our father and had turned bitter, using his fists to deal with his pain. I didn't want that for Letty.

So when she didn't answer right away I gave her waist a squeeze.

"It means, she did what she did. Everyone knows how she was; she didn't hide her bitchiness. She didn't hide that she hated me and my parents. Everyone knows she hooked up with one of the Horsemen and what that means. She associated with a prostitute for fuck's sake. I'm sure people think she was one, too. So, yes, people are talking and saying nasty shit. But, no, no one is saying it directly to me. I just hear the rumors. My customers come in and apologize to me about what they're hearing but really, they're being nosy, waiting for me to confirm or deny what they've heard."

She didn't hide that she hated me and my parents.

And there was Letty's real issue. It wasn't that she was grieving, going through the natural progression of coming to terms with a loved one's death—anger being a part of that. She thought her sister hated her.

"Kiki didn't hate you, Letty," I told her gently.

"She didn't?" Letty huffed a stilted, humorless laugh.

"She chopped my hair off when we were kids. She lied to my parents and told them I cut open her bear and ripped all the stuffing out. She shed actual tears when she told them. I didn't cut open her bear, she did. And it was her favorite stuffed animal—she ruined it just to get me in trouble. Who does that? Why would she do that? I can go on and on, all the shit she did to me when we were growing up, and it only got worse when we were adults."

I had to admit Kiki was a bitch, not only to Letty but her parents and Brooklyn, too. Though from what I'd heard she didn't behave that way toward Remington. She'd actually spoiled him.

"Jealousy makes people do horrible things," Rhode noted. "I've told you before but it bears repeating—she was blinded by her envy and she grew resentful. She didn't hate you, Letty, she wanted to *be* you. She wanted what you had with Brooklyn. She wanted closeness and attention but she never understood how to get it. She did nasty shit to you when you were kids because that was how she forced a reaction, and when she grew up, she never learned. She wanted all your mom and dad's attention she so forced that, too. It sucks, babe, but it has to be said; I didn't like your sister because I saw what she was doing to Brooklyn and to you and your family. But I will always be grateful for what she did for my boy."

Rhode paused and took a deep breath before he continued. "I'm not saying it should or that it does erase the years of havoc she caused, but Letty, her saving Remington's life counts for something. What she gave me and Brooklyn, the years I'll get to spend with my son, means a hell of a lot. Remy's alive today because of her and that doesn't mean a lot, that means everything. So fuck what anyone says. Kiki was a woman who lived her life selfishly but she died selflessly. Not one fucking person running their mouths has it in them to be as brave as your sister. Your parents understand that. They see her death for what it is—tragic. But out of that tragedy, they also got to see that the woman they raised had so much love inside of her that she was willing to die to save Remy."

When Rhode was done he looked ragged. Clearly, as it should be, he didn't like to think about his son getting kidnapped, held hostage, and almost shot. Yet he was willing to relive that time to help see Letty through. A testament to how much he cared about her. My respect for the man grew and I'd already thought highly of him. Not only for the way he'd stepped up for Remington when he'd found out that the one-night stand he'd had with Brooklyn resulted in a child, but also the way he'd handled the whole situation. A time when some men would be pissed and threw unwarranted blame on the mother, Rhode saw the situation for what it was—no one's fault.

"He's right, Letty," Cole added. "I've seen men full of ego, talking trash about how badass they are, so much bravado and bluster it's a wonder they didn't break their shoulder pattin' themselves on the back. Yet, those are the same men who during a firefight run the other direction and leave their buddies swinging. I've seen highly trained men freeze on the battlefield. But not your sister. She didn't run. She didn't save herself. She jumped in front of a bullet. She didn't hesitate. She didn't think. She did what she had to do. Anyone comes in here running their traps about who Kiki was or how she lived her life, you remind them of that, then you tell them to fuck off and mind their own business."

It was safe to say, I liked Cole.

"Got nothing to add to that," Wilson stated but continued. "Except to say, your sister has my gratitude. She didn't only save Remington's life, she saved Rhode's and I suspect Brooklyn's, too."

Rhode grunted his agreement. Letty's body sagged into mine and her face went to my chest. I heard her breath catch and her muffled cry as she pressed closer. I aided her in her endeavor and slid my arm up and held her to me. I did this thinking she was exactly where she was supposed to be, exactly where I wanted her to be. I was also thinking it had taken a long fucking time to get here. But it was worth the wait. She was worth the waiting.

My gaze went around the room, my eyes landing on each man. Not a word was spoken but they knew the depth of my appreciation and respect.

They all had Letty's back. Which meant they had mine.

Together, we'd pulled Letty through.

CHAPTER 19

Since it was a Saturday, Dulles had left shortly after my breakdown to go home to Brooklyn and Remy. Cole and Wilson were talking to River and I was wondering how in the hell my life had turned into...this. I was the very definition of a basket case. My emotions yo-yoed up and down depending on the minute. It was a miracle I hadn't given myself whiplash. It was a bigger miracle River hadn't run a mile. He was either crazy or he loved me as much as he claimed to. Another thing I'd spent a great deal of time pondering—why I couldn't say it back to him.

He hadn't shied away from his feelings. More than once he'd told me he loved me. More than once I'd wanted to say it back. More than once I'd thought about how many times over the years I'd wanted to break my promise that I'd never look him up and search for him. I'd dreamed about it for so long now that it had happened I was so terrified of losing him the words literally wouldn't come out of my mouth.

Another thing I was angry at my sister about. Since I'd spent years dreaming about River, I'd also spent years dreaming about how our first meeting would go. I'd built up the fairy tale—the long gaze across the room, the first kiss—which of course would happen right after I ran and jumped into his arms. What I had not dreamed of was River showing up in Idaho in the middle of me losing my mind. It was stupid and like everything else, I had to let it go. I was already buried under a mountain of shit, I was currently trying to work my way out from under. I didn't need to take on more.

I had to find a way to let it go—not the pain of losing Kiki, I didn't think that would ever fully go away but the anger. And if not for me, for my mom and dad. Brooklyn was right, I'd been hiding from everyone but most especially my parents. Instead of turning to them, I turned away. And since everyone was now talking about Kiki after months of the people who cared about me walking on eggshells, never bringing her up, I realized they'd been worried about me but didn't know how to broach the subject without causing me more pain. However, something had changed and I suspected that change was River. Even my dad had been different; at no time since Kiki died had he demanded anything from me. He'd put on his kid gloves and had handled me gently. But not after he met River. Only then did he order me to dinner, making it clear he was done with the distance I'd put between us.

I'd done wrong and I knew it. Now I had to find a way to repair the damage I'd done while I let go of the bitterness. Listening to Rhode, Cole, and Wilson talking about Kiki felt good. It wasn't that what they said was much different than what River had told me; however, they'd been involved in my sister's mayhem. Rhode intimately so, and if a man who'd almost lost his son due to Kiki's behavior could forgive her and move on, I had no excuse.

So what if I didn't have the perfect relationship with my

sister? So what if she'd been a holy terror when we were kids? So the fuck what if her jealousy had caused her to say mean things to me? In the end, she'd saved a life.

She'd saved Remington.

No, Wilson was right—she'd saved Rhode and Brooklyn, too. She'd saved them from a lifetime of hurt. The hurt my parents were feeling.

And what did I do? Turned my back on them when they needed me.

Not even I could twist that into being Kiki's fault. That was all on me.

Shit.

I hadn't yet come to terms with what I'd done to my parents, the unnecessary—albeit inadvertent—pain I'd caused them when Cole's voice cut through my thoughts and brought me back to the room. And that room was my awesome bookstore, where the walls were lined with hundreds of books—happily-ever-afters, steamy fantasies, worlds where anything goes, ups and downs, drama—but no matter what, everything ends the way it should.

In other words—fiction.

"Shep needs to give Letty a backstory."

"He's working on it," Wilson returned. "He said that's gonna take a few days."

That reminded me; I still didn't fully understand what was happening and now that I'd mostly got a handle on my latest freak-out I needed to start asking questions.

Starting with, "What's going on? Why does River need a..." I paused and tried to remember what they'd called what River needed and when it came to me I finished, "a new profile? And what's a backstory and why do I need one? And what exactly does a trade mean?"

It must be said Cole looked entirely uncomfortable

which was not a look I'd ever seen on him. Wilson looked thoughtful, which was always how he looked. The man took pensive to a whole new level. But it was River whose jaw clenched.

Since Cole and Wilson were getting ready to leave we were standing by the long, tall counter I used to check out customers. I was standing behind it, closing down the register, River, Cole, and Wilson on the other side. I was staring right at River, so I didn't miss the tightening of his jaw and I also didn't miss his flinch.

The jaw clench reminded me I was still mildly irritated River had come in and ripped into me. At the time I'd been too freaked out to throw my normal attitude and I'd quickly gotten over my drama due to the fact that I'd screwed up big time. River had also quickly recognized I was not going to back down and he'd obviously adjusted his plan on how he was going to handle the situation. The problem was, not only didn't I understand the situation, I didn't like plans were being made when I wasn't privy to what was being planned.

"I need a profile because I'm not letting you go into this without me at your back. Once I hit the scene they'll check into me and them seeing I'm a cop isn't going to get us an invitation to participate in their fucked-up game. And you need a backstory because once you meet with Dora they'll dig deeper. When they look, we need them to find something or they'll be suspicious. Not a lot, just a comment on message boards here and there. We don't want them to find too much but they have to see you've done this before."

I'm not letting you go into this without me at your back.

I would've balked at the implication that River had the power to *let* me do anything if my belly wasn't doing flip-flops.

"What River's trying to say is," Wilson started, "Dora's already done her homework on you. She wants to meet, which is a good sign. But you and River need a solid cover if we want this to work. The good thing is, you're clean—so clean that if you can convince her that you're in the life it will actually be beneficial you have no priors. It would mean you're careful. Obviously, she's never seen your screen name before, so we'll use that, too. Tell her that you change them with each transaction. But we also want her to see something, some sort of history, so Shep will insert some recent comments using the screen name on some other message boards he knows that deal with trading or buying."

At Wilson's explanation, my stomach pitched then twisted with revulsion.

That wasn't the first time I'd heard the guys talking about a trade.

"You mean they pass the kids around," I whispered.

"Yes, Letty. They trade or straight up sell for cash," Cole told me gently.

River made a sound between a snarl and a grunt, clearly conveying his displeasure.

He'd made himself clear he didn't want me involved, crystal clear he didn't even want me to know such things happened.

But now that I knew, he was right, I couldn't *un*hear. I couldn't *un*know that there were children, possibly a little boy somewhere close, who was being abused. He couldn't protect me against the mental trauma but I was counting on him to protect me against the physical danger.

"What do you need me to do?" I asked.

"Letty—"

"I need to do this," I interrupted River before he could once again tell me what a bad idea this was. I knew it wasn't smart, just like I knew making a comment on Reddit wasn't smart but I'd done it and I was doing this, too. "I need something good to focus on."

"This is far from good, baby. This is as bad as you can get."

Boy was he correct about that.

"You're right; what's happening to this boy is bad, so bad I can't even think about it without my stomach hurting. However, me helping you and the guys is good. It's right. It's what I need to do to focus on something else other than feeling sorry for myself and wallowing. I need to break the cycle of anger and guilt. I need to take a step in the right direction and part of that is doing good for a boy I don't know. So, please, I'm asking for you to help me do that. You've already—"

"Anything," River decreed.

"What?"

"Anything you need, anytime you need it, baby, it's yours."

I believed him and not just because his tone was fierce and his eyes were gentle as they held mine. It was because in all the years I'd known River he'd never let me down. He'd never failed to listen to my troubles. He never failed to celebrate my successes. He never failed to lift my mood, make me smile, make me laugh, or give me great advice.

He never failed—period.

I love you, I thought. The words bubbled up but got stuck in my throat.

"You know, right?"

River's face turned infinitely soft and his blue eyes became alert when he replied, "I know, baby."

That easy.

That was River. Until I'd started to pull away from him,

we'd never fought, never had disagreements, never even had heated words until I told him not to come to Kiki's funeral. He was laid-back to my high-strung. When I got into a snit, which happened often, he'd laugh it off and listen to me rant until I burned myself out. When I had issues at work, he'd lend an ear then give good advice.

He always gave and I always took.

I was thinking back, trying to remember if there were times I gave and River took, when Wilson's phone rang. I was still in deep contemplation when Wilson took the call. And I hadn't yet thought of a time when River needed me and I was the calm one who listened and gave great advice when Wilson's loud booming voice echoed through Smutties.

"Not good news, Shep." There was a pause then, "Yeah, you stepping this shit up would be good." Another moment of silence before, "Right. We'll get ready on our end. Good news is she wants to move fast. The question is why." I glanced at Cole and he was looking toward the front door. When my gaze went there I found my parents outside my store. "Thanks. I'll be in touch."

Wilson disconnected his call then declared, "I gotta get back to the office. Cole, you're with me. River, not that I have to say this but, Letty's not out of your sight. Someone's checking Letty's financials. Means we're moving fast on this. Also, it's likely someone's gonna be watching, so no more meeting in public, and before you come anywhere near the office check for a tail."

"What?"

"No time," Wilson answered. "Your parents are here and I've got shit to do."

Without further explanation, Wilson went around the counter to the door leading to the back of the store which had an exit that opened into the back alley. Cole followed close behind. River took a breath and on the exhale muttered a few curse words before he gave me tight smile.

"It's all good. Let's see what your parents need, then we'll hit the mall and get Remy's birthday present."

Holy crap.

I forgot.

With everything happening, I forgot about Remy's birthday party.

"I see you're gearing up for a meltdown, baby, but we don't have time."

I felt my blood pressure skyrocket along with my temper.

"Meltdown?"

"Fuck," he mumbled and looked at the ceiling.

"I forgot Remy's birthday," I snapped.

River dropped his gaze and pinned me with a stare. "Normally, you on a tear is hilarious. But right now, your parents are at the door. We need to see what they need, get to the mall, and we need to hit the grocery store before we go home. All I'm asking is for you to wait a few hours then I promise I'll grab a beer and you can let 'er rip and I'll gladly sit and listen."

He didn't need to promise to listen to me have a drama. I was over it as soon as he'd said "home."

But I had to save face so I hotly replied, "Fine."

"You just can't help yourself, can you?"

"What's that mean?"

River smiled and said, "I saw it, Letty, the moment you got over forgetting we needed to get Remy a present. But you're holding on to your attitude just because you're you and can't let shit go."

I shrugged and told him the truth, "That's just me."

His smile got bigger when he replied, "Yeah, baby, that's just you."

He looked amused and I wondered if his eyes lit up like that when we talked over the phone. I wanted to ask but unfortunately, my dad had run out of patience and knocked on the door.

"Crisis averted," he muttered and started to walk to the door.

He didn't stop when I announced, "Just so we're clear, if you ever say crisis averted again it will be crisis back on."

River's laughter filled my bookstore and I let that score through me. My insides heated and that hole my sister left when she died began to fill and I knew if I gave it time River would stitch back the tatters. That was his way, that was what he did for me. That was who he was to me.

I was still basking in the glow River created when I heard my dad's gruff voice filter through River's waning laughter.

"What's a man gotta do to be invited into his daughter's place of business?"

"Hey, Dad," I chirped, and I watched my dad's torso jerk back as if I'd punched him in the gut.

"Hiya, chipmunk, closed for the day?"

I ignored my dad's look of surprise which I was sure had to do with me smiling and answered, "Getting ready to go to the mall to get Remy's birthday present, then River and I are gonna pick up some groceries on our way home."

"Not like you to wait until the last minute to get that boy something for his birthday. Normally it takes you a month to pick up the twenty-five presents you spoil him with."

"Been a little preoccupied, Dad," I huffed and pointed to River. "I have an unexpected house guest."

"Right, a house guest." My dad chuckled. "Is that what we're calling River?"

I shrugged and asked, "What else would we call him, a squatter?"

Again my dad jerked and I ignored that, too. But I couldn't ignore his loud, boisterous laugh.

It sounded like music.

That, too, filled some of the hole in my heart.

But it was when I glanced at my mom and saw her standing proudly by my dad's side—a place I'd seen her millions of times over the years, a place I knew she loved to be—smiling at me I knew it was okay to heal. It was okay to be happy. It was okay to love my sister, and moving on didn't mean I loved her any less. But it did mean I could give my parents what they needed—to see me happy. It meant I could mend my family.

"Have you and Dad eaten?" I asked my mom.

"Nope. That's why we're here. We were hoping to catch you and River and see if you wanted to get a bite."

"If you're up for the mall we could stop after."

My father groaned an exaggerated breath before he grunted, "You at the mall is a form of torture. I'd rather have my leg hair waxed off than go shopping with you and your mother."

It'd been a long time since I'd heard my dad sound like his old self, a testament to all the ways we'd all been holding back.

I turned to River and said, "If you ever wondered where my flair for overstating the situation comes from, look no further." I tipped my head in my dad's direction and smiled. "Michael Welsh is the King of Drama."

My dad rolled his eyes and I watched my mom and River simultaneously roar with laughter. Okay, so maybe my mom didn't roar with it, hers was far more ladylike than River's. But it sounded magical, much like my father's had earlier.

Then it hit me; my family had been through a lot—the worst kind of tragedy, we lost something precious. My parents a child, me a sister. That loss would forever leave a mark and the scar my sister's death left on my heart was beautiful—a beautiful pain that meant she had lived.

CHAPTER 20

It was official—I'd been catapulted back to my teenage years. A time when I had no control over my dick. Throughout shopping, every time Letty joked with Michael or laughed with Tally I had to fight against my dick getting hard. Throughout dinner it was much of the same only worse because we were smooshed into a booth, and when she teased and smiled her body had been pressed against mine with her hand on my thigh.

Now we were in bed, Letty's head was resting on my chest, and she was in a nightie that had to have been hand-stitched by angels. There was no other explanation for the way the soft cotton clung to her curves and gathered tightly under her breasts. When she'd walked out of the bathroom my eyes glued themselves to the sway of her hips, I lost my breath, and I was close to losing my mind.

The room was quiet. The only light was a soft glow from streetlights outside and I was staring at the ceiling pondering how it was possible a woman as beautiful as Letty, as sweet and smart and funny and loyal, hadn't been snatched up. How she'd made it into her thirties without being married when her hand resting on my abs started moving.

"Letty."

I wasn't sure if I was attempting to convey a warning or a plea.

Her head tipped back and in the dim light, she held my eyes as her hand continued to travel down. When she got to the band of my shorts she didn't hesitate to slide her hand under.

"Baby."

Another warning.

Another plea.

Her fingertips grazed the head of my dick and she smiled.

Good Christ, she was beautiful.

Letty's thumb circled the sensitive tip of my cock and her beautiful smile turned wicked.

"You're playing a dangerous game, baby."

"Dangerous?" she asked and slid her hand down until it was wrapped around my dick.

There was no stopping my reaction to feeling Letty fisting my cock. My hips lifted and I thrust into her hand.

"Very dangerous."

Up and down her hand glided, my hips moving with every downward slide.

"I think I like this game," she whispered and tightened her hold.

"Time to stop, baby, or the games's gonna change."

Letty didn't stop. She continued to stroke until I was close to blowing—too close, dangerously close.

I knifed up, taking Letty with me, and twisted until she had no choice but to let go of my cock and she was on her back.

"Hey. I wasn't done."

"You were done," I told her and yanked her panties down her legs.

"I was having fun," she pouted.

"I reckon this will be more fun."

I scooted down the bed, spread her legs, took a moment to appreciate the beauty that was laid out before me, then I dipped my head. I was too far gone to ease her into what was about to happen. I'd waited far too long for a taste, I was far too hungry, so when my mouth hit her pussy my tongue speared in and I ate.

Letty communicated she felt the same way. Her hands went into my hair and she lifted one leg over my shoulder, planted her other foot on the bed, and rocked into my mouth.

Fucking perfect.

"River."

There it was again, that breathy moan that I'd longed to hear, and it was no less beautiful hearing this time than it had been the first.

Her heel dug into my back, her fists yanked my hair and I welcomed the pain. I listened to the sexy noises she was making until they became cries of pleasure and her excitement coated my chin. Only then did I free my tongue and lift my head. Her nightie was bunched up around her waist, her back was arched, her chest rose and fell with her heavy inhales, and her head was tilted back pressed deep into the pillow.

Fucking beautiful.

"River."

My name had barely left her mouth when I surged over her, freeing my aching dick as I went and by the time she righted her head the tip of my dick was sliding into her wet heat.

"Say it, Letty." I stilled and demanded.

"Honey," she moaned and hooked her leg around my hip.

"You want this to continue I need you to say it."

Her pussy clenched around the head of my cock and I fought against the need to take her—to finally make her mine. But this was too important. I needed her to understand what this was and what it meant. I'd never had sex with a woman I loved, never said the words—not during, not after, not anytime. Letty was my first, and I needed the words from her.

"You know I do."

"Yeah, baby, I know, but I want to hear you say it."

"Why?"

I brushed her hair off her cheek and let my fingers tangle with the strands until my palm cupped her jaw. I lowered my face until all I could focus on were her desire-filled eyes.

"I need you to say it so I can say it back," I told her. "In twenty years from now, I want you to remember our first time for what it is—us sharing something special."

I watched Letty's eyes become glassy and felt her hands go to my shoulders then glide up the sides of my neck until they made their way to my face and stopped.

"It's you. It's always been you."

Fuck, that felt good.

"Yeah?"

"I love you, River."

I let that slide through me, warm me from the inside out, sink in deep. Then I locked that feeling deep in a place I'd never forget and drove into her slick pussy.

"I love you, Letty," I groaned and felt her pussy ripple around my cock. "Only you. I've never loved anyone but you."

"River."

My name hadn't finished leaving her mouth when I kissed her. Tasting her hunger I deepened the kiss. Her hands moved to my back, then lower until her nails were digging into my ass cheeks and her moans turned desperate.

I disengaged my mouth and asked, "Can you take more?"

"Yes."

"Other leg around me."

Without hesitation, she swung her other leg around my waist and locked her ankles.

I slid in deeper and her back arched.

"More?"

"Yes."

Letty's knees pressed tight to my ribs. I gave her some of my weight and buried my face in her neck then licked from under her ear to her throat and continued to drive in deep and hard.

"River."

I was close but thank fuck she sounded closer. I shoved my hand under her ass and lifted her lower body off the bed and took more.

I heard the hitch in her breath and felt the contractions squeeze my cock.

"Ohmigod," she groaned and her back bowed.

"Christ, you feel beautiful."

"River, honey."

If she meant to say more she didn't finish. Her body went solid, her limbs locked around me, and her pussy spasmed.

"Let go, baby."

She shook her head in the negative but I felt the rush of wetness around my cock.

"Baby, let the fuck go."

Letty continued to shake her head and I could feel the tension in her body getting tighter and tighter until she was trembling, and with the shaking, trembling, and tension came her inner muscles squeezing until she was hugging my cock so tight I was gonna go before her.

I reared back until my ass was on my heels, taking Letty with me until she was sitting on my cock. One arm went diagonally across her back to brace her, my other hand went between her legs and I rolled her clit with my thumb, adding pressure until her head lulled to the side and a low mewling sound ripped from her throat.

And there it was. Her climax tore through her. And with my cock planted to the root with just the feel of her orgasm I came with her, looking right into her eyes.

Pleasure.

Letty's arms around me, her breathing heavy, her pussy clenched tight, love shining in her eyes—pure pleasure.

"Love you," she whispered.

"I know you do, baby."

Letty rolled her eyes and smiled.

No, this wasn't pleasure; it was heaven.

I came awake with my hand on Letty's bare ass and the sun shining through the window. Last night when we were done, she hadn't put her panties back on after she'd cleaned up but she left on her nightie. The thing was soft and sexy as hell so I hadn't minded. But this morning it was coming off.

We were also going to have to be quick seeing as Remy's

birthday party was that afternoon and we needed to be out at Rhode and Brooklyn's early so Letty could help set up. It was with that in mind, my hand left her perfect, round ass and trailed down the crease of her cheeks.

"River?"

"Roll over, baby."

"Huh?" she mumbled.

Fuck, she was cute when she was sleepy.

"Hands and knees, Letty. I'm gonna fuck you."

Her head lifted off my chest and she grinned.

I took that shot to the chest and committed the look of a sleepy, sexy, turned-on Letty to my memory then got down to the task at hand.

As she was rolling off me, I yanked the hem of her nightie.

"Take this off."

Her smile went wide and her eyes danced.

I committed that to memory, too, and watched as she got to her knees and ripped the material off over her head. And just like the first time she pulled off an article of clothing Letty wasn't shy with nudity. And she proved my theory right when she dropped her hands to the bed and wiggled her ass.

Sleepy Letty was obviously playful Letty.

Fucking brilliant.

I leaned forward and kissed her hip, lifted her up onto my knees so I could reach her lower back, and kissed her there, too. I moved behind her and continued to trail up her spine until she tipped her ass in a nonverbal demand.

"You wet for me, Letty?" I asked as I circled her nipple with my finger.

"Yes."

I rolled her already pebbled nipple between my fingers

and slowly started to pinch until I heard her inhale, then I went back to rolling.

"How wet?"

"I'm ready for you."

"Can you reach back and guide me in?"

She balanced on her left hand and used her right to reach between us. I hissed when her hand wrapped around my dick and she gave me a long hard pull. She didn't guide me in, she took this opportunity to stroke my cock as I pinched and pulled her nipple.

"Quit fucking around and guide me in."

"Um, I think I wanna play awhile."

"You can play later when we don't have to be quick."

"Quick doesn't sound like fun."

"It is when my woman's on her hands and knees in front of me with her ass tipped up wet and ready for my cock. Now, guide me in."

Letty gave me one last tug that had me gritting my teeth it felt so fucking good—that was, until the head of my cock notched inside her pussy. Then it felt fucking great and I had to inhale deeply to catch my breath.

Her hand fell away and I fucked my woman. Hard and fast with one hand cupping her breast and the other toying with her clit.

"River," she shouted.

"Too much?" I asked and slowed my pace.

"No. More."

I let go of her breast and planted my hand between her shoulder blades. "Cheek on the bed."

Letty lowered her upper half to the bed, resulting in her ass angling up allowing me to slide deeper.

"Holy fuck," she groaned.

"I'm gonna take you harder," I warned. "Tell me if you need me to stop."

"Harder?" She breathed and I smiled.

I gripped her hip and told her, "So hard you're gonna scream."

I felt her shiver, took that as my cue, and slammed home.

A few minutes later, Letty was screaming my name. A few minutes after that, she was screaming a bunch of incoherent shit but she was doing it while coming around my dick. I fucked her through her orgasm, then through her next, and only stopped going at her clit when she cried out her third, and I exploded with my own shout of ecstasy.

I was still coming when Letty start rocking back, slowly fucking herself while I closed my eyes and tried to recover from experiencing the longest orgasm I'd ever had. I'd barely regained focus when there was a loud knock at the door.

"Letty? Letty, dear, is everything all right?" Mrs. Simpson shouted.

Letty froze. I stiffened. Then her body started shaking and I groaned when the walls of her pussy tightened. Not a beat later her silent laughter turned audible and I groaned again when she fell to her side and my still-hard cock slipped out.

"Everything's great, Mrs. Simpson!" Letty yelled back.

"Are you sure?"

"Please, fuck, tell me this isn't happening," I muttered.

"Positive!" Letty returned, still laughing.

"For the love of God, please stop having a conversation with your ninety-year-old neighbor who lies and says she's eighty-three while my dick is still hard and I can see my come leaking down your leg, which is making me want to fuck you again."

Letty stopped laughing. Her eyes went soft, and her lips curved up into a smirk.

"I see you like that you can keep me hard after I just came harder than I ever have in my life when normally I need at least ten minutes before I'm ready again."

"Ten minutes?" she inquired.

"I'm not twenty anymore."

She rolled her eyes and said, "I thought guys needed like at least an hour."

One of the fucked-up things about being in love with a woman who was not yours to have, about being in the friend zone where she shared every aspect of her life, meant I knew about the guys she'd dated. I also knew about the ones she'd slept with. Further I knew that most of them had been shit in bed because she'd complained at length about how unfair biology was that a man could orgasm from crappy sex but a woman could not. Unfortunately, and at the time hearing her talk about a guy she cared about that was by her description great in the sack and gave good head was akin to having a dagger twisted in my gut while my heart was being torn from my chest. But at the time, she was not mine. We were nothing more than friends. Best friends who talked about everything including sexual partners.

But her question was telling. Good-in-the-sack Camron who gave great head had shitty recovery time. Normally I was not a man who compared myself to anyone. I didn't care enough to know how I ranked on a woman's sexual score-card. But Letty was different. It wasn't that I wanted the comparison, but it would suck if she was the best I'd ever had and I wasn't that to her.

"Letty?" Mrs. Simpson carried on.

"Everything's fine. I promise."

"Okay, dear. Just remember I'm right downstairs if you need me."

"You're moving," I declared.

"I know. I'm going to build a tiny house on Dulles and Brooklyn's property. Living off the grid with solar and hand pump from a well."

I did a slow blink and must've heard incorrectly so I asked, "Come again?"

"I've decided to be a minimalist so I'm building a tiny house."

"Baby, you have like a thousand books piled in your bookshelves. How are all of those gonna fit into your tiny house?"

"I don't know. I'll work it out."

"You're not building a tiny house."

Sleepy, cute Letty had turned into sexy, turned-on Letty, who had turned into hot-as-sin Letty who had not only let me fuck her hard but also had screamed three orgasms. Now I had narrowed-eyed, sassy Letty who was no less cute, sexy, or hot.

"I'm building a tiny house," she huffed.

"No, baby, you're not. I'm buying us a house that has a room big enough for you to turn it into a library. No way in hell is my woman stuffing all her books into a tiny house when I know because I've heard you tell me a thousand times that just looking at the spines of your books makes you happy."

The attitude left her eyes and tenderness crept in.

"You're buying us a house?" she whispered.

"What exactly do think is going on here?" Letty held my gaze but didn't answer so I reminded her, "I quit my job to come here. I would've already had my brothers pack my shit and ship it here if I didn't think you needed some time to—"

"Tell them to pack your shit and ship it here," she interrupted me.

I took that shot to my gut and let its golden trail of warmth fill my lungs until they burned.

"What?"

"I don't need time. I also don't need you to buy me a house with a room big enough for a library. All I want is you. So, if you'll give up your life in Georgia to move here with me that's all I need."

The timing of this conversation was absurd. Letty was lying on her side, hair wild and splayed out over the pillow, a just-fucked blush still visible on her neck and chest. I was up on my knees, semi-hard cock swinging out there, bedclothes messy, comforter half off the bed. An old woman may or may not still have been at the door after she'd come rushing—as fast as a ninety-year-old woman could rush—after she'd heard Letty's screams.

Absurd but perfect.

Just like everything else about us—from the way we met, to the friendship we'd created, to the way we'd fallen in love —it was unconventional but meant to be.

Before I met Letty, I didn't believe in fate. I hadn't even believed in love. I didn't think it was real and I certainly never thought about having a family, a home, a wife.

But Letty made me a believer.

"One day are you gonna marry me, baby?"

"Yes, with stipulations."

"Name your terms."

"I'll marry you if you promise to give me at least five beautiful boys all with your blue eyes."

She was making this easy. That was going to be my next

question, but it would've been rhetorical because I knew she wanted a big family.

"I can't promise you all boys or that they'll have my eyes, and I wouldn't even if I could. I want sassy little girls who are like their momma."

"You like me sassy," she reminded me sharply.

"Yeah, Letty, I like you sassy. I also like that you're throwing me sass now and I suspect I can get that attitude of yours to flare by telling you I've waited a long time to be in the position to find more creative ways to calm you down."

Her eyes dropped to my dick, then she slowly skimmed her gaze up my abs and chest until hers reached mine and she said with a taunt, "How creative can you get?"

"This round, it's not me who has to get creative."

"I think at this juncture I need to tell you that I lied. My vibrator doesn't have fresh batteries. They're dead. So I hope you weren't counting on my vibe to play a part in this creativity."

Actually, I'd forgotten about her vibrator altogether but now that she'd reminded me I scratched batteries onto my mental to-do list.

"How'd you run your batteries down?" I asked and dropped my hip to the bed and rolled to my back.

Letty rolled her eyes and I smiled.

"Obviously, they died from usage."

I reached over and plucked Letty up and pulled her over me. Once I had her sitting on my lap I asked, "What'd you think about while you played with yourself?"

"Wouldn't you like to know."

"Fuck, yeah, I would."

"*You* tell me what you think about when you're playing with yourself."

My eyes took in the vision before me. Full, perky tits,

soft stomach, flared hips, muscular thighs pressed close to mine, flawless skin, all of that my fantasy come to life.

"You," I told her with my gaze locked on my hard dick flat against my stomach, Letty's pussy resting on my shaft. "I'd lie in bed and jerk off thinking about what this would be like. I'd close my eyes and picture you riding me, you sucking me off, fucking you from behind, against a wall. Sometimes when I stroked my dick I did it thinking about how good you'd taste when I ate you, how you'd fuck my face and come in my mouth. I have hundreds of scenarios but they were always about you. But now, knowing what you feel like, what you sound like, what you taste like all of it's so much better than I imagined."

I finally tore my gaze away from our connection and glanced up to find Letty was staring down at the same thing I'd been.

"Hot, isn't it?"

She nodded her head.

"You ready to get creative?"

Letty rose up on her knees and I reached between us and lifted my cock. Once she lowered herself down I let go then watched as her pussy slid down my shaft then back up. Nice and slow, making a show of it when she swiveled her hips.

"I thought about you," she whispered. "I thought about this."

She slammed down hard but pulled up slow.

"I thought about teasing you until you were begging me to fuck you."

Letty continued to live out her fantasy by only giving me gentle upward glides but dropping herself onto my cock, making her tits bounce, then rocking before she started the glide again. Over and over. Up and down.

My hands tightened on her thighs and I thrust my hips in an attempt to make her go faster. But she continued to control the pace.

"Letty," I grunted on a glide.

"Beg me, River."

Christ.

"Fuck me, baby. Make yourself come."

I laid back and watched my woman fuck me harder and harder. She rocked back and forth on my dick. She lifted up and slammed down, fucking me wild. Her head was tipped back, her tits were swaying, her face the picture of rapture. I watched, thinking I was one lucky son of a bitch. I'd have this for the rest of my life. It wasn't just the phenomenal sex, but that I got to have it with my best friend.

It would be Letty riding my dick, bent over taking my cock, her mouth sucking me off, me returning the favor and eating her. But all of that came with her humor, her sass, her intelligence, her loyalty, seeing her smile, hearing her laughter, Letty taking my last name and having my babies.

Fuck, yeah, I was lucky.

I had it all.

"I'm close," I warned.

"You say that to me when I'm touching myself."

Fuck, she was killing me.

I cocked my knees and planted my feet on the bed and thrusted meeting her slide down.

"Yeah? Do I also tell you how good your pussy feels?"

"Yes," she moaned and I felt her clench around me.

"Do I tell you that you're so tight that as soon as I get inside of you, I wanna come?"

"River."

Fuck yeah, she was close.

"Tell me, baby, when you're fucking yourself with your

fingers and you've got your vibrator on your clit do I ever tell you how much I love you?"

"Yes, you always tell me you love me."

"Come with me, Letty."

Letty tipped over and I joined her.

"I love you, baby."

Her back arched and she cried out.

That time I didn't need the words back. Letty breathing my name while she rode out her orgasm was more than enough.

CHAPTER 21

We were going to be late. Normally this would piss me off and send me straight into a come-apart. I loathed being late and hated it even more when someone didn't value my time and was late showing up to something I had planned.

But after last night's and this morning's orgasms, which were so bountiful I'd lost count of how many River had given me, I couldn't give a flying flip when River drove around downtown Coeur d'Alene for thirty minutes until he was satisfied no one was tailing us. And even then, he'd taken two wrong turns down dead-end roads on purpose just so he could see if someone had followed.

My mood was mellow and happy and I was looking forward to seeing my family and celebrating my nephew's birthday so I was unprepared for my mood to shift so drastically when River's phone rang.

"Hey, Wilson, you're on speaker," River greeted.

"Are you still on your way to Rhode's?"

"Yep. We've got five minutes until we get there. I took a few detours."

"Good. A few things. Shep added your name and Letty's

to an account. There's a hundred K in there." My eyes rounded in shock that Wilson could get his hands on that amount of money in less than twenty-four hours. Unfortunately, he continued and my shock didn't wear off. "Reese and Jack are on their way to Wyoming. Yesterday, Rhode found something he didn't like and punted it back to Shep. There's credible intel that says the couple has two girls in their care, not enrolled in school, no sports, no medical records."

It didn't escape my notice that Wilson didn't say the name of the couple.

Interesting.

"Good that Shep could find something. Rhode wasn't pleased with what he'd found and less pleased when he hit a roadblock."

"Yeah, Rhode's good, but Shep's king. Also, Dora set a meet. Tomorrow three o'clock outside Hotel Coeur d'Alene at the walkabout around the docks. She asked Letty to wear a red scarf, so if she doesn't have one you'll need to get one."

River glanced over at me and I nodded. "I have a red scarf."

"I wonder if tomorrow Dora will come clean about looking into Letty," River continued the conversation.

"I wouldn't be surprised if tomorrow Dora starts with the threats. What will be interesting is if she brings the husband. Is this her sick game and she's got Greg cowed or is it the other way around?"

Personally, I didn't find anything interesting about whose idea it was to abuse a child. In my mind, they both had something seriously wrong with them and should spend the rest of their lives locked in a cellar being eaten alive by a million ants.

And part of me was still holding out hope that it was

not the Dora and Greg Thomas who'd lost their sons. However, the more I'd thought about the rumors the less hope I had. The talk about my sister was shitty, it hurt to hear, but I couldn't deny that it stemmed from a kernel of truth that had been embellished and twisted. Rumors about a girl being touched by her brother weren't far-out accusations; it wasn't something that high school students would make up. Unless someone had seen or been told something.

"Unless it's Greg communicating with Letty, Dora's a willing participant."

The thing was, Dora wasn't communicating with me, she was messaging Davis who was pretending to be me. I had yet to see a single message.

"Wouldn't be unheard of," I mumbled.

"What's that?" Wilson asked.

"I said, it wouldn't be unheard of for someone to pretend to be someone else over the internet."

River grunted next to me and despite the situation, I smiled at the memory of wondering if River was catfishing me. And that of course led me to remember the first time I called him and was half shocked he really was a guy and his name was River. From the beginning, River had never lied to me.

"You pushed your way into this meeting and in doing so you agreed to me taking your back. There are things you need to know, however chatting with a sick fuck isn't something you're gonna do," River told me.

"You know before I meet with the woman I've been supposedly chatting with I'll need to read the messages. Nothing screams set-up like Dora referencing part of the conversation and me not knowing what she's talking about. Or say, she tries to test me by saying the opposite of something she told me in a message. I understand you're trying to protect me but I can handle reading messages."

To my utter surprise, River agreed right away.

"I didn't say you couldn't handle reading the messages or that you weren't going to read them. You're right; tomorrow before we meet her you'll have to read them. What I said was, you weren't going to chat with her. It's one thing to read this shit, it's another to have to participate and think up replies to her disgusting questions."

Holy shit, I hadn't thought about that.

"What questions?" I squeaked.

"How about today we enjoy Remy's party and leave all this shit for tomorrow?"

That sounded like a brilliant idea so I quickly told him, "Fine by me."

"Well that's new," Wilson commented.

"What's new?" I asked.

"You being agreeable."

"Careful, Willy, or I'll cross you off my Christmas cookie list."

"As much as I love cookies I'll take my chances and tell you if you ever call me Willy again, River or no River, I'll spank your ass."

"If you try that I'll sic all six-foot-three-inches of my man on you."

"I have a feeling your man will understand."

"You'd think wrong, friend. Though, I do feel you on being called Willy. Thankfully out of the names my hippie mother named us, I got the best of the bunch. She calls you Willy again, I'll gladly spank her for you."

I vaguely wondered if he and his siblings had been teased about their names growing up. then I remembered Echo was an inch taller than River and Phoenix was only an inch shorter so I doubted the boys got made fun of. And Shiloh was a cool name but seeing as the woman was a badass I figured if someone was stupid enough to make fun of her name they'd only do it once.

"No cookies for either of you," I declared and crossed my arms over my chest.

"It'll be a shame if we miss out on Letty's cookies. Remy says they're better than Sadie's muffins and those fuckers are heaven in the form of a muffin, so it'll suck if I lose out on cookies. It's been a long time since I've tasted something sweet. That'll leave me stealing Cole's cookies when he gets his."

"No cookies for anyone this year," I amended.

River's deep chuckle filled the SUV along with Wilson's jagged laugh and I thought hearing that was a little bit of all right after the distasteful conversation we'd had. So I sat back and listened.

When River stopped laughing he said, "We'll see you at the party."

"You will."

The call dropped and River reached over and grabbed my hand, threading our fingers together before he rested it on his thigh.

"Wilson's right, baby, it would suck missing out on your cookies. Been waiting a long time for those, too."

I was already planning on making him a dozen of every kind.

But I didn't tell him that. Instead, I shrugged and said, "We'll see."

"Can't wait to spend Christmas with you," he returned and squeezed my hand.

I silently vowed to make him two dozen of his favorite kind—peanut butter with chocolate chips.

Two hours later I was standing in Brooklyn's kick-ass new kitchen helping her wipe down the counters while my mother loaded the dishwasher. All the men were in the backyard watching a gaggle of little boys run around. It was after lunch has been decimated but before cake and presents when I blurted out, "River's moving to CDA."

"Um. Duh," Brooklyn returned and my mother snorted.

"What does duh mean?"

"It means you'd have to be blind not to see that man is gone for you."

Well, she was right about that but it wasn't a given he was staying in Idaho.

"And he says he's buying us a house so I can have a library for all my books," I informed her.

"What?" Brooklyn stopped mid-wipe and gave me big eyes.

"And he asked me if I was going to marry him one day."

"He did?"

"He did," I confirmed.

Brooklyn slowly smiled, then she smirked, then her forehead crinkled and she burst out laughing.

"Took him long enough," she said through her hilarity, then once she got ahold of herself continued, "I was beginning to wonder what the hell was wrong with him. But then he shows up and gets all hot-possessive when he thought Reese was your man. And he wasted no time sorting out your head and giving you back to us." Brooklyn stopped and her smile faded. "He has, right? You're back to being you so does that mean he's given you back to us?"

I glanced over at my mom who was leaning her hip against the counter, one hand on the edge of the granite, the other placed over her heart. She was not smiling. Actually, she looked ready to cry.

"Mom?"

"Finally," she whispered.

"What?"

"We knew, honey," my mom said. "You tried your best but when a woman's in love there's no hiding it. So we knew, your dad and I."

That was news to me.

"You knew?"

"Letty." My mom shook her head and gave me a weak smile. "Every time he called you or you got a text your face lit up. You might've thought you were pullin' wool but you weren't. So, yes, finally, he's here and you can be happy."

I sucked in a breath and held it until my lungs burned. When I exhaled I felt no better. The guilt was creeping in no matter how hard I tried to push it out.

"I feel guilty for being happy," I admitted.

"Don't!" My mother's sharp command rent the air and slammed into my chest like a physical blow. "Let me tell you something. I lost one daughter and I'll be damned if I lose another."

"Mom," I whispered.

"You've been pulling away from us and your dad and I went into your bookstore that day because it was time we sat you down and talked about what was going on. But River was there and for the first time since Kiki passed we knew you'd be all right." My mom paused and took a deep breath before she told me, "There will always be a hole in my soul. I will always miss your sister. Kiki was not perfect, she had faults, as we all do, but one thing is for certain—your sister loved with her whole heart. She loved you deeply. She loved Brooklyn. And she adored Remington. She just never learned how to control her jealousy and when it got the best of her, she hurt those she loved the most. But I think we can all agree that in death she proved the depth of her love."

"Yes, Mom, she absolutely did."

My mom nodded and said, "Be happy, my sweet girl. Be happy with no guilt. I don't know how but I do know for certain that together as a family we'll get through this."

"I'm sor—"

"No, honey, today's Remy's birthday and it's a happy day made happier by the good news River's moving to town." My mom pushed away from the counter and came around the island and stopped in front of me.

Her hands came up and she grabbed my face like she'd done thousands of times since I was a little girl. I closed my eyes and soaked in my mom's love.

"You have nothing to be sorry for, so get that out of your mind. Enjoy this time with River. Be happy. Let us all be happy for you. And please, Letty, live your life. Live it and be *happy*."

I opened my eyes and found my mom smiling.

"I'm so happy for you, honey," she whispered and pulled me into her arms.

Nothing felt quite as good as a hug from your mom.

A few hours later I was setting down an armful of presents on Remy's bed when a picture on his dresser caught my eye.

Kiki and Remy at the lake fishing.

My throat clogged and my chest started to burn. Kiki was on her knees, her arm around Remy who was holding his pole with the tiny fish still on the hook. Remy was laughing, Kiki had a big, beautiful smile on her pretty face. A good day. Happy times. She and Remy sharing something special.

She loved with her whole heart.

My mom was right; Kiki didn't do anything in half measure. She adored Remington and always, but always, showed him.

I stared at that picture and began to fall into love with my sister, remembering the sweet times I had with Kiki. The time when Tony Bennet broke my heart in the seventh grade and Kiki climbed into my bed with me and hugged me while I cried. Her much smaller body wrapped around me from behind. Then there was the time I was in eleventh grade and some snotty bitch told the senior boys I was a slut and put out. I was horrified and locked myself in the bathroom. Kiki picked the lock and sat on the floor next to me and listened to me cry for an hour. She held my hand and threatened to beat up Penny. It was cute, it was sweet, it was my sister showing me she loved me. And when Brooklyn got pregnant and rumors started about who Remy's father was, Kiki put a stop to them. I didn't know what she said or did, all I know is from one day to the next everyone stopped talking about it. And that was after Kiki had been in my bookstore and overheard two customers whispering about Brooklyn. My sister loved Brooklyn, too.

How had I missed it?

Before I could start to dwell my phone beeped and I pulled it out of my back pocket.

Where are you, pop tart?

River and his silly nicknames.

I glanced around my nephew's kickass little boy room and texted River back.

I want all boys.

At least one girl. He returned.

I could totally do a little girl as long as she had big brothers to take care of her.

Deal.

I heard a noise and turned to see Brooklyn standing in the doorway smiling.

"Texting River?"

"How'd you know?"

Brooklyn shook her head and her smile faded.

"All these years and you really thought you had us all snowed."

"What?"

"Sister, we've been best friends since we were in diapers. You honestly think I didn't know you were lying."

Yeah, actually, I had thought that I'd hidden my true feelings for River.

And since Brooklyn was my best friend she could read me, thus, I didn't need to answer.

"It's in your face," she weirdly stated.

"What's in my face?"

My phone beeped again but I ignored it and Brooklyn chuckled.

"See, that look right there. You're dying to check that message. Same as always. When your phone beeps you get excited. When you see the message is from River your face lights up. And when you read the message your face goes soft and you get this little grin that says you just hit heaven and all is right in your world." Brook lowered her voice to a whisper when she said, "I love this for you. I love that he's here. I love everything about it. But mostly I love that River is exactly who you always knew him to be."

I loved all of that, too.

But Brooklyn was wrong.

"He's better than the dream," I told her.

"Right," she continued to whisper. "I love that for you."

I loved it, too.

"Now, not to put a damper on things, and I know River's wandering around looking for you so I'll make this quick. Rhode told me about what's going on and what you're doing. He also told me he asked you and the guys not to talk to me about it. He also told me that I wasn't to get involved and he told me in a way that I know if I tried he'd handcuff me to the bed and I'd have to have an uncomfortable conversation with my son about why Daddy has handcuffs. So I'm not getting involved but I want you to promise me you'll be careful and you'll listen to everything Rhode and River tell you to do."

Brooklyn wasn't getting involved, not because Dulles threatened to cuff her to the bed. She wasn't getting involved because when something was important to Dulles and he conveyed this to her, she never went against it and Dulles returned the favor.

"I promise."

"A real promise. Not a Letty promise that means you promise until you get a wild hair and go off to do what you think is right."

"I don't break my promises," I fibbed.

"You do when you cross your fingers which in your mind negates the promise. So show me your hands and promise me you'll listen and you'll be safe."

I held my hands up in front of me. At the same time, another text came in and I glanced at the screen to see River's name along with five devil emojis.

I smiled and said, "I promise I'll be safe and I'll listen."

"Good enough. Now answer your man before he thinks you ran off and left him."

I engaged my phone and read River's first text.

Time to go home, baby, I'm hungry.

I was pondering how he could possibly be hungry when I saw him eat two hamburgers a few hours ago...until I saw the devil emojis and I caught his meaning.

You've already eaten. It's my turn.

I sent my text and looked back at Brook.

"I could run to the ends of the earth and he'd find me."

"Damn straight," River said from behind Brooklyn. "Time to go home, Letty, say goodbye to your friends."

Brooklyn gave me an *eek* face and her lips pinched together.

"What if I'm not ready to go home?" I shot back.

"You're ready."

I narrowed my eyes and put a hand on my hip, but before I could get a word out River continued.

"Letty," River growled and I shivered.

"Oh, fine. I'll say goodbye."

Brooklyn giggled and looked at her feet. River's lips curved up into a sexy smile that held promises of good things to come. And since I'd experienced the goodness that River had to offer I shivered again.

But since I was Letty, I couldn't pass up an opportunity to give attitude.

"You don't have to be smug."

"I do when there's a lot to be smug about. This includes me knowing the only reason why we're not gonna stand here a year and argue is because you're looking forward to going home. And before you deny it, I didn't miss the tremble, and yes, I'm smug about that, too. Ass in gear baby, time to get home."

"You're annoying," I hissed but it was lacking heat.

"Annoying because I'm right?"

"Yes."

Brooklyn snorted then lost the battle and belted out a laugh. She turned to leave but paused at River's side and patted him on the shoulder.

"Good luck, Pen Pal, she's a handful."

River didn't reply.

"Well, are you ready?" I asked.

"I liked watching you with Remy," he said. "All day I was thinking if you give that much love and attention to your nephew I can't wait to see what you'll give our kids. Growing up I didn't have a mom and I had a piece of shit for a father. But I had a good brother who showed me how to be a man. I had a brother who taught me what it meant to sacrifice for family. I reckon since you had good parents anything I'm lacking you'll teach me."

Was he crazy?

"You're the best man I know," I told him. "I don't know if it was Echo or if your dad taught you what not to be, or if you were born the man you'd grow up to be. But what I do know, is there isn't a single thing you lack. Not one, River Kent."

"Christ," he grunted.

"I love you, River."

The words were now exceptionally easier to say.

"Home. Now."

I shivered.

Then we went home.

CHAPTER 22

I couldn't shake the bad feeling I'd woken up with. And I knew Letty felt it, too. She'd been quiet all morning. And when Mrs. Simpson called when we were driving into Smutties I could tell Letty was struggling not to lose her patience with the older woman as she answered questions about me, how long I was staying, where I was going to work, if Michael and Tally liked me, and so on. Letty had done her best to inject cheer into her voice but it missed the mark by a mile. When Mrs. Simpson brought up the Reddit post, Letty shut down that line of questioning by telling her that Takeback had taken over the case. Then she lied and told Mrs. Simpson that she didn't know anything else and would let her know if she heard anything.

It was the only play Letty could make, seeing as we didn't need a ninety-year-old woman getting involved.

Now Letty was sitting in the corner of her bookstore reading the messages Cole had sent to Dora using her screen name. Watching the disgust play across her face made my gut roll. This was a bad fucking idea. All of it. Start to finish this didn't make sense. It was too fast. Dora had pushed hard for this meeting to take place.

Something was wrong.

There hadn't been enough time to properly investigate the Thomases. We knew next to nothing about their son's murder-suicide. Their daughter wasn't returning Wilson's calls, and since this was rushed, there hadn't been time to send someone to Kentucky where Brianna now lived. There were no police reports filed against any of the Thomases, no recordings of callouts to their house. And when Wilson had talked to Detective Brasco about the Thomases he admitted to hearing the rumors but he wasn't a cop back then and neither could he find anything concrete when he'd asked around.

We had nothing.

Not a damn thing, and we were sending Letty blind into an unknown situation.

"Greg left the house with Dora," Wilson said from beside me. "Asher's gonna give it five minutes, make sure they don't turn around, then he's going in to search the house."

That was something but not nearly enough.

"What are the chances they keep the boy in their house?" I asked, not taking my eyes off Letty.

"In my experience, if they have the boy he'll be close. So either in the house or a nearby RV. Cole and Asher tagged some rigs that have power and water hookups but they look abandoned. Cole will look in those as well."

That sick feeling in my gut intensified.

"*If* they have the boy?"

"Shep went through that message board; it's new, posts only dating back a few months."

"I noticed that, too."

"There's only fifteen members on that board including the user name Cole set up for Letty. Dora Thomas is offering the boy to five of the members, not for trade, for cash. She's doing it sloppy, coming right out and saying it, and she's doing it in a rush just like she's doing with Letty."

"Hedging bets on who can come through with the cash the fastest?" I surmised.

"That'd be my guess, considering she only engaged with the five members who have the money to pay. The others she blew off."

I felt my neck muscles constrict and barely got out my next question without choking on the words, "But you're questioning if they have the boy to sell?"

A. Boy. To. Sell.

Jesus Christ.

"I'm questioning everything. First, because it's a smart way to run an investigation. Secondly, because I've seen a lot of fucked-up shit, I've dealt with the most vile monsters, and never have I seen one of them as stupid as Dora Thomas. There's zero chance she's this sloppy and hasn't hit someone's radar. No way in hell she's really and truly in trafficking and hasn't been caught. These people are disturbingly cunning as a rule."

I stopped watching Letty and turned to Wilson to find him frowning as he continued. "They get away with what they do for as long as they do because they don't do what Dora's doing. They don't get desperate and straight-up use the words, "you can have him for fifty thousand dollars" in a direct message for the authorities to read. The couple Reese and Jack are checking out in Wyoming deleted their account to the message board after their first interaction with Dora. That was the red flag the couple was legit. Shep looked further into them and found the girls. The other four people backed away, but not completely. They're playing dumb, saying they don't want money exchanged, calling themselves guardians and caregivers. Shep's digging into them further. The only person who they contacted through Reddit was Letty, but that's likely because Cole hadn't set up her username on the message board until after he deleted your account, and by then Dora had struck up a conversation with Letty on Reddit so she didn't see a point in moving their communication. Yet another fuck-up. If these people have the boy and they're this careless and haven't been caught there are serious fucking issues with a lot of agencies that oversee this kind of activity."

I had to agree with Wilson. There were highly intelligent criminals who were hard to catch. Then there were idiots who made police work a little easier. And we had to investigate both kinds.

"Scam artist?" I asked.

"That's the best-case scenario," Wilson said and tipped his head.

My gaze followed. Letty was walking our way with a look of stark horror.

That look on her face was one of the things I couldn't protect her from. The tightness in my neck intensified and along with that my jaw clenched. With effort, I pulled my shit together right as she stopped in front of me.

"When this is over, I'm throwing my laptop away." To punctuate her words she shook the machine in her hand. "I've never in my life read anything so absolutely vile. I have no words for how disgusting that was. She offered to sell the boy. *Sell him*. She said it right out. She didn't use any kind of code words or anything. I can't believe more of these people don't get caught. I mean, who offers to sell a human on the internet!"

I didn't answer her question because I wasn't about to further explain all the different kinds of sick, depraved scumbags of the world. I also wasn't going to explain to her that what Dora was doing was not how child trafficking was done. I couldn't protect her from much since she'd backed me into a corner but I was taking what I could and telling her more than she needed to know otherwise.

"Do you have any questions before you go?" Wilson asked.

Letty adjusted the red scarf she'd worn for the meeting and scowled.

"Yeah, what's the maximum sentence for murder if I plead temporary insanity?" she hissed.

"Why don't you stow your murderous intent, seeing as it would suck for River to move all this way only to have his woman in lock-up."

Letty was being cute, attempting to cover up her disdain, and if I had to guess a healthy dose of fear had crept in. She'd never say it and she'd still go through with this, but I'd bet she was rethinking her desire to meet up with Dora Thomas and wishing there was a way to back out.

I checked my watch and looked back into Letty's sad eyes.

Less than an hour and this would hopefully be done. Or at least Letty's part in it would be over.

"She's late," Letty mumbled.

Dora Thomas was indeed ten minutes late.

"It's all good, baby," I told Letty, not taking my eyes off the boats bobbing in the water. I was scanning the area, watching for Dora Thomas, when out of the corner of my eye I caught sight of a man with scraggly, shoulder-length brown hair that was five days past needing a wash. The same went for his beard. But what had the hair on the back of my neck standing on end was the beat-up leather vest and his fast approach. Letty clocked him, too; she scooted closer and her eyes went wide.

"Baby, behind me." I swept my arm out and Letty shifted immediately.

"What's—"

She didn't finish because the man stopped in front of us, did a quick scan of the area, then a pair of wary eyes locked with mine.

"Don't make the deal."

A chill raced down my spine and my hand went to my hip. The man's gaze dropped to my sidearm and his eyes narrowed. I took in the patch on his chest that declared him Butch and then the other side advertising he was a road captain.

A Horsemen.

Not fucking good.

"I think you've got the wrong person, friend."

"And I think you're a cop and Wilson's people did a damn good job scrubbing your record clean. Dora Thomas is gonna offer you up a boy for fifty large. Walk away from the deal and tell Wilson to back off."

Fucking hell.

"Unless you're gonna tell me why I should pass up gettin' something I want—"

"Dora Thomas doesn't have a fuckin' thing you want except a fuckton of issues with Zeus. Tell Wilson to stay clear."

Butch turned on his scuffed-up motorcycle boots and I got my first look at a Horsemen cut. Top rocker displaying

Horsemen MC, bottom rocker declaring they were the Coeur d'Alene chapter, and in the middle taking up the rest of the space a white stitched reaper. Generic.

"What just happened?" Letty asked.

"Just a second, baby."

I pulled my phone out and hit Wilson's contact.

"I saw him," Wilson said by way of greeting.

"Was that your man?"

"Yes." Some of the tension ebbed but that ball of apprehension I'd felt all day tightened. "What'd he say?"

"Not to take the deal and that Dora didn't have what I wanted."

"Fuck me," Wilson growled.

I felt Letty's hand curl around my bicep and I heard her whisper, "Dora's here."

"You got three seconds to tell me what to do."

"Goddamn it," Wilson spat. "Don't make any deals but keep her on the hook."

"Copy that."

"He say anything else?"

"Yeah, but I'll have to tell you later."

I disconnected the call and shoved my phone in my pocket just as Dora Thomas cleared the last set of stairs that would bring her to where Letty and I were standing.

I shifted Letty to my side and looked down to tell her, "Same plan, baby."

Letty nodded but couldn't hide the panic in her eyes.

"Calm, baby. Everything's good, yeah?"

"Yeah."

"Everything's good," I repeated.

I hooked my arm over her shoulder, hers slid around my waist, and she leaned into me. What she didn't do was relax.

Dora stopped close, glanced around the area, then her

gaze finally settled on Letty's red scarf and the woman became visibly wired. Either Dora was rethinking doing business with someone local who knew her or she didn't know the first fucking thing about doing business period. And the evidence was suggesting the latter.

"It's a beautiful day," Dora said.

"It's always beautiful this time of year," Letty returned the agreed-upon phrase, and once again Dora's gaze went to the surrounding area before it settled on me.

"Who are you?"

"I'm the man with the money," I told her and she nodded her head.

My answer was obviously good enough for Dora, which was another red flag this woman had not the first clue. Dora had set the meet with Letty and Letty alone; the message had been clear—no one else was to come. Yet, we'd taken a gamble and Dora wasn't balking. Anyone else would've seen me standing there and walked on by. But Dora Thomas stopped and she accepted my half-assed, bullshit answer.

"I have the guardianship papers," Dora started. "I'll sign them once the money's—"

"What's the rush?" I cut her off.

"We're moving and as I said, the boy's not a good fit."

"Where'd you get him?"

Letty swayed closer and that burn in my gut intensified.

"We...I...um..." Dora stammered. "On a trade."

Bullshit.

"My woman was under the impression you adopted him through legal channels."

"Yes, well, that's not the case."

I swallowed my disgust and seriously wished Letty wasn't present—not for any of it but especially not for this part.

"He's got no paper trail?" I asked and Dora shook her head. "Where'd he come from and is anyone looking for him?"

It took Dora a moment to think up a lie, and while she took her time doing that I watched agitation slide through her features.

This bitch thought she was going to walk away from today with fifty grand in her pocket. She wanted that money —no, she *needed* the money. Desperately so.

"Do you want him or not?" Dora snapped.

I leaned in an inch, taking Letty with me, and sneered, "What I want is not to buy trouble. What I want is to make sure I'm getting what I want. What I don't want is to complete this transaction then have the cops on my ass."

"No one's looking for him."

That was the first believable thing Dora had said. Believable because there was no boy.

"Good. We want to meet him. Tomorrow we'll come out to your place. If he's acceptable you'll get your money."

It was monumentally easier to negotiate buying a child when I knew there was no child to buy.

Letty's fingers bit into my flesh, reminding me she didn't know about Wilson's doubts, and she had no idea that Dora's actions had confirmed that the Thomases' sons might've been involved in some sick and twisted activities with their sister and the jury was still out on whether or not Dora and Greg knew or participated. However, I was positive they did not have a child in their possession.

Dora's gaze went to Letty, and in an effort to keep Dora's attention on me I asked, "How'd you think this was gonna go?"

It was a wasted effort when Letty joined the conversation.

"We'll be out at your place tomorrow morning. Eight too early for you?"

"Letty—"

"Eight sharp, Dora," Letty hissed. "Have him ready and I'll bring your money."

Off in the distance, there was a roar of motorcycle pipes and Dora's face drained of color.

What the fuck?

"I don't need this hassle," Dora huffed.

Letty's body went solid; she thought we were losing the boy.

"Wait—"

Dora halted and looked back at Letty, but her gaze quickly shifted back to the parking lot beyond the dock.

"Don't worry, baby, we'll find what we need elsewhere," I cooed and Letty flinched. "I think we're done, Dora."

I moved Letty and had to practically drag her to get her legs moving.

"What are you doing?" she seethed as I continued to pull her down the pier.

"Trust me."

Letty started walking, albeit stiffly.

We were back to the SUV when Letty tried again. "What just happened?"

"Get in, Letty."

I opened the door and waited.

"River—"

"In, baby."

My woman, never one to give up a snit, huffed an annoyed breath and got in.

My ass was barely settled on the driver's seat when she started in.

"Why'd we leave?"

"One more second."

I pulled out my phone, found Wilson's number, and hit call.

"I got Horsemen surrounding the back parking lot," Wilson said.

"I can't see 'em because the hotel's in the way but we heard them when we were out on the pier," I told him. "Dora did, too. Freaked her out, went pale. Haven't been around long enough to know if her reaction was fear because people are generally afraid of the Horsemen or if it was more."

"Seeing as you had a visit from Butch, I'd say it's more. Did she give you anything?"

"Confirmation Dora's an idiot. She asked who I was, I gave her a bullshit answer, and she didn't hesitate to tell us she had guardianship papers and wanted to make the exchange. The woman actually thought Letty was gonna bring the money and she'd be leaving with fifty large. There is no boy, Wilson."

"Agreed. Asher's had plenty of time to look around. There's no kid. He talked to some of the residents of the RV park; no one's seen or heard any children."

Thank fuck!

"There's no boy?" Letty asked.

"How you doing, Letty?" Wilson inquired. "That had to be tough."

"Tough? It was so disgusting I almost puked. Legit, I need a shower to wash off the filth."

My jaw clenched and I bit back my desire to remind her that was exactly why I didn't want her participating in the investigation in any way.

"Right, then I'll let you get home so you can do that. River, I'll be in touch later."

"Something else. Your man, Butch, knew I was a cop. Told me your people were good but he still knew. He also said to steer clear or there'd be problems with Zeus."

There was a beat of silence before Wilson growled, "I'll be glad when I don't have to hear that fucker's name again. And you've got nothing to worry about; Shep's good, there's nothing for anyone to find. Which meant Butch had you looked into the second you hit the scene."

"That doesn't make me real happy, Wilson."

"Give me some time and I'll find out why."

"That'd be appreciated."

"Talk soon."

The line went dead and Letty swatted my arm.

"You knew."

Not much got past Letty and I wasn't sure if that was good or bad.

"Wilson had his suspicions, and after he brought them up I agreed. But it wasn't until she showed up I had confirmation."

"How'd you know?"

Hell to the no.

Letty knew as much as she was going to know.

"Not gonna tell you."

I pushed the button to start the SUV and was putting the beast into reverse when she asked, "Why aren't you going to tell me?"

"Told you, once you got mixed up in this shit there would be very little I could shield you from. You know as much about how these sick fucks operate as you're gonna know."

"River—"

I was well-acquainted with that tone, it was the one Letty used when she was itching to argue.

"Did you enjoy that?"

"Enjoy what?"

"Listening to me talk to that bitch like I was haggling over a used car and not a child?"

"No," she whispered.

"Gutted me, Letty, having you hear me like that. Made me sick to think that my woman, who's good and clean and sweet and owns a bookstore, was standing at my side listening to that shit. I didn't want your mind cluttered with this, I didn't want it sinking in all the ways people are fucked. You horned in on it and there was nothing I could do to stop you. You weren't gonna back down so I did the only thing I could do and made it as safe for you as I could. But it ends here. You're done. All done. I love you and part of what I love is you'd see a child in danger and you'd step up. But from here on out, no fucking more. Wilson and the guys confirmed there's no kid and I'm sure they'll take it a step further and double-check. But whatever they find it's not your business, and if I have to cut off internet to your building to keep Mrs. Simpson clean I'll find a way to do that, too."

"Okay, honey."

No hesitation.

No attitude.

No arguing.

"That's it? Just, okay?"

Letty sucked in a breath and gave me a shaky smile.

"I didn't stop to think about how this would make you feel, what it would do to you having me at your side when you made the deal. All I was thinking about was the boy and myself. I wanted to help and I wanted the boy safe but I should've stopped to think about the rest and I didn't. So, yes, okay. I'll back down and I'll talk to Mrs. Simpson. I need you to help me come up with something to tell her. She's an old woman who sits at home bored and has nothing but time to look at the internet. And she's a little naive so she buys into every conspiracy theory and she's convinced herself that she's Sherlock Holmes and she's going to solve the mystery if there's really Big Foot." Letty stopped and softened her voice when she finished. "I'm sorry, honey; in the future, I'll think about you."

Letty's apology crawled over my skin and warmed me down to someplace deep. I didn't need her to tell me she was sorry, but I did need the assurance that in the future she wouldn't put herself in a bad situation.

"Thanks, baby."

"Can we go home now? I really do need a shower."

Letty's face scrunched up into an adorable scowl and now that shit with Dora was over, and Letty would be clear of any further knowledge of the case, I could fully appreciate how damn cute she looked when she was disgruntled.

"Absolutely."

An hour later I found a better way to get my woman's mind right. And I knew she was where she needed to be when she breathed my name while all four of her limbs held me tight.

CHAPTER 23

I covered a yawn with my hand and caught sight of Brooklyn coming out from the back of the store.

"Busy day," she noted.

The box of damaged books had been replaced and customers had been in and out all morning picking up their orders. And there'd been a steady stream of foot traffic between pick-ups.

"Did you get your book done?" I asked on another yawn.

"River keeping you up late?" she teased.

River had indeed been keeping me busy but that wasn't why I was tired.

"I was up late reading an ARC."

Advanced reader copies of upcoming releases were one of the perks of owning a bookstore.

"Lucky bitch. Who were you reading?"

"Olivia Michaels."

Brooklyn's eyes rounded.

"Her Watchdog Security series?"

"Yep. I'm gonna ask her if we can use her series for the book club."

I watched as my friend's smile softened.

"Have I told you how happy I am to see you happy?"

"You have."

"Have I mentioned that I love that you're starting the book club back up?"

"You're happy because if Olivia says yes and sends copies for the book club you don't have to wait three months for the book to release," I teased.

"That and you're not hiding anymore."

"Brook—"

"That's all I'm gonna say about that," she cut in. "But I'm going to add that I love that River's here. Has he decided what he's doing?"

River had decided a lot of things in the five days since we'd met with Dora. The first thing he'd decided on was an information freeze. I had no idea what was happening with the Thomases or if Reese and Jack had found anything in Wyoming. All I knew was that the guys still weren't home and it was weird not having them around. Especially Reese. He was the one, besides Rhode, who spent the most time at Smutties. It was mostly so he had an excuse to go to Treats and bug Sadie but he also helped me move boxes. Thankfully, River had taken over that chore but it was still strange not having Reese around.

River had made other decisions, besides the information blackout.

"Echo and Phoenix are packing up River's stuff and shipping it," I told Brooklyn. "He decided to sell his truck since he said he was ready to trade it in for something newer and it'd be stupid to pay to ship it here just to sell it. Echo called last night and said that he had someone on the hook to buy it and that the movers were scheduled for next week."

Brook made a silly face and clapped her hands.

"Yay!"

That was Brooklyn, always my biggest cheerleader. Always *by* my side and *on* my side no matter what. Always happy for me and celebrating when things went right. I'd made a promise to myself that I wouldn't dwell on the mistakes I'd made while I was out of my mind with grief. But it was hard during times like these when I was reminded how good of a friend she was and how I'd turned my back on her and shut her out. I had times like this with my parents, too.

We were a close-knit family and it wasn't unusual for my mom or dad or both of them to randomly show up at my store to say hello. The only time this had changed was right after Kiki's death and it had changed because I made it clear I wanted space. That space was no longer there and my parents had been by several times in the last few days. It stung knowing I'd pushed them away, but I didn't hide my feelings. I told River I felt bad for the way I'd behaved, and just like always he listened. Only now I had the added pleasure of him holding me close while I talked about my day. And I got to cuddle close to him when he made plans for the future.

River decided he was going to apply to the Coeur d'Alene Police Department. Wilson had offered him a job with Takeback and much to my delight he'd come home and talked to me about Wilson's offer and asked my opinion. It had taken me all of five minutes to suss out that River missed being a cop. And when I asked, he confirmed my suspicions and told me that he appreciated Wilson's offer, which to River was a sign of respect and acceptance. But despite the red tape and headaches, he loved being a cop. So that's what he was going to do. If there was nothing with the CDAPD he would apply to other local departments.

"Letty?" Brooklyn's voice pulled me from my thoughts.

"I've never been this happy," I whispered.

"I know."

"I didn't know happy could feel this good."

Brooklyn gave me a self-satisfied smile that bordered on conceited because she knew just how good being happy felt. First, she'd experienced it when Remington was placed into her arms and she experienced it again when Rhode came back.

"Enjoy it, sister. But just to say, it gets better."

"Better?"

"Oh, yeah."

I wasn't sure how much more happy I could take without spontaneously combusting but I was willing to test the boundaries of combustion if it meant I had River.

"Before I forget," Brooklyn continued. "When does Mrs. Simpson start?"

That was something else that had changed. River had come up with a brilliant plan to occupy Mrs. Simpson's time. She was now working part-time at Smutties. Not moving boxes or restocking the shelves but I needed help checking customers out. Brooklyn helped when her schedule allowed but she was busier than ever narrating and I was having a hard time keeping up with all the work it took to run a business. Having Mrs. Simpson sit behind the counter would free up my time to organize my office and maybe pay my bills during normal business hours, instead of bringing work home with me. I now had better things to occupy my hours at home.

"Next week," I told her.

"Cool," Brook muttered. "Break's over. I need to record the last chapter so I can get home to my boys."

I let Brooklyn go back to her recording booth but I did it smiling inside.

I, too, now had a reason to finish up my work and get home.

CHAPTER 24

I was studying the large whiteboard that Davis had meticulously organized when Wilson and Jet Brasco walked into the conference room.

"Anything new?" I asked Wilson.

His expression instantly went hard.

"Reese and Jack recovered six minors—four girls, two boys, and one nineteen-year-old who had been with the Schaubers."

The Schaubers were the couple from Wyoming.

"Holy fuck."

At least something good had come from the Thomases fucked-up message board. None of the other names Shep had given Rhode panned out but they were still looking.

"Never fails to make me sick," Wilson growled. "The team in Wyoming is taking over and Reese and Jack are on their way home. Told you I'd talk to Butch when he reached out about how he knew who you were. I met up with him this morning and he explained; he saw you and Letty together and sent your picture to his office and they ran you."

Unease coiled in my gut. I wasn't sure how I felt about an undercover DEA agent taking my picture, but more, I didn't like why he'd be watching Letty.

"There a reason he has eyes on my woman?"

"I already told you, Rhode made it clear the Welshes, Brooklyn, and Remy were off-limits. Lawrence is an idiot but he doesn't want the trouble so he's stayed clear. Me asking Butch to keep an eye out is a precaution. I don't want to be blindsided should Lawrence turn stupid."

"Good to know you've got a finger on Lawrence's pulse, however, that doesn't explain why he's taking my picture."

Wilson's lips curved up into an amused smile. "That was Butch doing Rhode a solid."

"Come again?"

"Butch knows Letty means something to all of us, especially Rhode considering her and Brooklyn are tight. After what went down with Kiki he feels bad about having to keep information that would've put the family's mind at ease about where Kiki was and what she was doing. So he was feeling protective and saw you and Letty exchanging words outside of Smutties. Butch said he didn't like the vibe and ran you to make sure you weren't some asshole who was gonna fuck with Letty."

Before I could explain to Wilson I didn't find a damn thing amusing about getting my picture taken Jet Brasco joined the conversation.

"Heard you're trying to take my job."

Since I didn't know where Jet was going with his remark I cautiously answered, "Put in for the job at the department but I haven't heard anything."

"Talked to Chief Buley. He called Georgia, asked around, talked to your old chain of command. Seems the Kent family's got a certain reputation."

I felt the muscles in my neck constrict and acid churned in my gut. Lester Kent. The stench I couldn't wash away was working its way to the other side of the country.

Motherfucker.

"Reputation?"

"Echo, Phoenix, Shiloh, and River Kent. All legends out there in the Peach State. I heard that your captain shed actual tears when you turned in your resignation. Also heard your chief of police called Chief Buley personally and begged him not to give you the job and send you packin' back home. Damn, brother, if you're half as good as the hype I'm putting in for a new partner. Mine's ready for retirement and that was fifteen years ago he shoulda put in his papers. Again, nothing official but I'm thinking your new desk is being spit-shined as we speak."

A burn in my chest ignited and finally, *fucking finally,* that nasty stain left by my piece of shit father melted away.

Jesus fuck, that felt good.

"If I get the job, be a pleasure to have a desk next to yours."

"You'll get the job, just try not to show me up when you do."

Before I could respond Asher walked in with a face full of thunder and a menacing stare.

"Ran that lead Butch gave you," he bellowed. "Thomases are into the Horsemen twenty grand and another local scumbag for ten."

"For what?" I asked.

"Greg Thomas likes to gamble. His problem is, he sucks at it. He was making payments to the Horsemen. The rent they collect from the RV park was barely covering the interest but Lawrence was happy to let Greg sink deeper. Then the asshole sits a game three weeks ago, thinks he's on a winning streak, not smart enough to know he's being hustled. Last game, pot's big, sixty K, Greg's problem is he doesn't have the cash to buy in. So he puts up the RV park thinking his problems are solved."

"Fuck," Brasco muttered.

"Fuck's right," Asher continued. "Greg loses the twenty K he won that night and the RV park, meaning he can no longer make his payments to the Horsemen. So seeing as the motherfucker is so smart, him and his wife come up with the brilliant plan to sell a kid thinking they can fleece some sick fuck, and what's the pedophile gonna do, report it to the police? Bet when Dora and Greg found out that Letty answered that post, they hit the motherlode. A local woman, they could get the money fast and skip town even faster."

I felt it happen.

Call it a cop's intuition.

The connection I had to Letty.

But my insides froze while my blood heated.

I was yanking my phone out of my pocket when it rang.

Letty's name flashed on the screen and I slid my finger over the screen to answer the call.

I braced.

"Letty, baby, where are you?"

"River?" Letty whimpered and my heart seized.

CHAPTER 25

"Talk to me, Letty. Where are you?" I asked and turned to run out of the conference room.

Wilson blocked my path and shook his head.

"Not smart, brother," I growled.

"River," Letty whimpered and a shiver of fear slid down my throat.

"Tell me where you are," I repeated.

"I don't know."

That fear intensified and I swayed on my feet.

"Tell me what you do know."

I tried to push past Wilson again but he held firm.

"Asher, get the team in here now," Wilson demanded. "Brasco, get your boys ready."

"I was..." Letty trailed off and hiccupped a sob. "I was going out to my car and something hit me from behind. I passed out. That's all I remember."

I gritted my teeth and glanced around the room. My eyes landed on the whiteboard and my heart clenched.

"Where are the Thomases?" I asked.

"No clue. They weren't at the RV park this afternoon when I went by."

"Did they clear out or was their shit still there?"

"Didn't go in but furniture's there."

"You think—"

"They think Letty's got fifty K," I interrupted Asher. "When I asked Dora why she was dumping the boy she said he wasn't a good fit and they were moving. They're into the Horsemen for twenty grand with no means to pay it back."

Asher went to the door and easily slid by Wilson, which only further pissed me off.

"Let me by, Wilson."

"Pull your shit together and talk to Letty."

"I need—"

"Where you gonna go? Drive around and hope to fuck she magically appears?"

Jesus, he was right.

"Tell me what you see, Letty," I barked and instantly regretted it. "Fuck, Letty, I'm sorry, baby. Can you tell me anything about where you are?"

"I'm in a container."

"A container?"

"A metal container. It's dark. I can't see anything."

Jesus, shit.

"She's in a shipping container," I announced.

A shipping container in fucking Idaho. Every fifth house once you got out of the city and into the woods had a shipping container on their property.

"They left you your phone?"

"It was in my pocket when I woke up so, yes."

"Can Shep track her phone?"

"Already sent him a message," Wilson answered and went back to looking at his phone.

"Are Brooklyn and Remy covered? Her parents?"

"Oh, God," Letty sobbed.

I closed my eyes and dropped my head.

I was fucking this up.

Wilson was right; I had to rein my shit in and clear my mind.

"Check your battery for me," I asked gently.

There was a pause then, "Eighteen percent."

Fucking hell.

"Okay, that's plenty of battery life. You're alone?"

"I hear something," she whispered.

"Put your phone on the ground near you face down. Don't disconnect the call."

"Someone's coming in."

I heard rustling then silence. I pulled my phone from my ear, put it on speaker, and muted the call.

"She said someone was coming into the container," I told the room.

"Do the Thomases have any other property? Someplace they could stash her?"

"You think this is a ransom?" Brasco inquired.

"Mark my..."

"Good, you're awake." A man's voice came through the line.

There was some murmuring that I couldn't make out and what sounded like metal scraping.

I turned to Wilson and asked, "Is that Greg?"

"Don't know."

Fuck!

"Brasco, record this call with your phone."

Without missing a beat he pulled his phone out and did as I asked.

"Come on, Letty, give us something," I muttered.

"The guys are coming in," Asher announced when he came back into the room.

Come on, baby, say something.

"Why isn't he saying anything?"

"Please don't!" Letty screamed, and I reached for the table to steady myself.

There was more scraping, then the sound of a train whistle.

"The train—"

"Two lines, one on the east side, one on the west. Hundred miles of tracks go through this area." Brasco halted my question.

"I left the store at four to come here. Letty closes at five." I looked down at my watch. "At most, they've had twenty-five minutes. With traffic, how far could they have taken her?"

"No!" Letty shouted and before I could catch my breath she screamed, "River!"

With that, my breath was gone, totally gone, and my eyesight had gone hazy.

Please, baby, give me something.

Anything.

Greg Thomas was strong for an overweight older man. My face was throbbing from where he'd hit me and my heart felt like it might explode out of my chest it was beating so hard.

He had one of my hands cuffed over my head and I was losing the fight to keep my other hand free.

"I told her not to pick you," Greg sneered and I flinched when spittle hit me in the face. "I told you and your family were bad news but she got impatient. Now we have nothing."

I struggled to keep my hand away from his but when he wrapped his fingers around my throat, instinctively my hand dropped to his and he seized my wrist and lifted it above my head. Before I could blink he cuffed my other hand.

Greg took a knife out of his pocket and real fear hit me.

"No!" I screamed.

"Shut the hell up," he growled in my face.

Greg lifted the hem of my t-shirt and in one quick cut, he sliced my shirt open.

Oh, God!

I didn't know why I did it but I yelled River's name and Greg's eyes lifted to mine and I saw it; lust.

"Don't know what you're screaming about, girl, but you don't shut your mouth you'll find yourself on the bottom of a lake."

He didn't know I was calling out for a person—my person, my River. The idiot thought I was talking about a body of water. Then I remembered River was still on the phone. I needed to get Greg to talk for a variety of reasons— the biggest being I didn't want him touching me—but maybe I could get him to tell me where we were.

"What do you want from me?" I asked.

Greg's eyes flashed in a sick way and I wished I could pull the words back and swallow them.

"Right now, while Dora's waiting for someone to pay us for your return, I'm gonna have some fun."

Ransom.

My parents.

Oh God, Dora's gonna call my parents and my dad's gonna freak the fuck out.

"My parents don't have any money," I told him. "If you

want someone to pay for me, you better call Rhode Daley. He's got money, he'll pay for me."

"Money's in your account, we already checked."

Goddamn, stupid me.

All of this because I made a comment on a stupid thread then I horned my way into an investigation that River had warned me not to be a part of. And because of that, Wilson put money in my account.

"That money's gone, Greg. We used it."

Greg reared back then leaned forward and got nose to nose with me until I could smell his putrid breath.

"You better hope it's still there."

It took me a second to pluck up the courage to continue. I was afraid that the turkey sandwich I had for lunch would make a reappearance when I said, "We figured out that you and Dora didn't have what we wanted. So we looked elsewhere and found it. He was more money." I stopped and attempted to shrug but since my hands were cuffed over my head it was more of a head tilt. "But you know how it is, you get what you pay for."

"Fucking whore!" he shouted and landed a punch to my stomach.

The pain stole my breath and I gagged until saliva filled my mouth. I vaguely wondered if I puked if that would be enough of a turn-off to get Greg to back away from me. I coughed and sputtered and even had to spit but unfortunately, I didn't throw up.

"Call Rhode," I wheezed. "And he'll get you your money."

It was then I realized I'd made a grave mistake.

Greg reached around me and patted my back pockets, then his face twisted with rage.

"Where's your phone?"

Oh shit.

"What phone?"

"The phone that was in your pocket!" he yelled. "That's what fucking phone."

Well, the jig was up. He obviously knew I had my phone. Which led to the question...

"If you knew I had a phone, you moron, why'd you let me keep it? What'd you think, I'd just sit here and wait for someone to come and get me?"

Two more blows to my midsection had me gasping for air.

The hit to my face had me seeing stars and all I could think about was how many times my dad had warned me that my temper would one day get me into trouble. But it was the second closed-fist punch to my temple that had me hearing my sister's voice in my head.

One day when I grow up I'm gonna be just like you and not let anyone be mean to me.

Kiki was six and had come home crying because a little boy had called her names. The next day at school I'd caught the little shit being mean to Kiki and I shoved him into the dirt.

I smiled at the memory and wished I hadn't when the small movement made my lips throb.

Greg moved away from me and I tried to draw in oxygen but my ribs protested each breath.

"I fucking told her you'd be a pain in the ass," Greg spat.

And in the dim light, I saw him squat and pick up my phone.

Shit.

What was I supposed to do now?

CHAPTER 26

"Does Shep have a location?" Asher asked.

You know I do, right?

Letty's sweet voice played in my head while I listened to the sound of her gasping for air and I prayed I wasn't hearing what I thought I was hearing but I knew that I was.

The tenuous hold I had on my sanity was slipping by the second.

There was a loud thud then a slap and an audible wheeze and that hold was gone.

"River," Wilson murmured. "Keep your shit together, brother, Shep's narrowing it down. We'll have a location in a minute."

Another minute meant sixty seconds more of Letty being hit.

Another minute meant Greg Thomas could do more damage.

How the fuck did we miss this?

"Who is this?" Greg's voice came over the line clearly and I unmuted the phone.

"Where's Letty?"

"Who is this?" he repeated.

"Who I am is either the man who's gonna deliver you the money you want or alternately if Letty's injured I'm the man who's gonna rip your fucking head off. Now, tell me where Letty is."

"I want fifty thousand."

He'd get fifty thousand dollars, never.

"Done. Tell me where Letty is and I'll be there."

My answer was met with silence and finally, the cocksucker wised up.

"I don't trust you."

"*You* don't trust *me*? That's fucking funny coming from you."

Wilson jerked his chin toward the door and started to move through it. I followed him with my phone to my ear. Since we were on the go I assumed Shep came through with a location.

"You've got thirty seconds to tell me where you are if you want your money. After that, I'm tracking you down, and for every minute it takes me to find my woman I'm gonna take that time to peel your skin off. Inch by inch, motherfucker. And you best believe you'll be wearing every bruise you leave on her. Every place you mark her, I'll mark you."

"I have a unit on the way," Brasco told Wilson quietly.

"I rerouted the team," Asher put in.

"Let me talk to Letty," I demanded.

"What? Why?"

God, this idiot was stupid.

"You want me to deliver you fifty grand in cash, without me knowing if she's alive?"

"I'll call you back with a location."

The line disconnected and I didn't bother calling back.

Wilson beeped the locks to his Suburban and we all filed in.

"Where are we going?" I asked.

"Hauser."

"How far away is that?"

"Ten minutes."

Fucking shit.

Wilson took off out of the parking lot and Brasco gave him directions from the back seat.

My knee bounced and I watched as the buildings flashed by, but I wasn't seeing businesses and restaurants; I was picturing Letty's beautiful face soft with sleep first thing in the morning. I was remembering the look she got when I said something she thought was sweet and how her eyes lit up when I told her I loved her.

All the years I wasted not coming to her sooner.

All the nights I fell asleep to her voice from thousands of miles away instead of beside her.

"Fuck," I snarled.

"Seven minutes, River. Hold tight," Wilson said.

I had no choice but to hold tight and wait.

Seven minutes felt like an eternity.

"Where are we going?"

I blinked into the bright light and tried to get my bearings.

The good news was I was out of the metal container. The bad news was I was still handcuffed and my shirt was hanging open. But I had bigger things to worry about than Greg seeing my bra. Whatever he'd planned to do to me he hadn't done so I wasn't going to gripe about a ruined t-shirt or a boob-shot here and there.

Trees for as far as I could see and a dirt lane.

That told me nothing. I could be anywhere from Rockford Bay to Sandpoint or anywhere in between the two.

"To get my money."

That sounded like a great idea but I didn't want to leave in case River had the Takeback team work their magic and they knew where I was.

"Why don't we wait here?"

Greg shoved me harder toward his Ram pickup and the too-tight handcuffs dug into the skin around my wrists.

"Shut the fuck up."

Maybe for once in my life I should do as I was told and shut up.

Nope. I couldn't do it.

"Just leave me—"

Greg grabbed a handful of hair and twisted until I came up on my toes to alleviate the pain now radiating over my scalp.

"I'm getting sick of your mouth, Letty. Shut up and get in the car or I swear to God I'll kill you and drop your body on your parents' driveway."

That shut me up. It also got me climbing into the truck.

I would endure anything he did to me as long as my parents didn't wind up childless. Kiki's murder destroyed them. If I died, too, they'd never recover.

And neither would River.

Why had I called him and not Dulles? Because I was selfish and if I was going to die I wanted to hear his voice. But that meant I'd done it again, I'd acted out and not taken his feelings into consideration.

He must be going out of his mind.

Dulles cared about me, but he cared because I was Brooklyn's best friend, not because he loved me.

Brooklyn.

The Ram jolted forward and I stopped thinking about my best friend and what it would do to her if my dead body was dumped on my parents' lawn.

"Slow down," I demanded when the back tires skidded on the dirt.

We came out of a clearing and my heart jackhammered in my chest.

"You're going too fast."

"Shut up."

We were high up on a mountain road with a sheer drop-off on my side of the truck. I would be silent for the rest of my life if he'd just slow down.

"Please," I begged. "Slow down."

"Goddamn it! Shut the fuck up!" he roared and slammed on his brakes.

From there everything slowed. We lost purchase on the dirt road and the truck broke sideways. I could see the bend up ahead and the tops of trees that dotted the side of the mountain.

This was it.

This was how I was going to die.

With Greg Thomas behind the wheel of a Ram truck careening over the side of a mountain.

I closed my eyes and thought about the first time I saw River.

I felt the truck jerk but I didn't open my eyes. I kept thinking about the bluest pair of eyes I'd ever seen.

An odd sensation came over me like I was weightless but I kept my mind on the only man I ever loved. Big and broad and handsome.

My body slammed into the dashboard just as I was thinking about how peaceful River looked when he slept. All that power shut down but still mighty. So beautiful. Finally all mine.

After that, everything sped up to warp-speed.

My last thought was of River.

Then everything went dark.

CHAPTER 27

"Sit the hell down," Echo snapped and my eyes sliced to my brother.

I ignored him and kept pacing the too-bright hospital room.

"Phoenix, turn off that light near Letty's bed, it's too bright in here."

My brothers shared a look before Phoenix reached over and pulled the cord to kill the fluorescent light above Letty's head.

The door creaked open and Sunny and Luke came in followed by Tally and Michael.

"We brought you back a sandwich and a soda," Tally said as she walked across the room.

I did my best to lose the crisp sharp tone I knew my brothers were getting tired of hearing from me when I smiled at Letty's mother.

"Thanks, Tally, I appreciate it."

"Then prove it by actually eating this one," she returned and slowly lifted an eyebrow.

I didn't grow up with a mother, didn't have a motherly

figure, or even a woman in the house who wasn't my sister, but I still recognized a mother's command.

"Leave the man alone, sweetheart."

My gaze went to Michael and I immediately averted my eyes. He was the picture of agony. If I'd thought he was in pain the first time I met him I'd been wrong—so fucking wrong—because now it flowed out of him and blanketed the entire room.

"No, Michael, I will not leave him alone." That brow arched higher and she finished. "I haven't seen him eat in five days and he's wasting away."

Michael looked me up and down, then turned back to his wife. "Think it'll take more than five days before that boy wastes away."

I couldn't remember the last time someone called me boy and I would've laughed at Michael saying it right then if I wasn't on the verge of coming apart.

Five days.

Letty had been lying in a hospital bed for five days.

By some miracle, she was breathing on her own with nothing broken and minimal head trauma. And by a miracle, I meant a tree.

A tree had fallen over and landed just right onto the tree next to it, so when Greg Thomas's truck slid off the road the bed of the pickup got hung up on the branches. Letty had miraculously been wedged between the dash and seat—with no seat belt on, she would've been thrown from the truck like Greg.

That was what had saved her life.

But she'd yet to wake up and now it was starting to worry the doctors. When she was brought in no one could believe she'd survived with bruised ribs, a swollen eye, a cut to her lip, and a bump the size of an orange on her forehead.

I was pretty sure the ribs, lip, and eye were from Greg hitting her but since she hadn't woken up I couldn't ask her.

I heard Sunny giggle and that, too, would've made me smile, since it wasn't until she met Luke that she'd done anything remotely girly like giggle or share her feelings. Now she did both regularly and my soon-to-be brother-in-law was the reason why.

"I seriously love Letty's parents," Sunny chirped and the sound of her happy voice made me cringe. "Has anyone else ever called River a boy? I think he came out of the womb a full-sized human."

"Smartass," I groused.

"And I love that Brooklyn calls you Male BFF or Pen Pal. How did I not know this?"

"Sunny—"

"Don't Sunny me, big brother. Do as you're told and eat. Tally's right; you haven't eaten since we've been here."

And they'd been at the hospital with me damn near around the clock for the last four days.

I let that sink in hoping it would calm my nerves, but all it did was serve as a reminder that my family had dropped everything to get on a plane and fly to Idaho because my woman had almost died.

Almost.

"I love you, Sunny. You have my heart, but how about I eat when my fuckin' woman's not lying in a hospital bed in a coma, yeah?"

"River." Echo's rumbled warning pissed me right the fuck off.

So I looked at Luke but I didn't need to say anything—he knew. It wasn't the same; Sunny had never slipped into unconsciousness for five days—but he knew my fear. He'd lived it when my sister had been held at gunpoint. I reckon the vision of the gun held against his woman's head was one he still dreamed about.

"Shiloh, baby, enough," Luke murmured.

Michael cleared his throat and my apology for my outburst died.

"All a father can ask for is that his daughter finds a good man. But what he hopes for is a man that would go five days without sleep to watch over her. What he wants is a man who would starve himself with worry. With that being said, son, you need to eat. My girl's gonna need you strong when she wakes up. And in case you haven't heard, she's a handful."

"I'd roll my eyes and deny that if it didn't feel like a thousand needles were piercing my skull," Letty croaked.

All the bodies in the room turned to face the bed but I was the only one who moved, and that was to take a step back as the force of her scratchy voice hit me like a physical blow.

"Holy shit," she whispered. "There's three of you."

Sunny chuckled. Tally sobbed. Michael cleared his throat again. Luke and my brothers stared at my woman like she well...bumped her head.

"Stand in a line," Letty continued. "From biggest to smallest."

"I take offense to that," Phoenix grunted.

"Yeah, it must be tough being the smallest," Sunny joked. "Poor little Phoenix only three inches taller than the rest of the male population."

I watched as Letty took in my sister. Then she blinked, and no sooner did she get her lids fully opened than she winced in pain but she carried on like she didn't feel it.

"I'd remind you that you're actually the smallest if I wasn't afraid you'd kick my ass. But since I'm guessing I'm already in the hospital, unless River's redecorated our house I might as well tell you now—there's no denying you're a Kent. You look like a miniature version of River, only beautiful."

What the fuck was happening?

Sunny let out a sigh then said, "You're taking the fun out of being the disapproving little sister. I didn't even get to give you gruff before I had to admit I liked you. And before you ask, I was planning on waiting until my brother busted you out of the hospital before I started putting you through my vigorous string of tests I came up with."

Letty smiled—and winced again.

"Will you forgive me for stealing your fun if I promise to help put any women Echo and Phoenix bring home in the future through your tests?"

"Forgiven."

My brothers groaned. I stared at Letty. Michael had his arm around Tally and they were both beaming at their daughter. Luke was standing next to Sunny shaking his head.

Again, what the fuck was going on?

"You done?" I growled.

Letty's face immediately gentled and she whispered, "Yeah, honey, I'm done."

My eyelids slowly drifted shut and for the first time in days, I could take a full breath.

"I'm okay."

I wasn't sure if she was talking to me or the room in general.

"Honey, come here."

My feet didn't move.

I'd waited fourteen years only to have it almost stolen.

"River, honey. Honestly, I don't know how but I feel okay."

I opened my eyes and looked over at Michael. It was easy to see he was feeling the same relief I was, but then again, he wasn't trying to hide it. Tally was in the crook of his arm. If her husband was near she was almost always burrowed close—something Letty did with me. Something she learned from her mother. Something I loved and hoped that in forty years she still did.

"I realize this isn't the way this is supposed to happen," I started and Michael focused on me. "A more appropriate time would've been out sharing a drink but I've waited too long already. I messed up and wasted years. I'll be the man your daughter needs and I'll work myself to the bone to be the man you hoped and wanted her to find. So I hope you take this as sincere when I apologize, but I'm asking now for your blessing."

Tally didn't hide her tears—not that she could with them steadily streaming down her cheeks—but I started to get worried when Michael's face turned red and he looked away.

"I sho—"

"No." Michael paused and coughed into his fist before he started again. "No need to apologize. It's always the right time to share what's on your mind. I speak for me and Tally both when I say we've been waiting a long time for you to show up, and you did when we needed you—when Letty needed you. But then, you've been there for her all along, haven't you? Of course you have our blessing."

There was a beat of silence before Letty spoke up. "Is this the part where River asks you for two cows or is it the other way around and he needs to give you three roosters and sheep?"

"It's not too late to change your mind, son," Michael quipped.

"A cow and a six-pack and I'll take her off your hands," I returned.

"I'll throw in a new fishing reel if you promise to keep her forever."

Forever.

That was the plan.

"Jeez, I've been awake for like thirty minutes do you think maybe I can get a..." Letty trailed off and glanced around the room.

I saw it happen when realization dawned. She'd woken up and immediately was her normal sassy, chock-full-of-attitude self; so much so that as the minutes slipped by and the joking had started I hadn't thought about this part.

Fuck.

I moved to the side of her bed and sat on the edge. Lightning-fast and with more speed than I thought was possible she nabbed my hand and squeezed.

"How are they here?"

"Letty—"

"How'd they get here so fast, River?" She shook her head. "How'd *I* get here?"

"Baby, calm down."

"*How* am I here? I wasn't wearing a seat belt. We went off—"

"Stop and take a breath."

Letty took a deep breath and flinched.

"Where's Greg?"

Shit. Fuck. Shit.

"He didn't make it," I told her softly.

"How did I?"

Jesus fuck, that was a day I never wanted to relive and I

sure as fuck wasn't telling her the details of the hour it took fire and rescue to secure the truck before they'd go out and get her. All we could see was the top of her head and for that hour I thought she was dead. It had taken Rhode and Wilson to lock me down and keep me from climbing the tree to get her out—which could've made the truck fall down the embankment.

"The truck got hung up on some trees."

"That's—"

"I'm begging you, baby, please, that's all you need to know."

She studied me for a moment and then she very quietly said, "Okay, honey."

I blew out a breath and went on, "You've been out for five days."

"Five?" she wheezed.

"You had some minor swelling on your brain, but yesterday's test showed the swelling had receded and the knot on your forehead has gone down. Your left eye's black and blue and your ribs are bruised. You still have a small cut on the corner of your mouth. No broken bones, no stitches. Your doctor said he expected you to make a full recovery. We've just been hanging out waiting for you to wake up," I finished lamely.

I knew my teasing fell flat when she frowned.

"And you didn't eat while I was out?"

"I've eaten, Letty."

Which wasn't a complete lie if you considered the candy bars Remy had brought in yesterday. I could easily reject food from the adults, but there was no denying Remington.

"Your family came all this way."

"Of course they did."

Something I didn't like passed behind her eyes and she didn't make me wait for an explanation.

"They came all this way because they love you and I'm taking you away from them."

"As you can see, since they're standing in the room, they're all capable of getting on a plane to come visit. Though Echo's a big baby and Sunny had to hold his hand during take-off and landing."

"Just because some of us prefer driving doesn't mean you get to name-call," Echo defended his sissy behavior.

Shiloh smiled. "Family doesn't take away from your happiness, Letty. They add to it. River's happy here with you and we're happy he's found you. You could take him anywhere and we'd still be family, we'd still be happy, and we'd still come visit."

Once again, I was taken aback by the changes in my sister. Pre-Luke Sunny would've scoffed at the mention of the word happiness. Now, she was throwing it out there left and right and doing it without choking.

I lifted my hand and gently traced the outline of her black eye. I didn't want to ask but still, I had to.

"Tell me how this happened."

Letty leaned into my touch and gave me a weak grin.

"Greg," was all she said.

I swallowed down the homicidal rage and remembered the cuffs she had on after her rescue. Her shirt had been cut open.

"Did he—"

"He scared me. He hit me. And let's leave it at that."

My neck tightened and my body went solid.

"He didn't touch me," she whispered, reading my thoughts. "Not like that."

"Your shirt—"

"I promise, I'd tell you if he hurt me. He didn't and now *I'm* begging you, please let me protect you from what happened like you're protecting me. He's dead, it's over."

He's dead.

The motherfucker certainly was that.

It was on the tip of my tongue to argue, to demand she tell me everything that had happened while Greg had her. Not knowing went against every fiber of my being. But I pushed those thoughts aside. For her.

"Okay, baby."

"Now do I get a kiss?"

I leaned down and pressed a gentle kiss to her temple.

"What? Does my breath stink or something?"

I smiled against her temple and gave her another kiss.

"You haven't brushed your teeth for five days, Letty."

Her eyes narrowed and she humphed a sigh.

I leaned back down and gave my woman a kiss, tongue and all.

In front of her parents and my family.

When I broke the kiss, Letty was smiling.

CHAPTER 28

Reese Turmel

My ass had barely hit the new obnoxious hot pink velvet overstuffed beanbag when Mrs. Simpson's shrewd blue eyes found me.

I'd never in my life been afraid of a woman and I'd served next to some badass women in my day. But the old woman had a way about her and that way told you when she spoke your ass better snap to or she was having your ass —verbally, of course. Though the way she was scowling at me right then made me wonder if she was hiding a yardstick behind the checkout counter.

"Mr. Reese," she called.

"What can I do for you, Mrs. S.?"

"Must you abbreviate my surname? It's truly not that hard to remember. Perhaps I'll speak to Letty and ask her to make me a name tag."

The old woman was a riot when she wasn't being a ballbuster.

"Yes, perhaps that will help me remember."

Mrs. Simpson looked to the ceiling and mumbled what sounded like a curse word.

"Such vulgarity coming from such a beautiful woman," I teased.

"You would test the patience of a saint," she returned and smiled sweetly. "Now, if you wouldn't mind there are some boxes in the back I need moved."

"You realize I don't work here, right?"

"Yes, Mr. Reese, I understand that you simply come in every day to harass Letty and Brooklyn. So while you're doing that you can also move some boxes."

It was the way that Mrs. Simpson pinned me with her stare that had me up and walking to the back room to move boxes.

I was passing by Letty's office and I stopped dead when she pushed away from her desk.

"Holy shit, there's a desk under all that mess."

"I know, right?" she returned. "And it only took me six weeks to get it clean. I should've hired Mrs. S. ages ago."

At the mention of six weeks, I felt my body string tight.

Six weeks ago we almost lost Letty.

The black eye and scrapes were gone. But the memory was fresh.

A memory that would fade for all of us except River. I suspected he'd never forget hearing his woman's screams over the phone, then witnessing her being lifted out of a truck dangling from a tree. Not that any of us would forget, but we wouldn't keep it forefront in our minds.

River was the kind of man who would and I couldn't blame him.

I glanced around Letty's now clean office and noted she'd also done some redecorating. There'd always been framed photos of her family on the walls, but it didn't escape my notice that she'd added a few more of her sister. Kiki with Remy. Kiki and Michael. And there was even one of Kiki and Letty—arms wrapped around each other, huge grins on their faces. They were standing in front of a lake but they were covered in mud.

Happy times.

"Like your new beanbag," I told her. "Color is horrific, but it was comfy until Mrs. Drill Sergeant told me to get my ass up and move boxes."

"It's not a beanbag. It's called a Lovesac."

"Nope. Not touching that."

Letty smiled and through her laughter, she sputtered, "You should get one."

"A Lovesac?"

"A what?" River said from behind me.

"Brother, I have no idea what the hell your woman's talking about. She got a beanbag—"

"A Lovesac," she corrected.

"Whatever the hell it's called. All I know is it's a big round hot pink piece of heaven. But there's zero chance of me buying anything called a Lovesac."

"You will when you lose our next poker game. Forget doing my laundry, we have a washer and dryer in our new place. New bet is you have to go to the Home Store and buy me a nice big electric blue Lovesac."

Letty thought she was funny and I had to admit I was thrilled that Letty was back to Letty after everything that happened with Kiki, then with Greg and Dora Thomas. As far as I was concerned, Letty was a rockstar. No one bounced back the way she did.

River chuckled and I figured it was mostly his doing— why Letty was free to joke and laugh less than two months after she'd been taken.

"You've got jokes."

"I do. But I also have the perfect place in my new library for a Sac, and since they're like two hundred bucks you're buying me one."

Two hundred fucking dollars. Was she crazy?

"Woman, your man just bought you a house with a freaking library, I think he can afford to buy you a Sac. Besides, now that he's gainfully employed I don't feel bad taking your money, which means this week I stop throwing games."

I was totally lying; I wasn't losing on purpose. Letty was that good at poker. She took my ass to the cleaners every time we played. The only person who could beat her was Cole.

"You're almost as bad of a liar as a poker player."

I ignored Letty's comment mostly because she was right but also partly because I wanted to move boxes so I could get home.

"Help me with some boxes, would you?" I asked River.

"Give me a minute to say hello to Letty then I'll be back."

I took that as my cue to get gone so he could properly greet his woman.

I had three of the six boxes moved by the time River showed up.

"I'd ask you how you're doing but it took you long enough to get back here so I'd guess you're doing good."

The smug bastard smiled.

Yeah, he was doing more than good.

"How'd today go?"

"Bitch pled guilty."

Dora Thomas had been picked up the night her husband had kidnapped Letty and she'd been sitting in jail awaiting trial ever since, which was due to start next week.

But on the advice of her attorney, she was supposed to plead out, which apparently she'd done.

"Good. Saves Letty from having to testify."

River grunted his agreement.

"New city, new job, new house. Shocked your hair's not on fire."

"No shit. We lucked out finding a house so fast." River hefted a box onto the shelf and said, "Butch reached out."

"What'd he need?"

"Wanted to let me know that Lawrence was going to call Wilson and request a sit-down. He's worried that Letty getting caught up with the Thomas shit will reflect poorly on the Horsemen. He wants to make it clear he had nothing to do with Letty's kidnapping."

"That sounds like bullshit to me."

"Agreed."

We finished stacking the boxes and were almost at the door when I said, "She's happy."

"Letty?"

"When I first met her, she was fire and attitude. Then Kiki died and all that fire died right along with her sister. But that fire's blazing again. I know I don't need to say it, suspect you know it, but I'm gonna say it anyway—never seen her happier. Not even back when I first met her. She had fire and more sass than any woman should have but she was missing the spark. Happy you're here, brother."

River gave me another smug grin and said, "Letty's got spark all right."

And for the first time, I experienced jealousy. Not because I wanted Letty but I wanted what that grin communicated.

River slapped me on the back and followed me out of the back room but stopped at Letty's office. I continued making my way out front, hoping I could slip by Mrs. Simpson just in time to see Sadie Pierce stomp into the store.

Goddamn, she was gorgeous.

And fire? The sexy baker had it in spades. She came off sweet and shy but with the tiniest provocation, the woman went electric. I spent more time than was healthy thinking about all the ways I'd like to explore igniting her temper.

I'd also recently learned she had money trouble. Something she was displeased I knew about and seeing her stomp into Letty's store I was fairly certain I was about to get a piece of sweet Sadie's fury.

I stopped where I was and waited.

If she had something to say she was coming to me.

In her current state, it didn't take her long to strut her jean-clad ass across the store. And since I'd already been in her bakery that day I knew those jeans had embroidery on the back pockets and they were my new favorite pair. Though I'd never seen her in anything that didn't showcase her long legs and great ass.

"Here," she hissed and held out a hundred-dollar bill.

"Why are you giving me money?"

"I'm not," she continued to hiss. "I'm giving you back *your* money."

I feigned ignorance and held up my hands.

"Why would you think that's my money?"

"Because I'm not stupid. No one in their right mind would put a hundred dollars in the tip jar, Reese."

I smiled, which only served to piss her off more.

"Oh, so you do know my name."

"I never said I didn't know your name. Here." She waved the bill. "Take it."

"That's not mine," I lied.

Or, actually, I didn't lie. The money was no longer mine since I'd given it to her.

The anger waned and hurt flashed across her face.

Fuck.

"Sadie, honey—"

I got no more out when embarrassment chased the hurt and my stomach curled tight.

"Please don't. Whatever game you're playing I want no part of it. I wish you didn't know but you do and since you heard you know how bad it is. I don't have time for bullshit. So, please, Reese, take your money back."

Now she was pissing me off.

"Yeah, Sadie. You're right, I heard. So don't be stubborn and take the tip."

"I don't need your charity," she whispered and dropped the money.

As it floated to the floor, I watched her turn and march out of Smutties.

Pissed no longer scratched the surface of what I now felt.

Furious was closer to the emotion.

But concerned was winning out. Since I hadn't actually known how bad her troubles were until now.

"Was that Sadie?" Letty asked.

"Yep."

"Is that a hundred-dollar bill on the floor?"

"Yep."

"Reese? Everything okay?"

Fuck, no, it wasn't okay.

"Nope. But it will be."

I left the hundred on the floor and went to find Sadie.

Next up is Reese and Sadie in Dangerous Games. Grab your copy here.

ALSO BY RILEY EDWARDS

Riley Edwards

www.RileyEdwardsRomance.com

Takeback

Dangerous Love

Dangerous Rescue

Dangerous Games

Gemini Group

Nixon's Promise

Jameson's Salvation

Weston's Treasure

Alec's Dream

Chasin's Surrender

Holden's Resurrection

Jonny's Redemption

Red Team - Susan Stoker Universe

Nightstalker

Protecting Olivia

Redeeming Violet

Recovering Ivy

Rescuing Erin

The Gold Team - Susan Stoker Universe

Brooks

Thaddeus

Kyle

Maximus

Declan

Blue Team - Susan Stoker Universe

Owen

Gabe

Myles

Kevin

The 707 Freedom Series

Free

Freeing Jasper

Finally Free

Freedom

The Next Generation (707 spinoff)

Saving Meadow

Chasing Honor

Finding Mercy

Claiming Tuesday

Adoring Delaney

Keeping Quinn

Taking Liberty

Triple Canopy

Damaged

Flawed

Imperfect

Tarnished

Tainted

BE A REBEL

Riley Edwards is a USA Today and WSJ bestselling author, wife, and military mom. Riley was born and raised in Los Angeles but now resides on the east coast with her fantastic husband and children.

Riley writes heart-stopping romance with sexy alpha heroes and even stronger heroines. Riley's favorite genres to write are romantic suspense and military romance.

Don't forget to sign up for Riley's newsletter and never miss another release, sale, or exclusive bonus material.

Rebels Newsletter

Facebook Fan Group

www.rileyedwardsromance.com

facebook.com/Novelist.Riley.Edwards
instagram.com/rileyedwardsromance
bookbub.com/authors/riley-edwards
amazon.com/author/rileyedwards

ACKNOWLEDGMENTS

To all of you – the readers: Thank you for picking up this book and giving me a few hours of your time. Whether this is the first book of mine you've read or you've been with me from the beginning, thank you for your support. It is because of you I have the coolest job in the world.

Made in the USA
Coppell, TX
27 October 2021

64747409R00164